Philanthropic Ways

by

Eugenie Laverne Mitchell

Published by: Uni-Tee Publishing

CONTENTS

Chapter 1

The people called them "Gods Three Little Angels" and they looked and sang as though they had wings and a halo. But at times when they were not gracing the altar at church on Sundays or at some other gospel concert or church event, the three friends were normal playmates – novice inquisitors who relished discovering the ways of the world through adventure, and often their behaviour could be more likened to that of mischievous minxes.

Sister May, who many considered highly spiritually astute and who professed to have the gift of discernment, compared them to *"Cherubs that hover around the Master's throne"* and she convincingly vouched to anyone that gave her an ear, that she could see a divine glow and perceive the presence of a heavenly host surrounding the Angels wherever and whenever they ministered.

Of a truth the Angels did carry a special anointing. Their ministration reached out to thousands in a way that only the most gifted and renowned gospel singers had ever done. They thrilled audiences up to 10,000 strong and equally enthralled those where two or three had gathered, for the same Spirit attended their performances wherever they went.

Many were positively affected by the ministry of the Angels as they delivered their renditions with full confidence in their abilities, belying their perceived naivety, and causing even grown men to weep and surrender all to the Lord. And many testimonies of great blessings, healings and deliverances taking place during their ministration drew the masses from far and wide to hear them sing in the hope that their lives too would be touched by a miracle.

The group had been the brainchild of Carly, the youngest of the three, who during the second week of the school Summer holidays of 1985, having become bored with performing to an audience of dollies, had put her name down to do a solo in church the following Sunday. And with only six days to prepare she had begun rehearsing "Count Your Blessings" in earnest, practising almost all day up to her bedtime for four days. But although her mother and father enthused about her efforts, Carly was not convinced that her rendition would be a good offering for, having been born with a well-tuned musical ear, she knew that something was missing. So although she feigned disappointment to her parents, she was secretly relieved when her performance had to be cancelled due to the fact that she lost her voice through overwork on the fifth day of rehearsals.

During the service the following Sunday Carly studied the worship leaders and church choir avidly; and it eventually dawned on her what was missing –

harmonies. So she tried to convince her best friends Avarel and Amelia to sing with her but neither showed any initial interest. Carly pondered how she might get her friends on board. She knew their voices would blend perfectly, recalling how they had sung in Sunday school and in the youth choir together. *"If I could only get Avarel and Amelia to appreciate how beautifully our voices will blend"*, Carly prayed that night. And her prayer was soon answered as an opportunity to do just that arose two weeks later.

Amelia Lanson was born on 12 August 1973, Avarel Andersen on 16 August 1972 and Carly Collinge on 17 August 1974. So each year the three friends held a joint birthday party, and this year, when they turned 11, 12 and 13, was no exception. The party was held at Carly's house.

It had been a glorious day of fun and frolic and after the games and merriment had ended and the celebrants had left one by one, only Avarel and Amelia, who were sleeping over, remained. Carly took a seat at the piano and her friends came to stand close by her, looking on as she begun to play skilfully – a favoured chorus. When Carly began to sing, her two friends naturally joined in, holding the harmonies to the popular refrain, and their voices blended beautifully. Soon they had an audience as Carly's parents came to stand by smiling at the three of them. This boosted their confidence and they sang with more vigour.

Auntie Belle was in the kitchen at the time, clearing up after the party. She thought she could hear singing and cocked her ear to listen to the melodic but barely audible strains. Wishing to hear more clearly, and as though instinctively drawn, Belle left the kitchen where she had been ensconced all afternoon helping out, and walked towards the direction from where the ethereal sounds emanated – the living room.

As Auntie Belle entered the room Carly continued to play and sing, but becoming aware of her presence, the other girls hushed, because they knew Aunty Joy to be anything but a happy soul. Her countenance was customarily as miserable as a prisoner on death row and the children were afraid of her. Unlike Carly, they did not realise that she had a heart of pure gold, or that Aunty Belle's facial expression had become sombre and her manner gruff due to the fact that she had lost control of the muscles in the right hand side of her face and most of the right half of her body as a result of having inexplicably suffered a stroke in her early thirties.

Belle was greatly loved by her family and dear friends but she was avoided like the proverbial plague by everyone else who did not know her story. She was given the name Belle because she was born beautiful and had brought great joy to Carly's Grandparents as their first child. But now only her name remained as a testament to that fact. No one would believe that she had been born beautiful because in addition to the disabilities brought about by the stroke, the sorrows that she had encountered in her life meant that she never smiled and deep furrows had become entrenched into her forehead as a result. The distorting lines around her eyes and mouth had completed the rearrangement of her beautiful features, causing her to look cruel – murderous even.

Children whispered that she was a wicked witch and often ran from her as though for fear that they would end up in her casserole pot, for she was equally famed for her excellent cooking.

"Don't stop singing", Aunty Belle drawled as Avarel and Amelia stood stricken with fear. Only their eyeballs moved as they glanced at each other, then at Carly who continued to play and sing unperturbed, then at Mr and Mrs Collinge, whose smiles were fixed in place; then back at each other and finally they stole another glance at Aunty Belle, as the biggest out of place crooked smile spread across her care ravaged face. The two girls' heads moved involuntarily to allow them to stare comfortably at Aunty Belle as though she were an exquisite treasure they had seen for the very first time. And then Carly also turned to stare in amazement for she had never before seen her Aunt smile quite like that, which caused her to hit the wrong notes, but she somehow kept on singing as her heart danced. The other girls gradually relaxed and re-joined her as Mr and Mrs Collinge and Aunty Belle smiled on.

Congratulations rang out following the rendition and Carly seized the moment to announce that they would be forming a group. Avarel and Amelia did not affirm or deny this statement – they did not wish to burst their friend's bubble and spoil the happy occasion.

For her birthday Carly had received a brand new computer games machine from her parents. She was the only one in the church who owned such a computer at that time and it was a big deal to her impressionable friends. And although Avarel and Amelia remained disinclined to be in a singing group with Carly or to meet for rehearsals, they were persuaded when Carly struck a deal with them – they readily agreed to go along with the "group" idea on the basis that when they met up, they rehearsed first before being allowed to play games on her computer.

It was difficult to get Avarel and Amelia to rehearse most of the time though – all they wanted to do was eat biscuits, drink pop and play computer games, and Carly had to put her foot down hard. Carly was spurred on by a new agenda – she wanted to make her beloved Aunty Belle smile widely again. So she pushed the girls to rehearse as hard as she could because she wanted them to be ready to sing a song at the up-coming church Family Day in mid-September. Auntie Belle always attended church on Family Day and the thought of seeing her smile again became Carly's all consuming passion. She pushed the others almost to breaking point, even when she herself would have preferred to do nothing but eat, drink and play. And they managed to perfect a rendition to her high expectation just in time for Family Day.

On Family Day when they were called up to perform Amelia and Avarel were so nervous that they almost peed themselves and it took much encouragement from the congregation to spur them into song. During their rendition Carly was playing the piano and strained her neck to watch Aunty Belle, who was seated two rows from the front with her parents, and as Belle smiled joy overflowed in her loving niece's heart.

After that first performance, many people came to congratulate the girls, referring to their sound as reminiscent of little angels singing. Bishop Holder, the head of the church at the time, was amongst those who hugged each of them and he commented jovially, "You three little angels – I would like you to practice a song to minister at the up-coming Youth Convention and this time I want you to practice with the church band". And that was how the group got their name.

At the Youth Convention Bishop Holder introduced them as "God's Three Little Angels" and following that Convention invitations for them to minister came rolling in. Soon they became hugely popular and wherever they went they commanded standing ovations and rapturous applaud.

The three had more than wonderful voices in common – each had demonstrative song-writing abilities and together they composed many simple but catchy choruses which they ministered to appreciative audiences. Another thing they had in common was that none looked their true age – many people hazarded guesses that they were in the age range of 9-10, and this common misapprehension added to their innocent charm.

To meet the demands of their ministration and performance schedule, the girls had to practise hard. They continued to meet at Carly's house each Tuesday, just the three of them, which more often than not turned into a social evening of fun and frolic and a little rehearsing. Bishop Holder had directed that they also rehearse every Saturday afternoon with the church band. This weekly rehearsal was in stark contrast to the meeting on Tuesdays, because under the ubiquitous eyes of music master Bro Darrell, they had to practise and that was where the real work was done.

For 5 years God's Three Little Angels was the name on thousands of believers' lips, and were the singers who had sung the songs that reverberated in as many hearts and spirits. Then suddenly, when they turned 16, 17 and 18 everything changed.

Chapter 2

God's Three Little Angels were the headliners, by special invitation from the new Mayor of Pembleton in North London to perform at his inauguration which was held at the local Town Hall. That night the Angels surpassed their previous highest mark in ministration and performance, and the standing ovations, rapturous tributes and joyous applauds drew them back on stage over and again, to appease a ravenous crowd whose appetite seemed insatiable.

After the performance, as they mingled with the crowd at the reception, Avarel, the eldest and more audacious of the three was approached by (and gave some of her time to) a young man apparently wielding the proverbial broom, manifested in charm, wit, beguiling words and a sugary sweet smile, who before she or anyone else realised it, had swept her clean off of her feet. He told her she was beautiful, a fact that even a blind man could not deny, for her physical beauty was complimented by a gentle spirit. Many if not most had commented upon her fairness in the past, but she had never before been told how beautiful she was by one as charming and stylish as Brendon Hurst and the compliment went straight to her head. He stole her away to a quiet corner of the large establishment, out of sight where they talked and she learned that he had connections and could introduce her to the right people in a whole other world, people who could take her places with his guidance and her looks and voice. He stressed that he was talking about big time wealth and honour she could only dream of and could never attain while she remained one of God's Three Little Angels.

Whilst Avarel loved the idea of fame and vast wealth she did not relish the thought of leaving the Angels behind – they were her sisters, her confidantes, sworn friends for life and she did not wish to break their strong emotional bond. But she did crave to see Brendon Hurst again, if only to look upon his face, (for in her eyes he had a most appealing countenance), and to drink in his seemingly limitless charm.

So see Brendon again she did – he met her after college most days and as she fell deeply in love Avarel devoted more of her time to Brendon. Soon she even began to miss rehearsals on Tuesday nights and Saturday afternoons just to be with him. Initially her parents knew nothing about her liaisons and by the time they found out, Avarel had become a prisoner of love. She confessed she would rather die than live without Brendon, swearing that her heart belonged to him alone. Her parents protested loudly, but were silenced and had to back down when she threatened to leave home to be with her beau. The following Saturday night, when she stayed out into the small hours, her strict father had broken his silence and sought to discipline her, which had resulted in Avarel absconding with Brendon the very next day. She wrote letters to her parents, confessing that she could not be parted from her love, and she also wrote to her group mates, apologising for jumping ship and wishing the Angels continued success.

Devastated by the loss of Avarel, the two remaining Angels picked themselves up, dusted themselves off and replaced her with Jenny Atkins, who was younger than Carly by two years. Jenny was at least as good a singer as Avarel and had a cute and endearing dimpled smile that they hoped their audiences would appreciate, but as if Avarel had taken all the angel dust with her when she left, robbing the Angels of all or most of their charisma, they were no longer as well received as previously. And the charm was never to return.

Next it was Carly's turn to depart from the group just over a year after Avarel left.

At 17 years old Carly was immature and impressionable to a fault – some would say that she was not very bright, but they would be wrong for Carly was a straight A* student in all subjects, except that of the heart apparently. Others still labelled her a "spoilt brat" – an only child who had gotten used to having her own way and they were probably right on that point. For it was too easy for Dwight Henry, a young 22 year old stallion of a young man with more brawn than brains, who visited the youth services on a couple of occasions, to talk nonsense to her, rush her off her feet (or as Sister Minns had said "tun har fool-fool"), deflower her and "drag har outta church", (another of Sister Minns' expressions).

Carly had been the singer with the strongest voice of them all and without her God's Three Little Angels lacked the necessary power to perform the boisterous up-tempo numbers that thrilled their more energetic audiences.

Days after Carly lost her halo and left the group, Jenny announced that she too was stepping down. The truth was that her initial interest in joining the Angels had been borne out of infatuation as opposed to true passion and as their popularity had waned substantially, so had Jenny's commitment.

So Amelia was left alone holding cherished memories of God's Three Little Angels. She nurtured those recollections of her group mates within her heart, for days, which turned to weeks, which turned to months, which turned to years, dreaming of the day when the other Angels would come home.

Chapter 1

True to his word Brendon's actions spoke loud and Avarel was immediately linked up with a recording company – Starline Records – that made her
an offer she could not believe, yet alone refuse. And less than three months
after the Town Hall concert, memories of the Angels had begun to fade fast as
Avarel embarked upon a new adventure in her life as a recording artiste.

Immediately upon receiving the news of her good fortune, Avarel had
sought reconciliation with her parents, wishing to share the news and gain
their support. They were quick to forgive her and became firm backers of
their daughter's venture, thanking God for his manifold blessings in choosing
to favour her with such a great opportunity, for not only were they a lowly
family that had known poverty and great lack, but they were also well aware
that Avarel was certainly the least talented of God's Three Little Angels. And
they were undaunted by the terms of her first recording contract, which practically amounted to her selling her very soul.

Chapter 2

Hi there – It's me – Avarel Andersen!

What did you say? Oh, you barely recognised me. No problem, I get that reaction all the time these days. Most people say I have changed a lot – I can't really see it myself though. But I guess it is true that my mode of dressing is very different nowadays. Instead of pretty little church frocks, I now wear risqué high fashion garments – some barely covering my curves, and a lot of make-up on my face. I guess it must be the make-up that causes me to look so different. Believe me, it's a relief to take it all off at night and give my skin some air to breathe.

Tonight after my make-up removal routine, I sit in front of the mirror a while longer, reminiscing about my life's journey so far. I pause to admire my reflection as a smile plays about my lips. Praise arises within my heart and for the umpteenth time I say "Thank you God for creating me so beautiful", and then a carnal praise of self arises from deep within as I appreciate just how beautiful I really am. Puffed up with pride, my smile widens – I rise to my feet to admire my standing reflection – what a body. My smile widens further, lightening my countenance even more, as I muse that I also have brain and a voice and I thank the Creator once again for His gifts – I am so truly blessed.

I am the first to admit that I'm no Aretha or Kim though, but I have made the most of the little talent that God gave to me. I guess you could compare me to the servant in the Bible who was given 10 talents and increased it by 10 more. But my transformation did not come about by my own efforts – no – I've got Brendon to thank for that. When I first met him he told me that I was the complete package and through good production and marketing he has proved it – the listening public have come to love me – they can't seem to get enough of Avarel Andersen. I chuckle to myself as I whisper my name. When I was born into near poverty and my family gave me that name, little did they know that it would one day be the name of a star. I am not joking – I am a superstar now.

Don't get the wrong impression because I am so confident about my looks and success, I'm not conceited, right – but I know what I've got. I'm beautiful and that's just how it is. My natural looks are those of an African Princess, my nose like a tiny triangular jewel upon the centre of my face, my eyes like those of an exquisite doe, fringed naturally with longer than average lashes and accentuated by well-defined yet delicately chiselled high cheekbones running above parallel and equally well defined yet delicately chiselled jaw line. My mouth is framed by perfectly well-proportioned upper and lower lips. At 5' 10" tall barefooted, I tower over Brendon by a full 5 inches in 3' heels and my limbs are slim, shapely and nimble, covered with unbelievably smooth luminescent chocolate coloured skin. My natural hair is short, like that of a boy's but this does not detract from my beauty, on the contrary, I have been reliably informed that my superb features are more prominent without hair to get in the way. Brendon was the first to tell me so and many others have voiced that same opinion since.

Brendon was spot on you know – he said that what I lacked in vocal ability I could make up for with good production and imagery and that is how I was marketed as an artiste – image first – talent second – but I don't mind that though, I'm rich and successful and that is all that counts at the end of the day.

Several well respected columnists have commented upon my "timelessly beautiful features", also remarking upon my physique, one likening my form to that of an elegantly carved stone goddess'. But some have sought to sexualize me in a degrading manner, by using raw animalistic terms when mentioning my bodily attributes, omitting to mention my endearing personality or my truly beautiful face. Thank goodness though for those who headline me in strong positive voices which has had the effect of quieting the negative comments to bare whispers.

One of my favourite columnists wrote of my ability to transcend races, and in truth it is difficult to say what my genetic make-up might be when I don one or other of my numerous hair pieces or hair weaves, and with application of the right shade of foundation and make up, I can cross many racial divides. With a long straight weave I am of Asian or European extraction covered in the deliciously rich African hue. On another day, I might favour an oriental – I am full of surprises – ultimately marketable – just like Brendon said I could be.

I'm not really certain who I inherited my incredible beauty from, for my mother, father and three siblings are not as well blessed in the looks department as I have been. However, there is some resemblance between my father and I – he has similar eyes and also my nose, albeit an oversized version of my exquisite jewel.

As I sit down again, I stare at my reflection and smile. I want to continue reminiscing. Would you like me to tell you more about what has been happening in my life since I parted company with Carly and Amelia? What do you say – yes? Okay then – won't you come and sit by me? Let us take a long journey over time together?

Well, within a year of leaving the Three Little Angels I had my first number one hit album – "Mercy" and my life changed dramatically. Worldwide fame came so suddenly – I found it hard to adjust at first. I was lucky to have Brendon on hand as my constant companion – he kept me grounded in a sense and guided me as my Manager. He saw to it that I was in the right places at the right time and ensured that I looked after my voice, figure, looks and my image, albeit in reverse order.

On the day that my album "Mercy" hit number 1, Brendon and I hit the town to celebrate and ended up at La Bon, the in vogue "place to be seen at", where Brendon surprised me by dropping to one knee and popping the big question – I was over the moon even if I had to turn a deaf ear to the malicious comments buzzing around that he was merely trying to protect his investment – to ensure that I did not leave him behind with my new found fame. But if Brendon was worried, I couldn't imagine why, because I simply adored him. He was beautiful in my mind – "beauty is in the eye of the beholder", so they say and in my eyes there was no man lovelier than Brendon. If there was one thing that I knew of a fact, it was that I loved him –I respected him too – Brendon was a real man – my knight in shining armour, for only a real man, one so assured in his masculinity could revel in his status as "Mr Avarel Andersen" – only a real man could appreciate that position without feeling threatened or side-lined.

I wanted to believe that Brendon loved the real me too, but it worried me sometimes whether he was just with me because of my beauty, the fame and wealth of which he earned his own fair share as my Manager. The fact that Brendon had a penchant for tall dark skinned, beautiful and successful model-like women just like me (most of his past girlfriends had looked very similar to me) was the source of my insecurity. And the fact that he once stated during an argument that he needed me to maintain my looks and figure or he might just begin to look elsewhere didn't help – I did not like that statement one bit.

Like I said my love for Brendon was strong, but it really got my back up when he made that comment about me maintaining my looks or he might look elsewhere. That was the first time it occurred to me that Brendon ought to be thankful to have me, for I could have had almost any man I wanted. Many wealthy and powerful men had tried to woo me behind his back, but I turned them all down – I only had eyes for him. But after he made that comment I looked at him with new eyes and thought – *"look at you – 5' 8" (short for a man), with less than average looks – a thin face, an extra-large aquiline nose, thin lips yet you dare to say that to me"*. His comment stung for many days and caused me to admit in my mind just how physically unattractive Brendon truly was. And when the hurt finally subsided, the realisation that my husband was not very good looking remained with me, but with the concession that he did have "to die for" smooth beautiful dark porcelain skin and the most unusual and endearing shade of hazel/green eyes, a testament to his Scottish/Ghanaian heritage. And he definitely had something special which kept me deeply in love with him.

We married days after Brendon proposed, exactly a year after having met – I was 19 years old and he was 30. Our nuptials took place on a sun drenched beach in the Caribbean – I cherished my vows and my husband became everything to me. We were inseparable – we slept together, woke up together, shadowed each other everywhere we went. People often joked that we were joined at the hip. I loved and trusted my husband with my life and I was ecstatically happy then.

Apart from the fact that Brendon could be a little controlling and a bit sharp with his tongue at times, he was a wonderful man. Actually, if I am totally honest I would say that Brendon was very controlling and his tongue had a lethal cutting edge, but true love overlooks otherwise fatal flaws. Brendon had been public school educated and having come from directly contrasting backgrounds we had little in common when we first met, but he found in me an obedient and eager pupil and very soon I came to appreciate most of the same things that he did. There was one subject on which we had starkly differing views, however – that was religion. We simply did not see eye to eye, and it gradually became apparent to me that Brendon hated God. I had known from the beginning that he did not like going to church so I never tried to force him to, but it was only after we got married that he revealed to me a new meaning to what he meant when he said that he was a *"believing sceptic"*. He had kept his baser thoughts on religion pent up inside his heart only to unleash them upon me in the very first week after our marriage. Then my husband made it clear to me that he had only tolerated me going to church on occasions while we were courting – he said that he would be happiest if I stopped going altogether. But although I was prepared to curtail my visits to church to twice a month, I would not be stopped.

After that, each time I readied myself to go to church Brendon would begin to grumble. His favourite words were "neglect" "neglected" and "neglecting" – he said them a lot and made me feel guilty so that I reduced my attendances even further – down to once a month which gradually dwindled down to once every two or three months. So anti-church was Brendon, however, that he remained dissatisfied even with my now random visits and he continued to discourage me from going to church at all.

Eventually Brendon succeeded in convincing me that I didn't need to go to church to be a Christian and that I could pray wherever I was and God would hear me – if there was such a being, he would always stress. I wanted peace to reign in our home, for I just couldn't bear the arguments that would kick off when I started to get ready to go, or upon my return, so as time passed what he was saying began to make sense to me and I relented.

I designated one room in our home as a prayer room and there I would commune with God. Initially I would set aside at least half an hour each day (usually first thing in the morning) to read the Bible, meditate and pray, seeking God in earnest for His guidance and protection. At first Brendon demonstrated respect for what he termed my "holy room" and my "holy half hour". But after a few months he began to grumble, about the time I was spending in my closet. He also made more and more demands upon me at times when I would normally be praying. And simply to keep the peace in our home I acquiesced to his wishes. I realise now that it was stupid of me to give in to him but that was what I did and my devotional time diminished on a declining scale – from every day to every other day, then from every other day to twice a week, then from twice a week to once a week and so on.

The quality of the time I spent with my Lord was also affected – I no longer prayed from the heart or spirit, but from my mind, often reading cursorily from purchased prayer books.

Then Brendon began to defile my prayer space by entering it and blaspheming or swearing and smoking in it. I could tell that he was doing so on purpose. This had a negative effect on me – I no longer felt that it was a holy space – I could no longer feel God's spirit there. And day by day my relationship with God deteriorated more. Soon my heart began to stray voluntarily and I no longer craved or cherished spending time with the Lord.

Once a month or so – then once every two months or so – then every three or four months or so, I still remembered to pray until I forgot to pray or read the Word at all. And gradually all interest in Godly things left me – I could not say exactly when that occurred but I was aware that other things crept into the space in my heart where God's spirit had once dwelt, notably a dark shadow seeped into my soul that would only be satisfied by sin.

Chapter 3

We were wafting on a very high and lofty cloud and life could not be better or more fulfilled, financially speaking. Brendon had delivered on everything he promised and he did everything he possibly could to make me happy – I reciprocated and we were the envy of all around us. But even so there was a void in my spirit – my soul craved more and more sin but was never fully satisfied.

The first number one hit was followed by several others in close succession – life was mostly busy, taken up with recordings, tours, live appearances, recorded appearances, interviews, sponsorship functions, etc., etc., etc.…… My life consisted of extremes – one minute I was busy beyond measure and the next we were jetting off to some exotic location where we would do absolutely nothing but lounge on beaches, drink elaborate cocktails and eat incredibly expensive food to our heart's desire for a whole week.

Sometimes I would still say brief prayers for protection and strength. When Brendon began to join me on occasions, introducing me to various chanting and rituals to encourage a positive aura, bring good luck and ward off evil, which often amounted to blasphemy, I did not object – I had lost my holy will and found myself being easily manipulated and sinking deeper and deeper into the miry sinful pit.

As time passed Brendon began to take on projects when we would otherwise be away together on vacation. He would spend one or two days of a one-week holiday with me before rushing off to oversee some important business. One such venture was a project with a female rap group. After he signed them, our time together diminished even more and soon he hardly ever came on vacations with me anymore.

"I've just got to give it a shot at making them a success", he would say excitedly. He had first heard *"Delicious"* (so called because the two founding members' were both called Delores), at a talent contest to which I had been invited as a guest judge – *"Fame Game"*. They were good though, and I could understand his passion to make them a success, but I did feel that he was neglecting me a little too much because of his new "baby". It wasn't the same lounging on a 5-star plus beach, staying in a 5-star plus hotel or eating in a 5-star plus restaurant, without my husband by my side. I had no-one I could really call a friend that was within my concentric circle. At those times I became lonely and longed for the friendships I had abandoned, those I had sacrificed at Brendon's will. At those times I would wonder about my friends left behind and what life had thrown at them. At those times I would regret not having kept in touch with Amelia and Carly. At those times I really, really wanted to call them but resisted. After all what would they think of me – I had simply disappeared from their lives – had broken ties and bonds asunder.

In the first year of my departure from home, both Amelia and Carly had tried to contact me on numerous occasions but for one reason or another I had never returned their calls, probably because Brendon did not like me to keep close friends, and I eventually lost touch with them. Now I regretted my callous and thoughtless actions. It was during such lonely times that I discovered new friends that filled the void. And I began to hang out with the two "Cs", Charlie and Champagne. They made me feel good about myself and helped to lighten the burden of loneliness – to fill up the void but eventually cost me more than money could buy.

Rumours floated around in the second year of our marriage about Brendon and the lead singer of the group he was mentoring, but nothing was substantiated. The first proven affair had come to light just over three years after we were married. She was one of my backing dancers who had had a rough childhood but who had been blessed with the face of a beauty queen. Her name was Hilary Watling and Brendon Hurst was the best thing that had ever happened to her. I knew something was wrong from the moment Hilary started to second guess me during rehearsals. For hitherto she had been respectful and demonstratively grateful to me for having personally selected her from thousands of other hopefuls who had auditioned to join my prestigious backing dance troupe. But now, having apparently forgotten where she was coming from, Hilary began to snap back at me when I directed the troupe to do certain dance steps.

At first I tried to ignore her but as this attitude continued I became tired of dealing with Hilary's insolence and decided to speak to Brendon about the possibility of replacing her.

"I am sick of her attitude – I just won't put up with it anymore", I said to him.

"Why don't you just talk to her", Brendon had responded agitatedly in a manner which had caused me to realise immediately that he thought I was making a fuss over nothing.

"Because that would make no difference whatsoever, that's why – I've already tried that – you try talking to her".

"Okay – I will".

But his tête á tête with the dancer had apparently made no difference either, as I observed at the next rehearsal.

"Okay, so this is it – to the right – arms over to the left, swagger, swagger then walk back", I had directed the Choreographer who had proceeded to interpret and perfect my requirements to the troupe who studied his moves and attempted to put them into practice – all except Hilary.

"Don't you think that swagger, swagger thing is a little outdated now, Avarel?" she had commented, daring to go above the Choreographer's head and address me by my name and in a demeaning voice and insolent manner.

"Whether the moves could be considered dated or not is not relevant, it's what I want for this particular track – in any case I don't consider them to be out-dated", I responded, my back teeth gritted.

"They are dated, man – we're supposed to move with the times, come up with new moves, not be stuck in the past", Hilary commented more insolently than before.

"I say we should do it like this", she continued, running through a routine that was tarty, slutty and debauch all at once, and so not what I wanted for that track.

The Choreographer stood by stunned saying not a word. His expression revealed that he thought Hilary was way out of order trying to tell the client what to do. I decided to ignore the ingrate and looking towards the Choreographer I said, "Jeff, can we get on please – run through the routine as I said", and Jeff obediently obliged, demonstrating the steps as he had done previously. Then he asked the troupe to copy what he had done, which they did expertly – all except Hilary who could be heard "kissing her teeth" (hissing air through her teeth) loudly, then commenting for all to hear, "This girl is brainless, man", as she looked directly at me. Her comment provoked an audible gasp throughout the studio.

"I beg your pardon", I retorted and continued without waiting for an answer. "This is the last straw – since you've obviously gotten way too big for your boots, young lady – just pack up you tings an' leave this instant", I lapsed into heavy Jamaican lingo a sure sign that I was mad as hell. "You' service is no longer required".

"I will do no such thing", Hilary had retorted, rendering me speechless for a moment. The tension within the studio was palpable and everyone except the two of us was so quiet that if a pin had dropped it would have sounded like a bomb exploding.

"You will do as I say – I refuse to continue working with you – go and pack you' tings and get out an' don' bodder to come back – you' service is no longer required", I repeated – I was livid.

Then a solitary whisper could be heard throughout the studio, followed by a chorus of whispered support for my position – Hilary had never been very popular.

But instead of doing as she was told or backing down, Hilary walked towards me in the centre of the studio (hands akimbo) and engaged me in a full scale "stare down" contest as all the other dancers and Jeff framed the studio floor. After a few seconds that seemed like long minutes, audible whispers again spread among the observers, just as Brendon entered the room.

"What's going on here? Brendon asked as he walked towards me.

"I just cannot continue working with this girl – she has to go", I announced.

Hilary said nothing but looked incredibly confident as she continued to stare at me with contempt.

"To think I dragged this rat out of the gutter because I felt sorry for it", I said with disdain. Hilary shrugged her shoulders and pouted insolently then hissed, demonstrating that she was unaffected by what I was saying.

After a beat Brendon pleaded "Sweetheart, give her a chance no – she's young". He spoke in the soft voice tinged with Jamaican lingo that he had picked up from me, my family and others that he had day-to-day dealings with. His command of the Jamaican lingo was haphazard and was often used by Brendon to bring a smile to my face – but it did not work this time.

"No – she has to go", I repeated adamantly.

"Look, fall back in line with the other dancers, will you Hilary", Brendon gestured with his hand.

"I said she has to go, Brendon", I almost shouted.

"Calm down sweetheart", Brendon said, "You're creating a scene"; he cooed quietly in my ear.

"No, I will not calm down", I shouted before stomping out of the studio, into my dressing room and bursting into tears. I just couldn't understand why my husband was so obviously siding with this insolent girl and treating me as though I was overreacting and the one in the wrong.

So Hilary remained with the troupe and continued to make it obvious that there was no love lost between me and her. I began to seethe inside constantly, realising that something was definitely not right – I suspected that something was going on between her and Brendon. And it soon became clear that my suspicions were not unfounded as I began to discover them in semi compromising positions almost every day. At first I kept my cool, wishing to monitor what was actually taking place, but when I lost my composure and reacted a few weeks later by asking Brendon what exactly was going on, my husband turned the blade around on me and accused me of being paranoid, jealous, overly sensitive – he even mentioned that I might be going crazy. That night I cried over and again and began to prepare my heart for major disappointment.

Just over a month after the first confrontation, I stumbled upon Brendon and Hilary having a full blown argument.

"I will not go down that road, Brendon", Hilary announced.

"Look – if you don't you'll be on your own then", Brendon had warned.

"Hey…..", I interjected involuntarily. I had not planned to do so. I had wanted to simply observe what was taking place but my emotions had gotten the better of me. Brendon almost jumped out of his skin while Hilary had glared at me in her usual manner and stomped off angrily.

"What was that all about?" I asked – the question had hung in the air for too long.

"Oh nothing to worry about – she has ideas about the dance steps for the up-coming show at the Crown Hall, that's all". "I was telling her she was on her own with that", Brendon said as he visibly squirmed. I didn't buy his explanation and made sure he knew it.

"Just watch you'self Brendon – I know there's something you're hiding from me about this Hilary "s**t but I'm on to you", I said before walking away. And it was just a matter of days before I found out what the argument had really been about.

The headline read "Avarel Andersen left crying as Dancer Snatches Husband", left me reeling. Then embarrassment overwhelmed, for there in full colour was my husband's infidelity plastered all over the best-selling thrash Sunday newspaper for all to see. Grabbing a copy of all the Sunday papers I drove to a hotel in suburbia and checked in – where Brendon would not find me. That afternoon I read the different versions of the scandal over and over and cried buckets of tears. It was the part about Hilary being 3 months pregnant that had hurt the most because it dawned upon me then the extent of Brendon's deception and what the argument I had witnessed was really all about.

The lies Brendon had told cut like a knife deep into my heart as I sobbed thinking about how he, who I had loved and trusted, had deceived me mercilessly. How my husband could have so barefacedly cheated on me was beyond my comprehension. I felt so stupid. Although I had suspected he was not being honest all along – I knew something was going on, but the truth was hard to digest. When I finished crying I got blind drunk on "room service" wine and fell into a fitful slumber. I awoke two hour later and scuttled to the bathroom where I caught sight of myself and I loathed what I saw. My beautiful face was marred by the puffiness of overindulgence and streaked make-up but I did not have the inclination to clean up or pull myself together. I stumbled blindly back into bed where I began to weep all over again and eventually drifted off to sleep again.

Next day room service came in the form of Anna, a trusty diamond of a girl who replaced my supply of room service wine with more palatable specially ordered Champagne and at my request, had scuttled off to the nearby shopping centre and purchased me a pair of stylist dark, dark shades, a small suitcase and suitably fashionable clothes and arranged a booking for me on a flight to a secret island location. She organised a taxi to take me to the airport and had also kept her lips firmly sealed.

I hid out on the island of Grand Cayman, staying at a member of Anna's family's guesthouse for just over a week, where I cried to my heart's content, became acquainted with the local bad men who supplied me with exotic cigarettes that almost blew my head off, and got drunk on locally produced over-proof rum every day. I finally pulled myself together good, good before making my whereabouts know to certain acquaintances that I knew would quickly divulge it to Brendon and to the Press who had all come looking for me the following day.

Brendon was a dab hand at apologising. He bought me flowers, fell upon his knees, cursed Hilary, blaming her for leading him astray, bought gifts, made promises and stated that he had asked her to have an abortion, cursed her some more, bought me a huge yellow diamond ring, cursed Hilary again and assured me that it had all been a big mistake that would never be repeated. Then after he had cursed Hilary for the tenth time, over five days of insistent grovelling, I finally gave in, having decided that I would never give

Hilary Watling the benefit of knowing that she had broken up my marriage –
not after the way that the little snake had insulted me. I had to show that little
scruff that she was really nothing to my husband, that she had gotten way too
big for her boots and that when it came down to the wire, I was the one that
called the tune that my husband danced to. But in spite of the circumstances, I knew abortion was wrong and encouraged Brendon to desist from that
action and to stand up to his responsibility to the child. But it transpired that
Hilary did not want the child without Brendon in any case.

What had also influenced my decision to give Brendon a second chance
was the fact that after a long and hard pondering it dawned upon me that
apart from anything else, I had done really well for myself because of his guidance. His management of my career had made me rich and famous beyond
my wildest dreams. I was riding high in the charts with my latest single,
"Treasure". And I still needed Brendon's help and support, for I knew that in
spite of everything, my husband was my most loyal fan.

So the marriage survived that first indiscretion, but after that first time
Brendon was to repeatedly breach his marriage vows with a series of beautiful
women, each resembling the other and me. But he became a lot more careful,
and although I suspected him many a time and there were whiffs of scandal averred to by the media, neither I nor the Press ever caught Brendon red
handed again.

That was until my husband began to play around with Marion Downs
– for then our marriage bore the brunt of his insatiable infatuation with this
new other woman and following a series of quarrels our foundation gradually
crumbled. I had been willing to keep on fighting, for when I had taken my
vows I had meant them to be for life, but Brendon had given up on "us". This
indiscretion was more than a mere fling and consequently, six years after we
got married he asked me for a divorce stating that he had fallen hopelessly
in love with Marion and wanted to be set free so that he could make her his
wife. I really didn't see why he wanted to substitute me for someone who was
almost my double but only he knew the answer to that question.

For three whole months I was inconsolable and went into seclusion on
my favourite island. My Personal Assistant, Anna, whom I had pilfered from
a hotel in suburbia had made all the arrangements and so I would not have to
be alone, she had also accompanied me, albeit that I wished to be left alone
most of the time to wallow in the pit of unrequited love and self-pity. Anna
was a wonderful confidante whom I could trust with my deepest secrets and
she was there when I needed to talk.

When I became tired of crying, I dried my tears and instructed Anna to
make arrangements for our return journey immediately. Back home I threw
myself into work and as a result of my hard work, following the divorce I
continued to enjoy success as an artiste. Brendon remained my Manager
but Anna became our go-between, having day-to-day contact with him, an
arrangement which worked very well for many years after our divorce – even

though it became a well-known secret that Brendon and I could not stand each.

Four months after my marriage broke down I met Leon Arcola. Leon was an up and coming rock star with even less talent then me, but with great looks. He was immediately smitten with me, as I was with him. He left his long term girlfriend to move in with me within two weeks of our first encounter. Two months later – less than two weeks after my Decree Nisi was pronounced, we got married. I was on the rebound and it soon became apparent that I had made a huge mistake. I should have realised that Leon was trouble when his ex-girlfriend made absolute no effort to fight for their relationship or to get him back. You see Leon was a sex addict who used his incredibly handsome Hollywood/Nollywood film star looks as a weapon of mass deception to lure women into our matrimonial bed – those same incredible features that he had used to bombard my mind and strike me blind with infatuation. He stood 6 feet and 2 inches tall and looked like a younger, darker, more exotic and handsome Brad Pitt – he had inherited his good looks from his Jamaican Grand Fathers and his Jamaican and Ghanaian Grand Mothers, and he boasted that he had a drop of every dominant race in him, for one of his Jamaican Grandfathers was of mixed African/ European heritage and the other one was part Chinese/India, English and African.

When we got married Leon had promised me the world but all he gave me were three things.

The first was a series of exotic venereal diseases that he had collected from all around the world. Luckily he did not give me the big 'A' though – phewww!

The second thing that Leon gave me was a headache of a divorce when he tried to steal the lion's share of my fortune after just one year and three months of marriage, most of which time he had spent half way across the world or in some woman's, or man's, bed, for I also discovered that Leon did not discriminate between the sexes when it came to physical gratification. And I learned from my neighbours that on the rare occasions that he spent in our matrimonial home, he converted our front door into a revolving one, for no sooner than I would leave for work, other women or men would enter my home. In the last two weeks of our marriage, on two occasions I had discovered Leon in our matrimonial bed – with another woman on the first occasion and with two other women the second time – that was the straw that broke the camel's back. So I did not fight Leon in the divorce settlement nearly as hard as I could have – I just wanted rid of him and his nasty ways for good.

But Leon's effect on my life did not leave entirely when the divorce became final, for the third thing he gave me was a raging cocaine habit that saw me go in and out of rehab time and again in the never ending battle against addiction. Granted I had been acquainted with drugs before I met Leon, but I had not relinquished total control then. It was the binges that he encouraged me to take part in with him during the early part of our relationship that had caused me to lose hold of the reins. I was in such a state that even Brendon gave up on me and informed that he would shortly step down as my Manager.

After Leon left taking his haul of my fortune, I found the strength, with Anna's help, to enter rehab and emerged some weeks later with an almost unblemished soul. I gave up on men and concentrated on my career which I continued to enjoy and threw myself into work. Brendon stayed on as my Manager for a time and helped me back. I channelled my ravaged emotions into writing captivating new songs, and my depleted fortune was soon restored and my fame maintained. I came to appreciate even more the privileges that were afforded to me as Avarel Andersen the singing star.

Following my second divorce, I had many loveless encounters. Then one loveless year later, during a time of deep contemplation, I realised that I needed someone special in my life, to fill at least part of the void within my soul. It was about that time that Brendon finally stepped down as my Manager. As though on cue, Simon Sanderson showed up for a job interview as my Manager the week after I made the decision that I was ready for romance again. I liked Simon on sight, probably because of my weakness for tall well-built men, and Simon possessed an unknown charismatic power that caused a lot of women (including me) to be drawn to him as though magnetically. What I liked the most about him was the fact that he seemed unaware of the effect he had on the female specie and his modesty made me fall deeply in love with him.

Simon was not conventionally handsome but came gift wrapped in a six foot, five solid muscle-bound package. He had a mop of honey brown bouncy curls atop his head with the sides shaven in a Mohican style, and a fixed easy smile that had etched laughter lines at the corners of his kind eyes. His plump cherry red lips and broad nose left no doubt as to his African lineage, for, like my first two husbands, Simon was of mixed heritage (English/Nigerian). Although he was strappingly built with huge hands Simon was a giant with a gentle manner. He reminded me of Denzil Washington with a lighter hue and although not as handsome as Denzil, he carried himself with the same debonair grace as the popular film star.

Unbeknown to Simon, I had singled him out as my next romantic conquest and I usually got what I wanted. It turned out that Simon wanted the same thing and we soon became an item.

Neither Simon nor I had any doubt that we would be together for life as we said our vows just 6 months after our first encounter – I was 28 and Simon was 31. We were ecstatically happy in the first year of marriage. It was as though Simon and I were meant for each other. With a shared vast experience of broken relationships behind us (for he too had been married twice before), we were well poised and committed to making our marriage work.

Chapter 4

So there you have it – now you know what I have been up to since leaving the Angels. Let me tell you some more about my marriage to Simon.

Simon and I have been married for 10 years now. We have had our ups and downs throughout our marriage. A true analysis of our relationship is that we now appreciate different things from our union. Simon enjoys our son Davy – he is his pride and joy – the apple of his eye. Don't get me wrong – I love my son too but I'm so busy pursuing my career that I don't get the chance to spend as much time as I would like to with him. For my part, I appreciate the freedom in my marriage to come and go as I please which allows me to pursue my career unfettered.

Our arrangement has worked very well. I enjoy the companionship when we are together, and the trust that Simon places in me when we are apart. I wouldn't say he is gullible exactly, but he does allow me a pretty free rein. That is how I have gotten the chance to "spice up" my life by entertaining the string of younger male lovers that I have become accustomed to. I keep my playthings a secret from my husband of course – he knows nothing of what I get up to. But although most of my religious conscience has been eroded by Brendon, I do sometimes feel guilty for cheating on Simon and I can just imagine that my parents and Bishop Holder would designate my lifestyle as licentious.

Let's get this straight right, my husband means the world to me and the little indiscretions are mere distractions that keep me amused when we are apart – right. So long as that is clear – I wouldn't want you getting the wrong idea. My marriage comes first, and if my indiscretions ever threaten it, I deal with them straight away, like I did with Max who had wanted more from me than I could give and wouldn't take "no" for an answer. I had confided in my PA Anna who had understood perfectly that Max had to go and together we had devised a plot for me to catch him red-handed with another woman. Anna had set it all up very well and though Max had protested his innocence, I had been inconsolable and would not listen. And I had sent Max packing as fast as a lightning bolt. For her diligence I had rewarded Anna well and she had enjoyed the beautiful new car that I had presented to her as a "thank you" for her loyalty.

Simon thinks the world of me, of that I am sure – he loves me so much that he wouldn't believe you anyway if you told him about my infidelity. I know how much he loves me because Simon keeps a diary. I read it once when we had been married for just a few months. But then Simon found out and locked it away from me. I had read the first page and intended to go back and read it some more but could not find it. This was what he wrote.

****

My wife is so beautiful – I am truly a lucky man. I love her so very much – she means everything in the world to me. Perhaps I love her too much. From the first time I saw her I fell deeply in love. It's easy to overlook someone's faults when you love them so much – it's not too hard to forgive their indiscretions either.

****

When I read that I was so touched and I wished that I had the key to his private drawer in the study where he kept his private stuff, so that I could read what else he had written. I checked from time to time to see whether he had left the drawer open, but he never did and he kept the key hidden.

****

I believe my wife loves me too, even though I suspect that she enjoys more than a little variety in our marriage – actually if I am really honest, I know that she plays around sometimes. I am more perceptive than I let on to her and everyone else – I recognised all the signs of infidelity from past experiences with my first wife, even though Avarel tries hard not to be found out. But I pretend that I am blissfully unaware. You see, when I was younger I could only dream that I, Simon Sanderson, would date, yet alone marry such an incandescent beauty and Superstar as Avarel Andersen. I am in awe of my wife and anything that makes her happy makes me happy too, even if it means that she steps outside of our marital bed from time to time. It's hard for her having all those admiring desirable men always at her beck and call. So as long as she shows me due respect as her husband and does not deliberately flaunt her affairs I can and do overlook her weaknesses.

It has occurred to me that I should engage the services of a private investigator to be really sure of what she gets up to – to get it in black and white – but so far I have not given in to that suggestive thought. I'm not certain how I might react if I saw it in black and white, so best to let sleeping dogs lie.

******

My husband is a wonderful man and I realise I am truly blessed to have him in my life. That is why I have tried my utmost to make my marriage work. I have gone out of my way to accommodate him because he is such a sweetheart. He is also my brick – I rely on him completely. He means so much to me that I have even been prepared to undergo pregnancy in order to keep him happy, because having Davy four years ago was not my choice at all, even though I now love my son to bits. Let me tell you how Davy's conception came about.

When we had been married just over two years Simon told me that he wanted to start a family. "Children ….. children…", I had exclaimed – I recall just how shocked I had been at the suggestion. We had never discussed having children before and now that he had mentioned it I had balked "Children, children – I don't want children", I had repeated over and again "At least not now". I did not want to even think of giving up my figure and my freedom – I couldn't do what I do with children – they would get in my way. My happiness was high on the agenda and children were way low on my list.

"Why don't we adopt a child?" I had suggested to Simon.

"Adopt – what do you mean adopt?" Simon had responded uncharacteristically gruffly.

"A-d-o-p-t, that's what I mean", I had spelt it out annoyingly.

"I want you to have my children, Avarel – you, no one else", he could not hide his anger. "You're the woman I love and there is nothing wrong with you so why should we adopt?" he said much calmer than before and looked into my eyes deeply with sincerity as he spoke, and touched my heart.

"I'll think about it", I had promised and I had thought long and hard then tried to forget about it.

A few months after our initial discussion about procreation my husband had broached the subject again and I had tried yet again to dismiss it, more vehemently this time. After that I noticed a visible change in Simon. For one he became a little aloof towards me and then he surprised me by stating that he wished to step down as my Manager. When I asked him why, he had responded that it was because he had been around showbiz people for too many years. I did not want him to resign because he was a good manager. Although not as robust as Brendon had been, he was diligent and meticulous, and more importantly, I knew he had my best interest at heart. After giving the matter some thought though, it dawned on me that it might be a good thing for us not to work together and that it would not be too difficult to find a replacement for Simon since I knew many competent people who could step into the role. Simon wanted to do graphic designing and so I had cut him loose.

****

I just couldn't stand the pain anymore – seeing my wife pretending that she was not carrying on with one or other of the young dancers or back-up singers or musicians or young fans. I just couldn't keep up the front, pretending that I was blissfully unaware. Over the past year, too often I had discovered she was carrying on with one or other young man, usually through whisperings amongst those that worked alongside us, some of whom could guess that I knew what was going on and I had become embarrassed to look them in the eye. I will always love Avarel and had married her for better or worse, but I have decided to step down as her Manager – it's the only way I can maintain my sanity.

******

Children – I thought about them for many months and Simon's desire to have a child was never far from my mind, but I could not change my mind. My figure was too important to my image, and my career – what about my career.

As the months past, we seemed to be growing more apart and in desperation to try and restore the status quo of a loving marriage I involuntarily brought up the subject again a few months after Simon's resignation. I hoped to make him see some sense and agree to a compromise. I hoped I could get him to appreciate my position and once again suggested that we adopt a child. But it was to no avail.

As the months passed the rift between us grew ever wider. Then one day, whilst searching the study for the key to Simon's private drawer, I found pictures of women with humongous bottoms stashed in his briefcase. One picture was of an African tribal woman with a large child strapped onto her back, balancing upon her unbelievably large buttocks. I pondered on the deepest level my husband's new found interest in other women's childbearing buttocks. I decided it was a manifestation of his longing for a child.

In the days following my discovery I surveyed my skinny behind from every angle in every mirror I passed by and each time I became more paranoid, fearing that I was in danger of losing my husband to some other woman with child bearing hips and buttocks who would willingly conceive and bear him a child, so wanting to stay in control I gingerly broached the subject of surrogacy to Simon. And there followed an almighty row. This happened over and over again for many weeks. I had thought I could wear down his resolve eventually but it was becoming obvious that the deadlock could not be broken.

What happened the tenth time I brought up the matter, however, although not entirely unexpected, shocked me to the core – Simon threatened to divorce me and marry someone else who would give him what I was refusing to – just like that. I was stunned into silence and could not utter another word on the subject. I pondered seriously my position – what would I do without my husband – he was my solid ground – I needed him. So that very night I reluctantly gave in to his request, closed my eyes, disabled my mind, and became pregnant at the age of 34.

And that was how my darling son Davy came about – I don't regret it now though. In fact I am glad I made the sacrifice. I was very happy and Simon was happy too. Although we have had our ups and downs, we get by – it all works itself out. But now and then Simon got really testy for no reason that I could understand.

******

My wife is a showbiz mum. After giving birth to our son, Davy, she could not wait to return to work. She worked rigorously to regain her renowned figure, and threw herself back into the old routine as never before. I had hoped that she would take some time out and that together we could spend some quality time with our son – we can certainly afford to do that, we don't need to work another day in our lives if we don't want to – but that looks unlikely now. I'm more like a mother to our son. Well he needs one of us to be there for him and if she won't that only leaves me. In all honesty, the love I have for my wife is diminishing every day and at the same time my love for my son is increasing – Davy is my life.

About a year after Davy was born Simon became really restless though. He wanted us to move out of London, so we bought a beautiful 6-bedroom detached family home down in Surrey and at first he seemed happier. But then he started moaning again about the fact that I continued to spend most of my time at the London House which I had convinced him we should keep. He just could not understand reason, that I needed to be close to my work and we began to argue a lot, especially seriously every time I left home to go back to London for work. This pattern continued for over two years.

Then Simon's grumbling took a more serious turn. "I do not wish for our son to grow up witnessing our frequent fallings out when we are together", he would say, or "I'm seriously considering that this marriage is failing". I must admit I didn't like the arguments either, but it just seemed impossible for us to stop. So I dealt with the situation by staying away even more. I was tired of the arguments when we were together, tired of arguing in front of our son who would burst into tears at our raised voices. But staying away didn't help at all and only made matters worse. It just seemed like a vicious circle.

When Davy turned 3 years old, Simon began to make threatening to leave noises, "I don't know how long I can continue doing this", was one of his favourite lines. "Doing what?" I would ask.

"What do you think?" he would stare deep into my eyes and raise his eyebrows. Of course I knew he was talking about our domestic arrangement. I was becoming more and more fed up of his moaning all the time and then he also begun to grumble that the house was too large. He wanted us to sell up and get a smaller place – a three bedroom house.

"A three bedroom house – we can't move to such a small place", I had countered.

"We can't, but me and Davy can", he had replied.

"What do you mean, you and Davy – what about me?"

"Well since you are never here – never around, I guess you can just live at the London house full-time", he had replied.

"What do you mean exactly – if you didn't keep picking arguments with me all the time….", I had accused, but even as I said the words I knew this was untrue. I knew that our problems stemmed from the fact that I neglected Simon – took him for granted. On many occasions Anna had advised me to take more time out and spend it with my family. I knew I was in the wrong but was not willing to accept it openly to myself or to Simon.

Lowering my tone to a dulcet serenade I said, "I was thinking we should get some counselling – darling I love you so much and really want to spend more time with you and Davy in future", I cooed.

"Well from where I'm standing I don't see any need for counselling – it is clear that the problem is that we come way too far down your list Avarel", Simon had replied looking deep into my eyes. I knew he was right.

But the effort required of me to work out our problems was just too much to ask. I had become spoilt – I had gotten used to living fancy free. I understood that Simon was asking me to make a choice, although he did not say so. But I was not ready to choose between the love for husband and son and the love for my career, etc. I wished Simon wouldn't make such a fuss – why couldn't he just be his usual supportive self – like he had always been in previously years?

Eventually I agreed to Simon's proposition – I understood that with me away so much he was probably lonely sometimes being the only adult in such a large house. So we purchased a smaller 3-bedroomed semi-detached house. I turned over a new page and endeavoured to make more time to spend with my husband and son. But not many months down the line, it was a case of "old habits die hard". My immorality got the better of me and I began to steal time away from my family again – I was a partying addict, and a devout philanderer. During times of deep contemplation I found the truth buried deep within my heart – I wanted to have my cake and eat it too.

Meanwhile Simon continued to mature as a parent and covered my role well. My dear husband worked from home so he could care for our son Davy. I was happy that it provided our son with the stability to develop into a well-adjusted young man. It worked well – I was free to continue pursuing my career. I was privileged to have such flexibility – the listening public have short memories and my short break away from the limelight to give birth meant that I had to work extra hard to get back to where I was before the break.

Things quietened down between us somewhat – the arguments became little niggles and we seemed to be getting over our troubles. My husband made no undue demands on my time and I was happy about that.

My perfidious ways became less treacherous for a time but an addict cannot be cured overnight and the demon lust would rise up inside of me from time to time, demanding to be satisfied. I felt more guilt laden following indiscretions though and at those times I would vow to give it all up and settle down with my family. But after the moment had passed I would move my day for settling down further into the future – I just wasn't ready to give it all up and so we eventually fell back into the old routine – me unofficially living in the London house and Simon in the house in Surrey with our son – me visiting them as often as I could, which amounted to not very often. Simon eventually gave up moaning – all was working well.

But recently I had begun to fret because Simon seemed to care less whether I came home or stayed away. I searched my soul and realised that I missed his whining, his constant demands for me to come home early and stay longer than I had planned. And I have been thinking about taking Anna's advice – maybe I should. What do you think?

What's that you say? You think Anna's advice is very wise. Ummmh – so you agree Anna then. Okay – I will think about it some more.

So there you have it my life so far since leaving God's Three Little Angels.

It's good to reminisce sometimes – looking back can make the way ahead much clearer. Our little journey has caused me to re-evaluate the important things in my life, especially because you fully agree with Anna's advice. Suddenly it has dawned upon me that there is nothing more important than family and I have started to miss Simon and Davy – like crazy. If I am really honest my career has hit a hiatus in any case – the demand for my music and personal appearances has diminished in recent months and there is no better time than now to go and spend some quality time with my family.

Chapter 5

Avarel gripped the steering wheel strongly as she propelled the limited edition MXLX sports car, eating up the miles on the easy Sunday morning drive home to her family. She smiled as she thought of the conversation she would have with her husband later and anticipated with joy the sight of his smiling face. It had been a whole month since she was last home and then for just one day. Suddenly fear wrestled her mind – a fear of relinquishing control – a dread of losing all the fame completely – trepidation that by taking more time out she would be hammering a nail into the coffin of her valued career. Was she truly ready for this? The question niggled at the fringes of her mind.

There was no doubt that she was missing her family more lately – over past weeks she had begun to feel lonely and the string of indiscretions could not seem to alleviate the void. She nodded her head as she affirmed that she needed more – "I need my family and I am going to tell Simon so today", Avarel verbalised her thoughts.

Pulling into the drive she caught sight of Davy's face pressed up against the bay – he smiled widely through the misty glass. Overwhelming joy gushed to the surface of Avarel's psyche and in an instant she was elated that she had taken the decision to come home. She hurried to exit the car, walked to the front door, opened it and reached down to hug her son as he ran to the door to meet her, "Mummy – I'm four", Davy said with a big dimpled smile. His words slapped Avarel across the face as she realised that she had forgotten her only son's birthday two days earlier. "Oh yes, you're a big boy now", she said seeking for redemption.

"Did you like mummy's present?" she lied, as she tousled her son's dark brown kinky curls.

"No – I no get a present from you, mummy – I no get a present from you", he replied wide eyed. Avarel felt a stab of guilt as she looked into the light brown eyes of her young son. It occurred to her that he was growing to look more like her every day and the blade twisted in her heart.

"But mummy did send you a present – a steam engine with bells – did you get it?" she continued to lie cruelly, already knowing what the answer would be. For a beat shame threatened to overwhelm Avarel's conscience but she quickly dismissed the emotion, which was just as quickly replaced by self-loathing. She had not intended to use her acting experience in such a callous way when she had started taking drama classes. It had been her intention to graduate from a singing career into acting – not this impromptu performance. She felt like the dirt on the bottom of her shoes as she removed them and walked into the living room after Davy.

"Noooo – I did no get it", Davy said shaking his head. Suddenly he turned and bounded from the living room and towards the back door. Avarel caught up with him as he struggled to turn the door knob – she ran to help him open it.

"Well it must have gotten lost in the post", the lie continued.

"Look what daddy got me", Davy enthused as he jumped onto a green and blue bicycle with detachable training wheels. As he pedalled down the long garden path chuckling loudly Avarel mused upon how handsome he was becoming.

"Be careful Davy", she guided.

"He's okay", Simon had appeared in the doorway. Avarel went towards him, hugged him and reached up to tousle his bounce curls. Suddenly he broke away from her embrace.

"You okay?" he asked.

"Yeah – I'm good".

There followed an icy silence broken only by Davy's infant chortling. Then they made small talk – it felt awkward to Avarel. A longing to go back to the way they used to be tugged at her heart. Before they had grown apart conversation and the show of affection had come so naturally to them. Determinedly she drew close to Simon again and placed her arms around his waist, whilst swivelling her body around so that she could face him. He avoided her direct gaze and she knew then that something was truly wrong.

"Aunty Lacy got me jammas", Davy said as he pedalled back towards the house. Avarel wondered who Aunty Lacy was but said nothing.

"Let me make you a cup of coffee – you've had a long journey", Simon said walking into the kitchen.

"Come on Davy – let's go inside with daddy".

Simon was on the 'phone a lot, as Avarel prepared lunch. When lunch was ready they ate heartily but the uncomfortable silence persisted.

After lunch Avarel took a long nap and dreamed that they were just like they were in old times. Her reverie was sweet and she was not best pleased to be awoken up from it. Davy shook his mother awake, "Mummy, mummy – its bedtime – come and read me a story – please mummy". Aroused from sleep, Avarel stretched her body. She smiled at her son and in a shot jumped out of bed and tottered along after him to his room. A sense of excitement came over her. She always enjoyed reading stories to Davy – she enjoyed the stories almost as much as he did, recalling them from her childhood. But her glee was soured when Davy mentioned that he was wearing the pyjamas that Aunty Lacy had bought him for his birthday – the same birthday that she had forgotten. Each time he mentioned it, a fresh wave of embarrassment slapped her across the face – she was failing as a mother – had failed, and she vowed within my heart to change for good.

"Who's Aunty Lacy", Avarel asked Simon as they sat in the living room after Davy had fallen asleep. He paused – looked her straight in the eyes and said "We need to talk". There it was again a red flag that waved "something is not right", Avarel felt like screaming.

"Okay", she replied as he went to put the kettle on.

Having placed Avarel's cuppa in front of her and set his own cup down on the coffee table, Simon took a deep breath and turned to look her in the eyes again.

"Avarel – you should know that I've met someone else – her name is Lacy", he said.

"Whaaa… aat", Avarel stuttered. Then she found her tongue. "I want to say something too Simon, I've come home for good because I want us to be a true family again – I'm ready to take time out", she paused and Simon spoke again.

"It's too late Avarel", he said simply.

"What do you mean it's too late – we're married".

"I've fallen in love with her – it's too late", Simon said sombrely.

"We're married for better or worse – for good – there's no going back now, Simon – you love me – you always said you would love me for life", Avarel gushed as realisation that she may be about to lose the best thing that had ever happened to her nearly knocked her for six.

"We have to make it work to have that little girl you always wanted – we'll spend quality time together", she continued. "We can fix this", she stood up to pace around the large living room, but as she looked at Simon's face, she feared that he was not willing to try.

"Sorry Avarel, I….I,,,,, let's talk – please try and understand".

Then Simon talked – he told Avarel everything that was on his mind. And as he spoke she recalled that in addition to his modesty, it had also been his honesty that had made her fall so deeply in love with him, that caused her to love him still – so very much.

Simon informed that he had met Lacy Daniels soon after they moved into the big house. She was a single mother whose daughter attended Davy's nursery and was now in his class at school. For a year and a half they had simply been acquaintances, but very recently, with Avarel gone so often and for so long he had become lonely and she, having been a single parent for over three years, was lonely too. They had found comfort in each other's company at first just as friends. But over recent months they had fallen deeply, irreversibly in love.

Simon did not apologise to Avarel – quite unreasonably she expected him to. He did not seek to apportion blame either. She knew deep down that it was her own fault – but she would not accept it. She was not willing to give up on her marriage so easily and resolved within her heart to put up the biggest fight.

Walking into the kitchen, Avarel immediately telephoned Anna and asked her to cancel all her commitments for the next two months – she had intended to spend two weeks with her family but now what had seemed to be an impossible length of time away from work, seemed grossly inadequately short in which to sort out her marriage problems.

Avarel vowed within her heart to do all that she could to save her marriage – it would be worthwhile to miss out on a few shows, TV appearances, or interviews if she could save it. She was ready to give her all, to sacrifice to win the battle that she was facing. She sat down at the kitchen table – stunned. She could hear Simon skulking around from the living room to the bathroom where she knew he would be deep in thought too and she got up to and pace from one end of the kitchen to the other but found no relief. So, grabbing her car keys, she headed out the front door – she needed to be alone to think things through.

Chapter 6

Having driven blindly for many miles, it suddenly dawned on Avarel that she didn't know where she was. She drove on and each turning looked familiar – yet alien. But she could care less, she wanted to get lost – trying to find her way would give her something other than the agonising pain of a breaking heart to occupy her mind. There was enough petrol in the tank to take her a hundred miles and back again.

Suddenly she had the urge to find a secluded spot where she could stop, park up and ponder her dilemma. Nowhere seemed ideal so she drove on and on until she approached a dual carriageway and joined it. The road was quiet and Avarel drove at a snail's pace as she mused upon the recent shocking revelation. "But why didn't I see this coming", she said loudly.

"See – that's the problem with Simon – he is far too secretive – if he had said something, we could have avoided this", she said with yet more fervour.

"Who are you kidding, Avarel?" she soliloquised then laughed mirthlessly.

"If you were around looking after your family instead of playing Miss Diva, Prima Dona and HARLOT (Avarel shouted the last word), this would not be happening".

Realisation refused to give her mind a break – it hammered home the fact – she was losing her best friend and confidante, her soul mate, her dear faithful husband, and Avarel burst into floods of tears. As the flow blinded her eyes she struggled to leave the carriageway at the next exit and drove on until she came to a large supermarket which was closed. She parked in the darkest corner, switched off the car lights and began to sob in earnest. She cried until her tear ducts were empty. The pitch blackness of the night began to yield shadows as she stared blankly ahead and her eyes became accustomed to the blackness. Fear was a welcomed friend then Avarel felt numb for a time.

Suddenly a wave of emotion slapped her back to consciousness and it dawned fully upon her just how big a fool she had been. This happened over and over again until Avarel felt she might be losing her mind. She fought to return her thinking to normality and began to strategize how to win back her husband's heart. It occurred to her that the first thing to do was to stop running away, so setting the car into motion she manoeuvred in the direction that she had come – it was after midnight now. It was late and high time for her to start being the mother that her son needed and the wife that her husband deserved and she would start by trying to seduce Simon back tonight and then she had to get some sleep if possible, for she needed to get up early in the morning to take her son to school like any good mother should.

When Avarel arrived home, Simon was frantic. He was peering through the curtains as she pulled up in the front driveway and hurried to open the front door to let her in. "Where have you been Avarel – I was worried silly you might do something stupid", he shout-whispered not wishing to alert the quiet neighbourhood. "Why didn't you tell me you were going out?" Then Simon said nothing else – he turned and walked into the kitchen where Avarel could hear him brewing a fresh cuppa. She knew he would be making one for her too – Simon's mum had taught him that all problems could be solved over a cup of tea.

At 2 am Simon retired to the guest room. Avarel followed him and crawled into bed beside her husband. Wrapping her lithe body around his she tried to seduce him but he pushed her gently away uncompromisingly.

"Avarel – no please – I'm sorry, I just can't do this", Simon said, and then he got up, left the room and went to sleep on the couch in the lounge.

"Mummy, why are you taking me to school this morning?" Where's Dad?" Davy questioned. Avarel said nothing but smiled at her inquisitive son. He continued unashamedly. "Will you be taking me to school tomorrow as well mummy?" "Mum, why haven't you taked me to school before", Davy continued to chatter. "Taken Davy – not taked – you say why haven't you taken me to school before?" Avarel corrected, thinking of how she could get Davy's mind off the subject. "Mum why haven't you taken me to school before", Davy repeated and looked at her questioningly.

"Because mummy was very busy, Davy", Avarel replied and smiled uncomfortably.

"Oh – are you still very busy, mum?" Davy's boyish curiosity was beginning to annoy but Avarel quickly pushed peevishness aside as she recalled she was endeavouring to bury her past selfishness.

"Not so busy".

"Oh – that's good – that means Dad won't be lonely anymore when I go to sleep", her son's words cut a swathe through Avarel's breaking heart and guilt copulated with pain and gave birth to deep remorse. Avarel felt overwhelmed and tears pricked the back of her eyes again. "Okay Davy – we're nearly there now", she said – a tremor was evident in her voice. She was relieved that the school gates loomed at the end of the road. Although the school was only a 5-minute walk away from home, because it was on a steep incline, Avarel was out of breath. "Ooh, I didn't realise I was so unfit", she puffed as Davy ran ahead. Something had caught his attention – Avarel soon realised what. A gorgeous little girl began to wave and smile at Davy as he quickened his step towards her. Her hair was in two large plaits adorned with various hair ornaments and her face was fresh and storybook pretty. It occurred to Avarel that the little girl would make the perfect sister for Davy – they looked so alike.

Avarel wondered whether Simon was in fact Emma's father. She quickly calculated that if Simon was to be believed, he had not met Lacy until three years ago so the dates did not add up. "There's Emma and Aunty Lacy", Davy ran ahead and Avarel puffed along behind him. Her eyes rested upon the pretty but grossly overweight woman who was vying for my husband's affection. Even though she was pretty, she looked ordinary and Avarel was tempted to think that she could never compete with her, but then she did a reality check – although she was infinitely more beautiful, Lacy was the one holding the trophy – she had stolen her husband. Knowing Simon as she did, Avarel doubted whether she was able to compete with Lacy now. Simon was a one woman man through and through and Avarel knew that his heart was now firmly within the palms of Lacy's hands. And she had placed it there herself on a plate.

"I just hope it's not too late" Avarel mumbled.

"What mum?" Davy

"Oh nothing Davy".

"Hi Emma" Davy gushed as he sprinted to his playmate.

"Davy we're nearly late – let's run – Mrs Morgan will be angry with us for being late", Emma said in the most adorable 4-year old voice Avarel had ever heard.

Lacy looked at her and smiled timidly but Avarel was in no mood to be friendly – she replied by casting daggers at Lacy.

"Be careful – don't run too fast or you may fall down and injure your-selves", Lacy cautioned as she ignored the hostility of her rival and walked quickly to catch up with the youngsters.

Avarel walked quickly to try and keep up with Lacy but could not. She found herself glaring at her rival's large behind which bounced rhythmically as she walked. Jealousy festered within her heart as she recalled the photos of large-bottomed women that she had discovered in Simon's briefcase so many years before – not only did Lacy's rear resemble theirs, but she had stolen her husband too and to make matters even worse, she was also fitter than she was in spite of her obesity.

Anna ran back and kissed her mother goodbye, "Bye mum – see you later then", she said adorably. Davy did not offer a kiss so Avarel hurried towards him and seized one. "See you later, son", she said. "See you … ma..a..mum", he replied. Was it Avarel's imagination or did her son appear uncomfortable to address her as mum in Lacy's presence?

Walking slowly back into the playground Avarel looked back over her shoulder to where Lacy was, to see that her rival was walking at a deliberate snail's pace. But she wasn't about to let her off the hook. She had delivered her son to school with an agenda and now it was time to table it – so she walked back towards Lacy. "Hi Lacy – it's so good to be able to drop my son off at school – you know my work is so demanding that I have not been able to spend quality time with my son or my husband", Avarel looked straight into Lacy's eyes as she spoke. "But all that is going to change now – I fully intend to give my husband and son my undivided attention from now on – I've been working far too hard and you know what men are like – if their wives are away for too long they soon begin to sniff around like dogs at anything that is available", she said bitterly and added, "It would be a mistake for any *****
to mess around with my husband though and if they ever did they should definitely watch their eyes – I don't keep my nails one inch long for nothing",

Avarel presented her highly glossed talons close to Lacy's face for emphasis.

As she ended her message she saw Lacy's eyes overfill with tears and felt a sudden but fleeting pang of guilt for her cruel words and harshness. Lacy was obviously a very decent, homely young woman who just happened to have fallen in love with the wrong husband.

A vengeful smile crossed Avarel lips as she walked back to the house. She felt happy that Lacy seemed like a pushover – she did not anticipate that she would put up much of a fight. And as she shooed away a passing thought that she would not be in this predicament had she been taking care of her family as she should have been, Avarel sought to justify her position with the words, "Simon and I are married for better or for worse".

Simon was waiting at the kitchen table with a freshly made cup of tea when Avarel returned from Davy's school. "Avarel, we need to talk", he said without hesitation. "You had words with Lacy, didn't you – what did you say to her?" he said angrily.

"What do you mean – I merely told her that I would be around more often from now on".

"Look Avarel – I don't want any trouble from you – I told you that I love Lacy and I won't stand by and watch you hurt her – we can do this civilly or it can turn nasty but Avarel – it's over between us – just understand that – there's no going back".

Avarel was rendered speechless. The knife wound deepened and an overwhelming desire to embrace her husband bombarded her mind.

"Please sweetheart – Simon, please – let's try and work this out – save our marriage", she blubbered.

"No Avarel, no – it's over – I'm tired of you taking me for a fool", Simon said as though he had taken on board new fuel. "Do you think I wasn't aware of all your philandering ways – do you Avarel?" He was furious now. "All the nights I slept alone while you were warming other men's beds – younger better looking men than me", he thundered.

"I have never been unfaithful to you Simon", Avarel lied. "Never – why on earth would you think that of me – when …. when …. all I was doing was working – how could you think that of me?" for a beat she believed the lie. Then her mind strayed briefly – it was definitely the right time for her to explore new avenues as an actress – her performances were not at all bad.

"Do me a favour – I am not your fool anymore, Avarel – I played the idiot for too long because I loved you so very much". "But you despised my love and now I have been blessed with someone who truly loves me for who I am – and you know what Avarel, I don't care about this mess of a marriage anymore – I can't go back now", Simon sneered. "So please leave Lacy alone – you don't need me but she does – none of this is her fault", Simon said alluding to the fact that it was Avarel's fault.

"Please Simon – I'm sorry for any hurt I may have caused you", Avarel was weeping again.

"Your tears don't move me Avarel – my mind is made up now".

"What about Davy – let's think about Davy", Avarel clutched at straws.

"Davy is the reason why I put up with your rubbish for so long, Avarel, but no more – Davy stays with me – I'm all he knows". "He will be happiest with me". "You can have access whenever you like because in spite of yourself I believe you truly love Davy." "What are you crying for – now you can have what you have always wanted – all the freedom you have ever craved – you can sleep with whosoever you please now – shove whatever you like up your nose without worrying that I might find out", Avarel was surprised – she was unaware that Simon knew of her occasional drug taking.

"It won't be hard for you to find husband number 4 – you've probably got him all bagged up and labelled already" Simon said rancorously, and then he left the kitchen slamming the door deafeningly behind him. Avarel had never known her husband to be so decisive in all their years together – and in that instant she knew there was no use fighting – she had lost him for good.

For the first time Avarel faced up to the fact that her conduct during her marriage had been totally unacceptable. And she regretted her actions as it was now evident just how much pain she had caused Simon with her philandering ways and she began to weep in earnest. "I'm so so sorry, Simon".

As Avarel wept she heard the front door shut and Simon's car engine ignite. By the time she reached the bay window the red Mercedes was out of sight.

That day Avarel used up all the coke that she had brought home with her before crawling into bed with a bottle of vodka for company. Although she hated spirits, there was no wine or Champagne in the house and she needed to deaden the pain. After getting drunk as well as high she fell into a fitful slumber. When she awoke many hours later, she struggled to unscramble her thoughts and then began to ruminate upon the path of her life as a third divorce stared her square in the face. She pondered upon the causes and effects, musing that although she had realised her wildest dreams in having become vastly rich, famous and successful doing something that she loved, she had lost sight of what was truly important in life. And with all the fame and wealth that she had amassed, she lacked personal peace and true joy.

After some time Avarel reached for the bottle again. With each swig she hated the taste upon her tongue and throat more and the stench of the innocuous looking yet powerful liquid made her nauseous, but she craved for yet more of it. She punished herself by guzzling down the hated brew, contemplating the years past between mouthfuls. She embraced regret tightly as it dawned upon her just how stupid she had been, firstly in losing her faith, then by leaving her true friends and family behind and finally in putting her career before a family that truly loved her – a family that she had now almost certainly lost to someone who had taken the time to care.

Suddenly tossing the bottle aside, Avarel clambered out of bed and stumbled towards the full length mirror where she stared at her reflection and detested the egocentric fool that stared back at her. But how could she have changed so much from the untainted young girl that Brendon had discovered at the age of 18? Even in her drunken state her mind had a ready answer – she had gotten her priorities wrong – had headed down the slippery slope that had led to a Godless life.

Crawling back towards the bed but not quite making it, Avarel was aware of a pain that engulfed her head before she escaped into a dead slumber sprawled upon the carpet and there she lay for countless hours.

Avarel awoke in bed the next morning – she guessed it was about 5 am as the July sun had not yet risen. "My beloved must have tucked me into bed", she mumbled, still under the influence of sleep and alcohol. She wrapped her arms about herself as she imagined Simon's large loving arms around her, lifting her up. She smiled stupidly as the warmth of love surged throughout her mind and body. Then suddenly, like a bullet fired from a sniper's gun, reality hit her, "Ooh – my beloved is no longer mine", Avarel whined and as the sense of loss overwhelmed her once again, she began to weep with renewed verve. A clanging headache added to her total misery as she prayed for sleep to come again. But it did not.

After an hour she stumbled down to the kitchen where she brewed strong black coffee and drank several cups of the sobering brew. Not wishing for Davy to see her in that state she escaped back into the bedroom before he awoke. From there she listened to her "soon to be lost" family pottering about from room to room. Simon made breakfast and brought her a plate. "Avarel, please try and eat something – you don't want to make yourself ill", her "soon to be lost" husband said sensibly. Avarel sat up and looked at him pitifully, hoping to tug at the strings of his heart but he simply turned and left the room with the passing admonition, "Eat up".

As she picked at the sumptuous breakfast Avarel heard the front door shut. She continued to pick at the beautifully prepared first meal of the day and hoped that Simon would return after dropping Davy off at school so that she could beg him once again to give their marriage another chance, but he did not come back. Avarel guessed he must have gone to work from Lacy's home.

Chapter 7

Tuesday followed the same pattern of the previous day, as Avarel sought to drown her sorrows and searched her soul. Wednesday was a repeat of Tuesday and Thursday of Wednesday. Then finally, on Friday it dawned on her that now that her world was beginning to unravel out of my control she needed to pray – but sadly she realised that she had forgotten how to.

"How could I have drifted so far away from God – so distant now that I have forgotten how to talk to Him?" "How could I have wilfully neglected to observe God's fundamental commandments – how could I have lived a life filled with such debaucheries?" "How could I have forgotten what Sundays are for?" "How could I have forgotten who I am – a church girl brought up to honour God and embrace His ways". "How could I have allowed myself to drift so far away from God to have become a completely new creature – one reborn into sin after having been born again?" "How could I?" Avarel asked herself, before beginning to sob bitterly all over again. Then through her sobs she heard the still small voice she had known so long ago, ***"come home my child"***.

Immediately encouraged that God had not forsaken her, Avarel dried her eyes and spoke from her heart, "Help me God, please", she cried out repeating the same four words over and again, and after many minutes it occurred to her how to find her way home. She would go just as she was and seek for God's compassion.

That afternoon Avarel did not drink anymore but remained sober. She had a long hot bath, applied some make up and prayed a series of simple prayers before putting the depth of her thoughts to God in the verse of a song that arose effortlessly from her spirit. And as she sang she began to weep silently – tears of hope.

> "I've walked through far desert places unknown.
> Squandering wealth I'd not sown
> Just like the Prodigal son – so unworthy of your grace and love, I am,
> Yet I see you standing in the distance – bidding me to come
> To return into your loving arms' embrace
> To the place of holiness where I was safe
> Just like the Prodigal son
> I'm your Prodigal daughter
> Just like the Prodigal son
> I'm your Prodigal daughter."

Avarel sang the verse over and over again, searching her spirit for the chorus, the bridge, the hook, the next level, but try as she may she received no inspiration. She could not hear anything else – just the same verse – so she sang it over and over again and felt encouraged and motivated to begin planning her return home to the place where she had known God and his love – Born Again Church of God.

Chapter 1

Dwight Henry was a sweet-talking fool, an impresario of the spoken lie (or a jinal (conman) as Sister Minns used to call him). But he was evidently not such a fool since he had managed to influence me, with my five A* A-Levels and fixed reservation in one of the country's most prestigious universities, to take my life out of the hands of God, out of the hands of my parents, into my own hands which I had then placed firmly into his, willing for him to change its entire course from that of a promising young professional into that of a potential no-hoper. He had somehow also managed to talk me, (who was then the most devout of Christians), into leaving behind my conviction, abandoning my moral standards and setting up home with him without even the mention of a ring of any calibre.

I became besotted with Dwight Henry the first moment that we met, not that he was an Adonis or anything – I just loved his style – his swagger. His 6' 4" stature was impressive, complimented by his silky smooth coconut cream enhanced waist-length dreadlocks. His gold tooth to the front of his mouth and his sly crooked smile added to his street credibility. And his cheeky personality completed the whole package – to say he impressed me was an understatement. As an only child who had had a privileged and sheltered upbringing I found Dwight very exciting indeed. I was able to overlook his acne scarred skin which rendered his caramel hue unattractive. And I was blinded to fact that his eyes were squinty and his nostrils far too flared for his long face, for Dwight had been over-blessed with the gift of the gab and sweet talk flowed like honey from his thick, chapped and uneven lips. Beauty is in the eye of the beholder so they say and I must truly have been blinded by love to have exchanged my hopes of a bright future for his lies and single parenthood. Now each night after having tucked my children into bed, I lay awake reminiscing upon the path my life has taken.

When Dwight had first approached me at church, I was a young and impressionable 17-year old. My oval face comprised a straight unobtrusive nose, full eyes and cherry ripe smooth lips which I customarily enhanced with lip gloss. My cheekbones not well defined enough to set me apart as a classic beauty but some would say that my full brow, reminiscent of a black Barbie doll's enhanced my features so as to place me in the above average category in the looks department. My appearance was complemented by a fresh rich cinnamon complexion. I was a little on the plump side, (which turned out not to be puppy fat because as the years rolled by I maintained the same curves) but

Dwight told me he liked what he saw – he said I had the face and voice of an angel. He introduced himself as a reggae music producer/promoter and promised that he would produce my first hit album and make me rich and famous. I remember how excited that had all sounded to me – I was actually going to follow in the footsteps of my ex band mate Avarel who was at that time riding high in the charts with a big number 1 single.

The notions with which Dwight filled my head were vivid and so well implanted, of world class recordings, live vibrant stage shows, beautiful clothes, jewellery and makeup, recognition and fame, accolade, wealth and riches beyond measure. And I had fallen hook, line and sinker for his lies.

But within two years of our first meeting I began to have my doubts and as time passed I had a gradual and rude awakening, eventually having to face up to the fact that all Dwight's promises were at best fanciful and at worse, cruel and callous deception. And if only I had not refused to take off those rose coloured glasses, I might have been spared my further downfall.

At first I truly believed that Dwight would deliver on his promises – he did take me to the studio like he said he would, but the studio turned out to be an ill equipped basement of a friend and all that was achieved was a badly produced demo of three songs with badly arranged and performed musical accompaniment. But he had convinced me that the demo was not really that important – it was merely my stepping stone to fame and wealth beyond measure. Dwight had been completely convincing when he told me that with the demo he would impress his "connections", that upon hearing my dulcet tones they would without hesitation open doors to the next level, which he assured me would include well kitted out and luxurious recording studios where well-known music stars created their masterpieces.

On the strength of Dwight's promises I had postponed my university studies for a year, during which time I expected, with Dwight's guidance and direction that I would have achieved fame and fortune as a singer. Dwight and I were in love and an item and I believed my man with all my heart that he would not disappoint me, even when he had started to behave rather inconsistently by urging me to become pregnant with our first child (a boy whom he named Gregory).

Dwight said getting pregnant was the right thing to do although my intelligence had dictated to me otherwise, since I was still only 18 at the time and giving birth could surely only hamper my goal of becoming a worldwide soul singer or reggae superstar. But my man had a way of getting me to relinquish power, leaving him to make all decisions, even those concerning my own body, and before I knew it I had one baby and another on the way.

So fame and fortune was put on the back burner, as were my university studies. My parents were outraged and tried to talk some sense into me. They told me to leave Dwight and come back home. They offered to take care of the babies while I resumed my studies. But I did not listen – I only had ears for Dwight. Before long I behaved as though I no longer had a mind of my own.

I called my second baby – a girl – Dwightene after her father. She was born on the day after I received the letter confirming that my university place had been forfeited.

The following year there followed a third baby a boy called Dennis. It was about that time that I became so busy with caring for my growing family that I stopped dreaming altogether. Dwight began to spend less time at home too, blaming work commitments, while at the same time he brought home little money from his earnings as a producer/session musician. Although he did not smoke around the house, I became aware that the stench that emanated from his clothes was not recognisable as cigarette smoke, but was no doubt narcotic based. This odour grew stronger as the months past and coincided with Dwight's degenerative behaviour, for my man became virtually incoherent and unsteady on his feet most times.

My parents still urged me to return to my studies, but by that time my pride would not allow me to even consider their generous offer to return to live home where they could help me care for the children while resuming studying at evening classes. You see, I was not ready to admit to them that I was wrong.

As I turned 24, Dwight was hardly ever home. I got on with life the best I could, and by now had no choice but to swallow my huge lump of pride and accept the financial assistance that my parents offered, without which we could not have survived.

Depression was knocking at the door of my soul but was kept at bay by my preoccupation with the children. I did not have time to wallow in self-pity. I was somewhat relieved when my then youngest son, Dennis, started school. However, my jubilation did not last for long because in that very week I discovered that I was pregnant again with my fourth child.

When Dwight found out about the pregnancy he began to argue with me constantly. Even when he was not at home he would telephone to deride me upon my propensity toward maternity. He argued that it had not been his decision to have a fourth child; that I was "trying to trap him"; that it was my body and I should have made sure that I used contraception. However, Dwight and I had never practised safe sex and contraception was an alien concept to us both – it was a miracle in fact that I had not gotten pregnant more than once in four years which was probably due to the fact that Dwight and I were not often intimate as he would flit in and out of my life as he pleased, often leaving for months on end and simply resurfacing out of the blue when it suited him.

During my third month of pregnancy with our fourth child, Dwight decided it was time for him to pack up and leave us all behind without the little support he had hitherto provided. And so I was left to single-handedly rear my brood. After he left I contemplated the chain of events that finally led to his departure: we had had a huge argument when Dwight brought up the question of abortion for the umpteenth time but my stance had been unflinching, I would not kill another of my unborn children. Not after the depression that had almost swallowed my mind when Dwight had convinced me to abort my second girl child two years previously.

So I gave birth to my fourth child, another baby boy whom I called John, and pressed on with life as a single parent. I lived each day as though I had encountered an irreversible shock, getting on with life as though I were a semi-conscious zombie on auto pilot. I stopped dreaming and became more melancholic – I did not expect anything good to happen for me and nothing other than the mundane ever did.

Chapter 2

Being the best mother became my sole purpose in life. Each day my children received my undivided attention – they were well cared for and people often commented that I was a very good mother. But at nights I cried – I missed my man so very much, although in truth in the last two years of the relationship he had hardly been there. When John turned six months old realisation fully dawned on me that apart from our occasional sexual relations, we had become virtual strangers and had very little in common, so missing Dwight was truly a fallacy – all in my head really. And for the first time I admitted the truth to myself – he had never really been there.

A true analysis of the situation was that since the birth of Dwightene, Dwight had become consumed with "business", which had intensified after our third baby, Dennis, came along. This was a "business" that apparently yielded little or no financial fruit – he had never efficiently supported us. I also had good reason to suspect that he was busily preoccupied with other women – some had even dared to turn up on our doorstep to ask to see him. And so I dried my tears realising that Dwight really wasn't worth the heartache.

Initially I resolved to get Dwight to contribute financially towards his children's upbringing. But all my efforts yielded little. He was in fact happy to contribute what he could afford towards the rearing of his offspring, but since he did not work officially, such contribution amounted to little more than pocket money. It angered me that he drove around in a very flashy car and wore the most expensive clothes and jewellery, yet pleaded near poverty, but I could produce no documentary proof that he was not destitute. Whenever I confronted him about contributing more towards his children's upbringing, Dwight had the nerve to inform me that his girlfriends were the source of his good living – and believe me when I tell you that that statement eroded most of the little respect that I had left for the man.

It was obvious that my parents were gravely disappointed with me and the path I had chosen to take, although they tried not to show it, and I thank God that they did not turn their backs on me. Without their help I don't know what I would have done. They helped me out with money, although having had me during their forties they were both pensioners by the time I had John and their finances were limited too. Mum and dad even rented out a room at their home to bring in extra cash so that they could help me out.

It was hard for me not to harbour bitterness towards Dwight, a man who had taken my promising future and dashed it to the wall, who had kept me constantly pregnant in my early youthful years only to abandon me as unwanted goods at what should have been the height of my prime youthful years. By my twenty-fifth birthday, I felt constantly exhausted, I looked haggard if not bedraggled and many commented that I was growing to resemble my Aunty

Belle (God rest her soul). I looked into the mirror and saw that they were right, not only had my features changed, but my skin which had once been a beautiful flawless cinnamon had been marred by the ravages and stresses of life, and was now more reminiscent of slightly crumpled mid-brown autumn leafs.

Men no longer paid any attention to me, although that did not trouble me much for the last thing on my mind was finding a substitute for Dwight Henry. My thoughts were preoccupied with getting through each day and providing enough food, support, care and attention to my brood. Although I loved each of my children, there were times that I had to struggle not to resent them due to the fact that I could not pursue my dream of becoming a famous singer or a doctor, the latter of which, with my straight A* academic record, my school headmaster had assured me was well within my capability. But at times I would thank God for blessing me with my gang of four (my term of endearment for them). All I was going through seemed worthwhile just to see their toothless smiles.

But the burden of being a single-parent is a heavy one indeed and I was often overwhelmed by the sheer weight of responsibility. I thank my parents' for their unflinching support – they took the children off of my hands two afternoons/evenings a week and I was able to work part time as a receptionist at a doctor's surgery which provided me with some sense of independence if not much financial assistance.

When I was 29, my youngest son John turned four and started school. I felt like a caged bird that had been released. I got a full time job as an Assistant Manager in a firm near home. This worked well – I dropped the children off at school early and mum and dad collected them after school and looked after them until I finished work. I earned a good salary and could provide adequately for their needs. And for five years we were able to live relatively well. Then four things happened to set me back to square one.

The first misfortune was that Dwight Henry came begging me for forgiveness and professing undying love.

The second was that I made the mistake of taking him back. I must have been so desperately lonely and frustrated to have allowed that man back into my life. And he must have thought me a right idiot when I made just one stipulation – that we got married immediately. I wanted to be married – I craved validation for myself and the children. Looking back now I realise just how stupid that was but I told myself that I was doing it for the children because I wanted them to have their father around all the time. That would have made sense if I was not previously aware that Dwight was accustomed to going AWOL more often than not. I also conveniently forgot about his propensity to lie, cheat and be generally unaccountable and irresponsible. My mind was blinded to reality and I truly believed that being married would put everything right.

At first Dwight looked to have changed and appeared to be living up to his promises – he played his role as a father very well, and even though he was not really contributing financially, my salary was enough to support us all. The only thing was that Dwight never honoured his promise of marrying me and we fell back into the destructive pattern of co-habitation which I had wished to avoid. I reminded him often about the promised nuptials, but he would expertly dodge the subject or turn a deaf ear to me.

I even got my parents involved, nudging my father to broach the subject over and again but Dwight stiffened his neck the more, refusing to budge. And soon the rose coloured glasses that I had put back on started to become misty and cracked through and through.

The third misfortune that took place was that after seven months of living together again, at thirty-four years old, I found myself pregnant yet again. I could say that it was all Dwight's fault – he was the one that kept on insisting that we have unprotected sex but it's my body and with the experience of his past abandonment, I should have taken control – what a complete fool I felt. I fretted and hid the pregnancy from Dwight, whom I was certain would want it terminated. At the same time I intensified my efforts to get him to walk me down the aisle – any aisle. I was even willing to forego my treasured dream of a white wedding in church for a quiet registry office do, but all my efforts were met with more empty promises. Before my pregnancy started to show I even began to arrange the nuptials by myself only to find that my efforts were stymied due to the fact that Dwight's involvement was required.

When I found out I was carrying twins, I worried even more, became gaunt and began to look unwell. I didn't want Dwight to leave us again because his presence was having a great effect upon the children who seemed to be developing more positive mental attitudes about themselves. But in my fifth month of pregnancy, Dwight noticed my swelling belly and confronted me, and I was forced to admit that I was expecting not one but two further babies. Dwight did not argue with me for fear that "… the children might hear", he stated in the letter he wrote to me instead. In his letter he wrote "I am disappointed in you for your act of dishonesty in keeping from me the fact that you are pregnant….." He went on to say that he could no longer trust me and added, for good measure, that he could never have married me in any case because I was not marriage material and had no prospects. And he left before I returned from work the day following my admission that I was pregnant.

The fourth misfortune happened three and a half months later when I was in the eighth month of pregnancy with my twins – mother became gravely ill and was rushed into hospital with a stroke. I was on maternity leave by then and spent most of my time at the hospital.

Two weeks after mother's admission, I too was rushed into the maternity ward at the same hospital where I gave birth to the twins – a boy and a girl. I called them Kira and Kiran and divided my time between the new-borns in the maternity ward and mother in intensive care. Then two days after the twins were born mother had a second stroke and died.

Chapter 3

Dad fell apart when mum died and I found myself caring for three new-borns, for it was as though he had regressed to babyhood in the first few months of her death. It was a good thing that I was on maternity leave at the time otherwise I could never have coped with the pressure. I did not even have the opportunity to grieve my mother's passing properly – I had to be the strong one. Luckily the older children were well trained and able to take care of themselves and all looked out for John, and helped out with the babies too. But I still found the arrangement physically taxing. So I decided that it would be best for me to give up my Council flat and move back home to live with dad. I asked the older children what they thought of the idea, and the responses I received were surprisingly well reasoned.

John, the ten year old wanted to stay at the flat as all his friends were nearby. Dennis the fourteen year old wanted to move to Grandpa's because it was closer to his school and had a large garden where he could play football. Dwightene and Gregory, fifteen and sixteen years old respectively reasoned together that it made financial sense to give up the flat and move in with Granddad because it was costing a lot of money going to and fro; that the combined bills would be more beneficial to all; that Granddad needed constant care and attention not just at various times of each day; that the four bedroom house was way bigger than the three bedroom flat. Dwightene also cited the fact that the dining room could be used as a fifth bedroom and that there were three toilets counting the en suite to the master bedroom. And Gregory contributed further to the debate by stating that there was also a conservatory and the cavernous lounge was big enough to accommodate a dining table as well and leave ample space to be utilised as a living area; and Dennis observed that the garage which was currently full of old furniture, could also be cleared out and made into living space.

Proving that he was wise beyond his years John gave further food for thought when he asked, "Mum – what if we hate it living at Granddad's house – can we come back home?" The question hung in the air as I directed my mind to fashion an appropriate reply. "There's," was all I could say. Then I conceded, "I'll have to give it further thought, John – good point".

The next day I telephoned the Council to find out whether I could in fact rent out the flat during our absence and was pleased to be informed that I could do so for a period of up to six months and then seek further permission when that time had elapsed, so I wasted no time in contacting a letting agency and within two days they had found four potential tenants. We selected a nice Asian family who had suffered a fire at their own home and needed somewhere to live for some months.

Then we began to pack up for the move to dad's house. It felt good to be going home to the house where I had spent my childhood.

Dad was a shadow of his former self since the death of mum three months before. He wanted to wallow in sadness and self-pity and it was as if he had made a silent vow never to embrace true happiness again in his lifetime. But within a few weeks of us having moved in to live with him, he started coming out of his shell. My concern that he would be annoyed by the children's continuous bickering and fighting seemed unfounded – dad apparently thrived on the mayhem and I was relieved that he began to interact with the children in a positive way. And as the days passed he seemed to grow happier and happier and I could tell that he loved it when the boys looked up to him for manly guidance in place of their absent father. As for Dwight, it seemed he had completely abandoned his children once again.

It touched me how dad began to put the children's needs before his own. I could not understand why I found myself with such a low life as Dwight, because girls are supposed to end up with men like their fathers, but my father was nothing like that deadbeat. He had more integrity in his little finger than Dwight had in his entire body.

After we had been living with dad for a while he began to insist that the children attend Sunday school every Sunday, not occasionally as they had done in the past. Father was strict about that and Gregory began to make noises about being forced to do something he didn't want to – he wanted us to go back home. But dad thought of the perfect solution – he bought Gregory a guitar and enrolled him in the music classes at church and soon my first son became enthusiastic about going to church, not just on Sundays, but also in the midweek services. He learned fast, demonstrated that he had inherited mine and dad's gifting for music and before long he was drafted in as a full time member of the church band.

Dad also expected me to attend church but I resisted, asking him to allow me a little time to recover and adjust after having given birth, mum's death and the upheaval of the move.

"Dad, look how out of shape I am – I want to get into shape – sort my hair and skin out – when I come to church again I want to look my best and at the moment I look my worst", I pleaded time and again. And dad did not force me – instead I overheard him praying for me some nights – he prayed that I would find my way home. He also prayed for me to overcome fear and embarrassment. When I overhead that prayer for the first time, I realised just how much my dad cared for my soul and I knew that he did not insist that I return to church as he had done with the children, because he understood my feeling of shame at the way I had conducted my life since leaving church. I mused that dad did not even know the half of my separation from righteousness. And although I doubted whether God would ever forgive me, I began to pray for myself too, often shedding tears during my prayers.

As the weeks passed, I analysed my true feelings and realised that I was not and would never be ashamed of my children – I considered every one of them a gift from God. But I felt ashamed of myself – when I thought of my upbringing and how far I had deviated from my parents' expectation and the moral standards that they had instilled into me while I was growing up in church – I felt ashamed of me.

When the twins turned six months, I received a letter from my workplace asking me if and when I would be returning to work. They stated that my services were needed urgently due to a new and lucrative contract that they had obtained and they offered me an incentive to return sooner rather than later – a substantial raise in pay. So a family meeting was convened to discuss the subject of me returning to work and once again I was surprised by the wise dialogue of my children. Gregory, Dwightene and Dennis were in favour of me going back to work. However, Dwightene tabled that I should return in a month's time, because I needed a good rest first. She also proposed a pampering rota. "Nice" – I voted for that, and the motion was carried.

During the month before my return to work Dwightene saw to it that I received the pampering of my life and I loved every minute.

John was not in favour of me returning to work at all though, stating that "I like it when you are there when I get home from school, mum". However, he rather maturely stated that he was aware that I had to work so that they could have nice things and, belying his years, provided me and my dad with further food for much thought when he stated out of the blue. "I like it living here at Granddad's house, but I like to live at our home too – my friend Louie has got two homes". "Mum, can we have two homes?"

The day after the meeting, having informed my workplace of the intended date for my return, I also contacted the Council Housing Department to find out how much it would cost to purchase the flat. Listening to John speak favourably of the flat made me realise that our home held many favoured memories for our family and I did not wish to let it go. After speaking with the Council I spoke to dad who was willing to try and raise a small mortgage on his house to enable me to pay the deposit on the flat so that I could buy it and continue to rent it until such time that we wished to return home. A friend and neighbour at the small estate where the flat was situated had purchased her flat recently and I anticipated that the Council would sell my flat to me at a similar price. I worked out that my salary would adequately cover both mortgages and with Dwightene and Gregory helping out one of our neighbours at a local indoor market and earning their own pocket money, I only had to worry about buying food, paying for the utilities and supporting the younger ones, which with Dad's co-operation was manageable.

Chapter 4

Life as a single mum was hard, but with dad's help and now that the children were growing up it was getting increasingly easier – I was getting better too – much better. I was doing really well. I held down a responsible job, was earning a great salary and bringing home a disposable income far in excess of that available to many if not most two-parent families – my family was blossoming, and I had now become a property owner. Yes, life was good. But there was still something missing. I needed companionship and more.

Then Dwight came begging again one Saturday evening and nearly floored me with shock.

"Hello Carly – I went to the flat and the tenants told me you were here – please can I see the kids?" he asked sheepishly.

"Kids – what kids – do you have any children – Dwight Henry – let me ask you again – do you have any children?" I rammed the words home.

"Carly, please I know I haven't behaved right towards you and the kids but please give me another chance to make it up to you – no one is perfect", Dwight had the nerve to say.

"Another chance – another chance to do what – mess up my head – mess up their heads before you decide that this family is not worth your time, nor worthy of your love and disappear again?" I could feel tears queuing at the back of my eyes.

"Please Carly – it will never happen again I promise – I'm truly sorry – you know I love you and the kids – I'm sorry", Dwight pleaded.

"Sorry Dwight? Sorry – you have never even seen your 18 month old twins since they were born – sorry Dwight – sorry – do you know what the word sorry means?" I lambasted him with my tongue on the doorstep, causing the rest of the household to come and check out the reason for the commotion. "I'm the one who is sorry", I stated.

The tears at the back of my eyes gave last warning that they were about to spill and I was just about to slam the door in Dwight's two faces when John (now 11 going on 30) intervened, "Dad – hello – good to see you – come in, come in", he invited and Dwight did not hesitate to accept the kind invitation, much to my chagrin. John ushered him into the living room where one by one the other children thronged him with hungry smiles and ravenous hugs – all except Gregory who had grown to loath his father. Gregory went upstairs and closed the door to his bedroom.

Retreating to the solace of the kitchen I closed the door and sat down stunned as I fought back the tears and began to ponder my life and circumstances over. After a few minutes I was joined by Dad who offered to make me a cup of tea. Dad then sat down with me and we discussed the situation. "Dad, what does Dwight want from me again – what does he want from us?" I asked.

"My dear, I can imagine how you are feeling after all this time but you can't stop him seeing his children", Dad countered, as I wished he would get up, go into the living room and order Dwight out of his house.

"Why not – why not Dad – it's not as if he cares for them – he couldn't care less if they live or die – all that sorry nonsense is just an act", I said angrily. Then I burst into tears. Dad drew near and put his arms around my shoulders. "Never mind dear, never mind", he said.

I could sense that Dad wanted to try and convince me some more but he refrained from doing so as the tears flowed unchecked down my face. He arose from his seat and crossed the kitchen where he peeled off two sheets of kitchen towel from the roll and handed them to me to dry my tears. I took them gratefully and took deep breaths in an effort to calm myself down.

Becoming aware that Gregory had entered the kitchen, I stopped crying and immediately sat up straight. I did not want my son to see me in tears, although it dawned on me that it may be too late to prevent him from doing so. "You alright mum?" Gregory asked as he came over and bent to give me a hug and a kiss on the cheek. I marvelled at how my first son had grown – he was now almost a man – he would turn 18 years old in a few months.

"Yeah – I'm okay", I lied as Gregory took a seat at the conference table.

"Mum, I know how you feel – I don't like the way that Dwight has treated you at all", Gregory said. It immediately struck me that he had referred to his father by his given name.

"Look mum, if you want me to, I will go and ask him to leave right now", Gregory said in a no nonsense manner.

"Carly, you need to think carefully and make the right decision – I believe that you should give Dwight a chance to see his children", Dad interjected. "I am not saying you should take him back, but you can't stop him seeing his children – they need their father", Dad continued.

"Mum – I don't need Dwight – I don't know about the others, but for me – I don't need him. But mum I will understand whatever decision you make", Gregory said – I could sense the restrained anger behind his words.

"Carly, even if you refuse him access to his children, he could take you to Court because he is their biological father", Rufus cautioned, then continued, "But I understand you are hurting and may need time to consider the issue". "I know he is not the best father for the children, but he is the only father they have", Rufus rested his argument.

"You're right about that dad – he isn't the best father but as for taking me to Court – there is no chance of that ever happening – where would he get the money from?

"Granddad – you have been a better father to us than Dwight", Gregory said then hissed air through his teeth.

"I hear what you're saying son but nobody is perfect and he is your only father so try and forgive him if you can", Rufus said gently as he cradled my shoulder. "I hate to see you in pain Carly, but life is based on choices we make

– you had these children with Dwight and must face up to the consequences" Dad said.

Soon after that I retired to bed with a headache and did not see Dwight before he left. As I lay awake I contemplated the circumstances. Dad was right of course, I was caught in a trap of my own making. I had not one or two but six children with this man, and they needed their father – especially the boys. "So I have no choice but to allow Dwight to see the children – but no way will I ever go back to living with that creep", I spat the words out angrily, then curled my body into a protective ball and promptly fell into a deep slumber brought on by emotional exhaustion.

And Dwight was true to his word, after that first visit he saw the children at least once a week and usually brought them some goodies too. On a couple of occasions he even surprised me by handing over some cash to the children to give to me as I invariably stayed out of his way when he called around. It wasn't much but it provided sufficient evidence that Dwight appeared to be keeping to his word of trying to make up for his past delinquency. This arrangement seemed to be working well.

When I unexpectedly ran into Dwight near my workplace during my lunch break three months later I wondered whether he was stalking me but was civil towards him although anger towards him at the many years of neglect still stirred deep inside.

"Hi – you okay? Dwight smiled the warmest and brightest he could manage upon seeing me. He was looking smart and smelling as though he had used at least half a bottle of expensive cologne – I wondered briefly where he had gotten the money from to buy it.

"Yes thank you – and you?" I replied, and immediately wished I had not added the last question – I should simply have walked on.

"Yeah – I'm good – can't complain", he replied.

I was just about to say – "I'll see you then", when he added, "So are you on your lunch break then?" and looked me straight in the eye.

"Yes – I must rush", I replied and hurried away. But Dwight was not easy to shake off and he quickened his step to catch up with me. "What's the hurry – can't we even talk for 5 minutes?" he asked to which I replied. "I really must rush back to work", and hurried on.

"You know that's not true – you're only trying to avoid me", Dwight countered. "Dwight – what do you want from you?" I stopped walking and faced him – I felt exasperated.

"Nothing – like I said – just glad to see an old friend but the way you are treating me is bad man, after all we have been through together we cannot even exchange pleasantries nowadays", he said as I cast my eyes towards the sky, recalling how Dwight had always had a way.

Dwight ended up walking me back to work "So this is where you work now"; he smiled charmingly as he viewed the opulence of the building's exterior.

"Yes – it's the headquarters of Cheritas Group International", I replied thinking of how well I had done for myself.

"Nice, nice", he said appreciatively – then he changed tack – "I realise that I have neglected the children – but I am ready to start making it up to them, you'll see" he said soberly

"Okay" I said and smiled.

"I'll pass round and see the children on Saturday – around 2 pm – I want to take them out to the park if it is good weather so please make sure they're ready", he said then he surprisingly attempted to kiss me on the mouth. I skilfully turned my face just in time to prevent him from doing so. "What do you think you're doing", I said furiously.

"It's just a little kiss for old times' sake", Dwight said and winked.

"Look – you stay away from me, right". "Don't ever try anything like that again", I said before bounding up the steps. I felt Dwight's eyes trailing me as I entered the building and I knew he was up to his old tricks again.

And nothing had changed – after that first encounter Dwight kept on popping up outside or near to my workplace. And though I hate to admit it, very soon he had me eating out of his hands again like a puppy – just like old times. We had started out as old acquaintances but soon we were holding hands and kissing again and before I knew it the butterflies were back in my stomach – I had fallen under Dwight's spell yet again. Dwight engaged my thoughts – all I could see was his smile – all I could hear were his words – all I could feel was the warmth of his comforting arms around me, protecting me. He made me feel truly alive again. But I was determined not to lose myself completely to hold on to just a little bit of common sense.

Then when three months had passed since we started meeting for lunch or dinner four things happened to demonstrate to me Dwight's heart and convince me that we were destined to be together.

The first thing that happened was that Dwight confessed to me that the reason he wanted to move back in with us was that he had left his girlfriend some weeks previously just so he could spend more time with the kids because she had objected to him spending a lot of time with them and that he had been crashing on a friends couch at night which meant that he was effectively homeless. And he had added that the reason for leaving her was because he had realised just how much he loved me and that I had always been the only woman for him. He said he had been so blind but now he could see clearly what a fool he had been. Dwight had never been so candid with me before and he touched the depth of my heart.

Secondly, I began to relax in Dwight's company and to trust him again. My spirit was perfectly at ease when he was around – he made me feel that everything would be alright. Having shown me just how much he had changed I was willing to give him another chance, after all I had six children for the man and it felt so much better when he was around than when I was raising them all by myself. He was so good with the kids and they, even

Gregory, were once again relating to him as their father. But when Dwight suggested that we move back into the flat together I resisted. To try and persuade me, Dwight stepped up his efforts. He repeatedly telephoned me three or four times every day – he bought me flowers – he sent me love notes – took me out for romantic dates and treated me like royalty. He also began to treat the children extra special which touched my heart – I love those kids so dearly and I decided that they deserved to have their father living with them.

Dwight affirmed my decision that we were meant for each other when he did the third thing – he got down on one knee in an overcrowded burger bar one lunchtime and proposed marriage to me – he had never done anything like that before and I was knocked out by the gesture. We set a date for our wedding there and then – it was to take place on my birthday, six months from our engagement. He sealed his promise to marry me by presenting me with an engagement ring – the first he had ever given me and I was overcome with joy.

And the fourth event that convinced me that Dwight and I were destined to be together was that the tenants decided they wanted to move out of the flat earlier than expected – I decided that it was time for us to move back in together and live as a family again.

Having taken the decision to move back to the flat with Dwight, I informed dad and the kids. Dad was not best pleased and tried to talk me out of it. He didn't see why we couldn't just wait for six months and then move back after the wedding. "What's the hurry – why not just wait until you are married". "You know that as a Christian I cannot condone you living in sin", Rufus said. He rarely got angry with me but I could tell that he was livid – I did not feel he was overreacting for I too felt that Dwight should have married me a long, long time ago but even so my mind was not swayed.

All the children were in agreement – all except for Gregory who wanted to remain living with his Granddad. "Granddad will need some company", he said and I agreed that that would be the best arrangement. Later Dwightene and Dennis also wanted stay with Dad and I agreed because the three bedroom flat was not really big enough to accommodate all of us and there was so much room at Dad's house.

An overwhelming feeling that I was doing the right thing propelled me on with the moving plans, and it was finalised that the move back to the flat would be three weeks later, a few days after the tenants vacated. I prayed that Dwight wouldn't disappoint me again, because if he did I would be totally broken, for I had fallen back in love with him more deeply than ever before and if he let me fall again, I would fall hard.

Two days before we moved Dwight came to meet me for lunch. He had already moved back to the flat the previous day when the tenants left, and had begun cleaning up and decorating in readiness for our return. Lunchtime had been very exciting for us as we looked ahead – we felt like young lovers again, about to embark on a life together for the first time.

Dwight walked me back to work as he was accustomed to doing and kissed me deeply before leaving me to watch him walk away, as I was accustomed to doing. He would usually glance back at me over his shoulders and wave goodbye over and over again until he was out of sight, as though he were embarking upon a long journey and as if we would not be seeing each other for many months if not years. I watched him walk away and we waved at each other as was usual, but just before I lost sight of him, I was surprised to see a female figure approach Dwight. He stopped walking and they appeared to be arguing as she started tugging at his clothing and gesticulating wildly. I could hear their raised voices but could not make out what was being said. And Dwight never looked back or waved at me again but having become preoccupied with arguing with the woman, they walked out of sight.

That evening when I finished work, I went straight to the flat to help Dwight with the decorations and was pleased to see that he had almost finished and we were on course for moving day. As I surveyed the work he had carried out, I marvelled at how beautifully it had been finished – I was surprised, I was not aware that Dwight was so gifted – he could easily have been an interior designer. And I surmised that Dwight had matured into a real man at last.

Before I broached the subject of the woman I had seen arguing with him at lunchtime, without prompting Dwight began to recount the incident and explained that he had been accosted by "a mad woman", who had demanded money from him and tried to attack him. Apparently she had only left him alone when he threatened to call the Police.

"My goodness – what is London coming to – there are some crazy people around these days", I commented.

"You're not wrong there", Dwight had concurred.

The day before moving day I was early for work – I wanted to get up to speed since I would be taking two days' annual leave on Monday and Tuesday the following week – I needed the time to settle into the flat after the move on Friday. As I began to climb the steps of the building I heard someone call out to me, "Excuse me miss – is your name Kylie". I spun around to look towards the direction of the voice and saw the same woman that I had seen remonstrating with Dwight the previous day.

"Why are you asking my name?" I asked, feeling somewhat threatened as I recalled Dwight's report that this woman was crazy.

"My name is Alesha", the woman replied sharply.

"Oh – what can I do for you? I asked.

"So you are Kylie then, are you? Alesha asked – I said nothing and she continued.

"I have seen you with Dwight a few times and I am here to ask you to leave him alone", "SLAP" – this blow caught me in a most sensitive spot, stunning me momentarily. As my mind returned to relative normality I asked the stranger standing at the bottom of the stairs, "Who are you, anyway – are you his ex-girlfriend?" "He told me all about you – he told me it was over between you two", I babbled.

"Is that what he told you?" Alesha asked then hissed air through her teeth. She put her hand akimbo then continued, "Well, it's far from over between me and my 'usband my dear – I am not ready to give up on my marriage so easily – I married for better or for worse", "TOTAL KNOCK OUT" – I was emotionally floored by this revelation, mentally incapacitated and physically weak at the knees which felt as though they were buckling.

"Your what?" I questioned disbelievingly – then laughed bitterly, "ha ha ha ha – do me a favour".

"Oh – you tink seh its funny – well the laugh is on you darling – yes, my dear Kylie, Dwight and I are 'usband and wife – I bet he didn't tell you that eh?" Alesha said triumphantly.

"No – that can't be true?" I said shaking my head as it occurred to me she might be speaking the truth. "Why do you have to make up such lies anyway – what's the matter with you?" I asked in denial and becoming angry.

"Sorry luv I am not telling any lies", Alesha replied, a tinge of sympathy in her voice now. She continued "I've got to go now but you can give me a call later this evening if you want to talk about it", she offered.

I thought quickly and concluded that if there was any truth in what this woman was saying I should find out, so I replied. "No, if you wish to talk, you give me a call", in a tit for tat fashion as I wrote my mobile number on the back of my business card and handed it to her. "Please call any time after 6.30 pm", and I turned and walked up the steps, my mind in a quandary.

Somehow I managed to get through the day although I did not get nearly as much work done as I had hoped to. That evening I went home instead of to the flat where Dwight was expecting me to help with the final touches in readiness to move back in the next day. I ignored his calls which came at 10 minute intervals. As I pondered Alesha's revelation and searched my memory it dawned on me that people had tried to tell me about Dwight's nuptials. I recalled my cousin Vidalyn who had informed me 9 years before that she had seen wedding pictures of a friend's friend and that the groom had looked exactly like Dwight and coincidentally had the same name too. But I had dismissed that comment because I thought it impossible – in my mind if Dwight was getting married surely he would let his children know at least. I also recalled hints from acquaintances along the same lines when Dwight had come back to live with me before the twins were born.

At 7.30 pm Alesha telephoned – I picked up eagerly. "Hello, is that Kylie?"

"Carly – Alesha, my name is Carly", I corrected her. We proceeded to talk for over an hour and I learned that I did not know Dwight nearly as well as I thought. I found out that for the greater part of my turbulent on/off relationship with him he had also been having a relationship with Alesha. They had met 15 years ago, which I calculate was when I was pregnant with Dennis. I also calculated that he must have been carrying on with Alesha when he had forced me to abort what should have been our fourth child who would have been a girl. Alesha informed me that when Dwight had left me 11 years ago (which I calculated was just before John was born), he had gone to live with her and that they had gotten married less than a year after that. Alesha spoke and I mostly listened as she confirmed that their marriage had yielded two children – Jane and Jenny. She informed me that she was previously aware that Dwight had only one son named Gregory, and was until now unaware of the other five children. And by the time our conversation ended, I felt emotionally drained and totally confused mentally. I locked my door switched off my telephone and wept bitterly.

The next morning I arose bright and early not having slept for more than three hours all night. I fixed breakfast for the children and steeled myself to break the news to them that we would not be moving back to the flat after all. Then I committed to the telephone – the first call I had to make was to the removal people to cancel. And the next was to the locksmith – I would need to replace the locks at the flat. The next call I made was to the letting agents – I could rely on them to find me reputable tenants within days if not hours.

Surprisingly the children took the news really well. They immediately set about unpacking and settled back into the usual routine. Dad was pleased that I had reconsidered moving back in with Dwight before our wedding. I did not have the backbone to divulge the full facts to him or to the kids – I needed time – time to get over the shock myself – time to refocus – time to re-evaluate – time to heal.

It was not easy to convince Dwight that the move had been re-scheduled to the following day due to the fact that the removal people had double-booked. He wanted to call the firm and argue it through with them and I had to work hard on him to make him see that an extra day would not hurt. I arranged to meet him for lunch at 12.30 pm, and I also arranged for the locksmith to arrive at the flat at the same time. I asked Gregory to meet the locksmith at the flat at 12.30 pm in order to oversee the work. We always used the same locksmith and Gregory knew him well. I was aware from past experience that it would take no more than an hour to replace all the locks.

Dwight was on time for our lunch date and by 1.00 pm we were eating our lunch. It was difficult for me because I didn't feel hungry at all – I picked at the food on my plate and smiled weakly. At 1.30 pm I received the pre-arranged call from Gregory to inform that the work had been successfully completed.

When I ended my conversation with my son I stared long and hard at Dwight, discomfiting him, "Why are you looking at me like that?" he asked between chomps. I did not reply and he proceeded to cram his mouth full of delicious rice and peas before repeating the question, "Well, why are you looking at me like that – do you love me?" he asked, as a grain of rice coated in spittle flew from his mouth onto the table. Then he smiled and licked his oily lips.

"Yes – I do", I said. Dwight swallowed, rose from his chair and leant across the table. As he searched for my mouth I turned my head to one side. "Yes, I do love you Dwight – in spite of everything I still love you", I said in a sad monotone as I pushed Dwight away from me. A look of confusion crossed his face.

"So, what's going on now then?" "Why are you pushing me away from you?" Dwight asked soberly.

"Dwight, I have always loved you", I droned.

"And I love you too sweetheart", Dwight reciprocated his voice noticeably softer. A soft smile brightened his face as he remained blissfully unaware of where the conversation was leading.

"But Dwight my love was never enough for you – was it?" I asked and continued. "I was never what you truly desired".

The smile was immediately wiped from Dwight's face as he sensed for the first time that there may be trouble brewing.

"Sweetheart, remember we are not looking backwards we are moving forward". "I admitted to you already that I used to be a fool, but I'm a new man now and I won't make the same mistakes ever again, I have made you a promise and I will definitely keep it". "From now on we will stick together through thick and through thin", Dwight said and smiled nervously.

"The fact is Dwight that we cannot move forward in the future if we cannot even be honest about the past – is there something that you need to tell me, Dwight", I asked as I studied my one and only lover's reaction.

"Baby you and me go back to teenage days – you know everything about me and I know everything about you – I hope", Dwight said and chuckled uncomfortably.

"But I don't know everything about you though Dwight – do I", I mocked. Dwight hesitated. I watched as his eyes darted from side to side like those of a trapped animal.

"What do you mean – who you been talking to – don't listen to any malicious rumours – who you been talking to?" Dwight appeared to have suddenly lost interest in what was on his plate.

I paused for effect then said, "Does the name Alesha ring any bells Dwight. [Pause – no response]. "Does the date 30 July ring any bells" [Continued Pause – coughing fit]. "How about September 9 or better still October 31", I continued. Dwight took a gulp from his glass then a deep breath, "Oh man – what's this?" he seemed lost for anything else to say. "Or better still, how about Jane or Jenny?", my voice was sombre. "Do any of these facts ring any bells Dwight?" I asked then fell silent. Dwight gasped another deep breath before attempting to reply.

"I was going to tell you about Alesha – but I didn't want to hurt you", he finally confessed. "I can explain everything – I can….."

"Forget it Dwight – I don't need to know now, I know already", I snapped.

"Carly – take it easy, baby – I'm getting a divorce", Dwight pleaded loudly as all heads in the tiny restaurant turned towards us.

"You should know that I've changed the locks at the flat and your two bags of clothes will be waiting for you outside the front door". "Please collect them and rest assured that I will never again in my life have anything to do with you". "We have six children together and I will, of course, deal with you civilly for their sakes". "But apart from that, Dwight Henry, anything else we had is history – please never bother me again in my life", I spoke above Dwight's pleas and the sniggers of the other restaurant patrons. And as I rose from the table and walked out of the restaurant, leaving Dwight to settle the very large bill, I felt like a butterfly emerging from its cocoon into its new life form. "Sweetheart – don't go – listen will you?" "Okay – go on then you fool – stupid gal", I heard Dwight say as I walked away, but I was not affected, after all, I could not expect anything better from that pig of a man and I smiled defiantly in spite of the pain.

As I made my way home I vowed to be strong as I fought back tears and forced my mind to think about other things, things like food, as it suddenly dawned upon me that I was hungry – I had not eaten most of the sumptuous meal that I had ordered for lunch and I allowed my mind to regret that.

When I returned home I locked myself away in my bedroom and contemplated my life and the present circumstances. I found solace in reading the Psalms of the Bible – and then I prayed – my prayer consisted of just eleven words. "Lord help me find my way back to you – back home". And by home I meant "Born Again Church of God", where I had been safe, before Dwight Henry had come prowling around and stolen me away and changed the course of my destiny. And as I ended my prayer a new chorus arose within my heart and for the first time in many years I began to sing.

"I want to come home
I want to come home
Two long I have wondered from the succour of your bosom
Two long I have roamed
Drinking of pleasures that could never satisfy my soul
I'm so much wiser now
Father this prodigal daughter wants to come home"

I anticipated inspiration to write the verse or bridge or middle eight of the song by singing the chorus over and over again but none came – just the chorus which resounded clearly in my spirit.

Chapter 5

Rufus and the children planned a surprise birthday party for Carly which saw her come out of the "funk" that had covered her mind and spirit since the discovery of Dwight's duplicity. Having invited almost everyone that they knew their mother would like to have at the party, the children, under the direction of Dwightene Gregory and their Grandfather, worked tirelessly to make the party an unprecedented success. They each bought their mother presents, having saved up their pocket money for weeks. Carly cried tears of gratitude and joy when they sang "Happy Birthday", Stevie Wonder style. The little ones danced as they sang causing all in attendance to smile, laugh and comment variously at their boldness and dexterity. And Carly felt her spirit healing as she appreciated how much loved and truly blessed she was.

As soon as the party ended at just before midnight all the children crashed into bed – they were exhausted. Rufus stayed up to help Carly finish tidying up before she insisted that he also go to bed and leave her to it. After half an hour, Carly heard her father's mild snore and knew he was fast asleep. Now that she was certain that everyone in the house was asleep she took a seat at the piano and began to play pianissimo and adagio and she sang – her voice almost a whisper.

"I want to come home
I want to come home
Too long I have wondered from the succour of Your bosom
Too long I have roamed
Drinking of pleasures that could never satisfy my soul
I'm so much wiser now
Father this prodigal daughter wants to come home."

Then Carly made a commitment to return home – back to the beginning when she had known innocence – before she met Dwight Henry – back to church where she had known the goodness and grace of the Lord. She was ready to surrender all for she had tried to live her life without God's guidance and integral presence. Her life was by no means a total failure but she was missing the joy that comes with an intimate relationship with God. Although He had never left her completely, for she had sensed God's constant presence around the periphery of her life to where she had relegated Him. She longed to return to the place of her youth when she had ministered as part of God's Three Little Angels. She knew that there was so much more to life than she had experienced without God. So she repented completely within her heart as she sang her prayer.

The following Sunday 21 August 2011 Carly got up early and readied

herself to attend church with her family. She was ready to swallow her pride
now – she was ready to hold her head high, to walk hand in hand with her
father and her six children, to enter the sanctuary with disguised shameless-
ness, but deep inside feeling like goods put out on "sale" – already used up
and returned – slightly damaged but greatly reduced". But nevertheless she
was going home.

Chapter One

Hello there – this is Amelia – you remember me from God's Three Little Angels. I know I look a little older now, but apart from that I am still the same Amelia Lanson – I have not changed one bit.

It's been a long time since the break-up of God's Three Little Angels. It really hurt me when I lost my friends the way I did when the group broke up – but then I eventually picked up the pieces and moved on. I have other friends now, though none as close as Avarel, Carly and I used to be.

When the other Angels went away, I missed them beyond consolation – and when it became apparent that they had gone for good, I mourned their loss as though they had departed this life – for over a year I cried most days. And the sadness remained with me for many years. I would lock myself away every chance I got and go through photo albums, reliving our journey togeth-er and praying that they would return. It caused me pain each time I recalled our parting of ways, but I nonetheless recounted those events time and again, for I loved to remember my friends.

After Avarel left she soon made it clear to me and Carly that she did not wish to keep in contact with us. At first we had employed strenuous efforts to stay connected to her but it eventually dawned upon us that Avarel was simply not interested so we finally let her go. Carly and I became closer then, clinging together for comfort. But sadly that wasn't to last long, for Carly too would soon be enticed away from me.

Just over a year after Avarel left, Dwight Henry came sniffing around and stole the mind of my remaining best friend. I tried to tell Carly not to have anything to do with him because I could tell he was bad news but she didn't want to listen. And it became apparent to me that she thought I was jealous of their relationship. So I gave her some space for a time. Then a few months after she left church I tried to make contact with her but Dwight got in the way. He would answer the 'phone whenever I called. I left numerous messages. Carly did call me back a couple of times but it was obvious that her heart was not in our friendship anymore – she changed drastically in the blink of an eye from my once gregarious companion to one that was introvert and secretive. Where we had once shared our deepest thoughts, Carly now had very little to say to me and I suspected that our conversations were being monitored by Dwight.

When Carly became pregnant she grew even more distant and stopped returning my calls altogether. I missed her so terribly that one day, in des-peration, I took it upon myself to go around to their flat, a studio that they had moved into together in the face of Carly's parents' protestations. Dwight opened the door and told me that Carly wasn't at home. But I was certain that I heard her voice inside before I rang the bell and told him so.

"Are you sure she is not in – I thought I heard her voice before you opened the door".

"Well you must be hearing things then – SHE'S NOT IN RIGHT", he shouted and as he made to close the door unceremoniously in my face I put out my hand to stop him.

"Please could you ask her to call me", I pleaded.

"Okay", he said then slammed the door with attitude.

But Carly never called. I heard from her mother that she had given birth to a son and went to visit her in hospital. Dwight wasn't around at the time and Carly was overjoyed to see me. She asked me to be Godmother to her son and I joyfully accepted. When I left I told her that I would visit her again when she got out of hospital. But a week later when I called at her flat Dwight opened the door and informed me that Carly didn't want to see me. So I called out to her because I heard the baby crying inside – if it was true that she did not want to see me I wanted her to tell me so herself, "Carly – Carly, are you okay?" I called.

"Yes, of course I'm alright", Carly replied brusquely as she came to the door. "Why didn't you call before you came".

"I did call but you never answer your 'phone anymore and when I leave messages with Dwight you never call me back – I thought something was wrong with you", I said, sounding concerned.

"Look – I will call you when I'm ready right, but I don't feel like speaking to anyone right now", she replied then added, "And Amelia, please don't come round here again without speaking to me first".

And after that Carly never telephoned me again – I heard through the grapevine that she had had her baby christened in another church somewhere in South London and someone else had stood as Godmother. I cried a lot. After that I never tried to contact her again – I knew when I wasn't wanted – and I never heard from her either. It hurt me a lot.

In the first five years after Avarel's departure, you couldn't switch on the TV without seeing her. She was riding almost as high as her skirts, on a very big wave of success and I would smile each time I saw my old friend recalling our happy times together – times that would never come again.

My colleagues at work, in the office where I got a job after leaving school did not believe me at first when I told them that Avarel and I used to be playmates – but when I showed them photos of us as toddlers, juniors and teenagers, they soon changed their minds. Many of them wanted me to fix up meetings with Avarel, mostly for their children who were fans and some of the men wanted to meet her personally for their own interests. But, of course, I couldn't arrange any meetings with her because I did not even see her myself anymore. So I stopped talking about Avarel. I became tired of the questions from my colleagues to which I had no answers.

Chapter 2

When the girls first left I gave up my song ministry for a time, but then I pulled myself together realising that I did not want to abandon God's work – so determinedly I began to sing solos every chance I got. Such opportunities were few and far between back then. It was scary ministering alone at first – each time I stood upon the altar or stage demanded a mammoth effort – luckily the nerves did not affect my voice.

A turning point came one night when I was given a 100% confidence booster that made me stand much taller than my 5' 3" stature. It was at a charity concert where the proceeds would go towards building a school in a remote African village. At that function I was introduced as the lady with the beautiful face and the golden voice – I will never forget that night. I had never before thought of myself as being beautiful and the compliment caused me to undergo a personal re-evaluation.

When I sat in front of the mirror in my bedroom that night, I saw me in a whole new light. I now appreciated that my large almond shaped eyes, full naturally pouty lips and soft chin complemented my round face, that my snub nose accentuated my features as did my soft cheeks which were dimpled on each side. I smiled at my reflection and my face was instantly illuminated. My face was framed by lustrous shiny jet black hair which I customarily straightened and wore in a bob that rested just above my shoulders – my crowning glory. And I agreed then that I just might be beautiful in the eyes of some, but not be so perceived by most. A natural beauty though for I have never worn much make up, as evident from my flawless brown-honey coloured youthful skin.

Initially defiant at the way in which I had been abandoned by Avarel and Carly I dubbed myself "God's Angel". Then my anger dissipated as I matured in ministry and I dropped that moniker and called myself simply "Sister Amelia". I worked hard on building my spiritual standing with God, and received the reward for my efforts – God opened His hand and poured out a strong anointing upon my ministry and it grew from strength to strength as He also opened many doors.

Recently I read an article in which my singing ability was likened to many of the great singers past and present. I want to stress that although the promise of greatness was always present in the early days when I sang with God's Three Little Angels, my gift had not then been perfected. Then one day I heard a preacher say that to settle for mediocrity was a sin that we should thrive for perfection in ministry and I became driven. I worked tirelessly on building my voice and developing my ministerial ability. And I prayed, asking God to perfect my gift – and he did just that in the most spectacle way. God endowed me with divine determination so that I did not relent in my quest for excellence. I worked tirelessly to develop my gift, in the same way that a musical impresario might work to master their instrument or as one of the great artists of all times might have worked to create one of their masterpieces. Where my voice was once weak in parts and lacking in volume it has been honed until it was now as strong, powerful and self-assured as I willed it to be. Yet, if I commanded it, it could be soft, gentle and emotive as can be.

Where my diction was once poor, it has been developed and now it was effortlessly fluent, rich, clear and easily deciphered. The ethereal tone of my natural voice has also been enhanced by coaxing it over many years with the aid of various vocal exercises, until it now flowed sweeter than honey mingled with rich cream.

And I worked hard to gain full control of my voice so that no inflexibility remained now and there is no vocal feat within 4 scales that I cannot accomplish. From a range high, high down to mid-range or low, low my voice retains its strength and agility.

My breathing, an area in which I once struggled, has been perfected too. My diaphragm now pliable yet strong, supports my voice to glide effortlessly through sophisticated rifts and thrills, confident in its integrity to hold up against all challenges. I am not showing off – just stating a fact, because I am myself amazed at what has been accomplished through prayer, hard work and dedication.

Many have commented upon my ability to interpret a song and deliver the required emotive accompaniment – they say that it is legendary, likening me to Mahalia, Nat or Elvis. Some say I would even have received props from such legends, going on to say that none of the most famous songstresses or songsters past or present have ever possessed such God-given ability. I try not to allow the accolade heaped upon me to go to my head and pray daily for God's humility to dwell within.

In those early years I came up against much discouragement mostly from within myself. I also struggled with the temptation to compromise and had to reach out to God in prayer and pull down divine strength and courage. And I made the following confession daily:

"I have made my choice and I will never turn back from my decision". "At the age of ten I asked you Lord Jesus to become my Lord and I will never change course – I'm going all the way with you".

And suddenly my heart would overflow with the presence of God's Holy Spirit and divine strength would flow into me. And I would be empowered to keep my vow never to part from Him – through thick and through thin He has been faithful and so have I. Even when the going got real tough and the last thing I felt like doing was serving, when I would remember how my best friends left me behind and I would feel betrayed, marooned, lost and question why. Even in the darkest of circumstances I held fast to Jesus' hand and I survived.

I also began to focus upon my song-writing ministry more, developing the raw talent that God had given me. And over the years the songs I have written have been my closest friends. They flow from my spirit, each one arising from the depth of me, formulating a novel praise or a new context of worship for my Lord, bringing comfort, bringing joy, greeting me with a "hello, it feels like I've known you all my life", and I welcomed every one, becoming familiar with their curious twists and turns, harmonies and rifts, flats sharps and tempos, from adagio to forte to staccato to pianissimo. And I would drift away as I sang them in private worship to my Lord and they would cheer my heart, strengthen my spirit, sooth my mind and satisfy my soul, depending upon the mood of the day.

Chapter 3

"Sister Amelia" is who I am – a Christian – a humble servant of God whose faith is built up unshakeable – I simply believe in the Word of God and in His promises and His infinite abilities and I am wholly accepting of God's laws. As a result of my efforts to constantly seek and stay close to Him, I share a privileged personal relationship with my Lord and receive guidance and revelation from Him through His Holy Spirit. God has never failed me and I know that He will never let me down – I have a strong foundation. I accept with humility everything that life brings my way, and trust – yes trust – that all things will work out for my good. And they mostly have done.

But there is one area of my life where I remain unfulfilled – that is in my love life, for I need a husband and family of my own and have been praying for many years about this. But, apart from one strong revelation in my early twenties and a few rather confusing dreams, God has been mostly silent. In the revelation God showed me that my prayers had already been answered. And I remain expectant – simply trusting Him.

But as the years pass by, I won't tell a lie, it has become harder to keep on believing in what God promised. Often doubt overwhelms, and it would be only too easy to believe that the man that God told me was on the way had in fact lost his way. Others also make it difficult for me to keep on believing, and it doesn't help that the chief protagonist happens to be a member of my very own family.

Of my three siblings, two have also embraced the faith – my brother Kirk, who is thirty five, and an ordained Pastor, with a beautiful family of two handsome boys – one thirteen years old and the other fourteen, whom I adore. My younger sister Alison is also a Christian. Alison married the first man that she ever dated. They went on only two dates before he popped the question and she accepted without hesitation, and in the face of much criticism, they were married only four months after their first meeting. That was ten years ago when Alison was twenty-three, and she and her husband Harry have been blissfully happy, having been blessed with three beautiful children, a boy aged 6 and two girls aged 8 and four, whom I also adore.

I admire Alison's bravery, but I don't think I could ever marry a man I had known for less than 2 years. Alison defends her decision – she says she just knew that Harry was the right one because God had told her so and she encourages me sometimes when I am down – she tells me not to lose hope – that God is still in the business of providing wonderful spouses, which always makes me smile. I love my sister Alison – she is an awesome woman of God

My other sister Gemma, the youngest in the family is the wild one – she flew the coop as soon as she turned seventeen, with her big dreams. And having attended Fashion School and developed her natural gift to create beautiful garments with a distinct cut and style, she worked for some years with one of the most renowned fashion houses. She looked to be fulfilling her dreams and was doing pretty well for herself as an in-house designer then as a freelancer. But only too soon the fickle fashion industry had turned its back upon her to embrace new talent, dubbing her cuts and style outdated. So at twenty-two wishing for security Gemma had married her boyfriend of five years, Norman Shivers, who was from wealthy stock. Their union had provoked many protestations from his family, most of whom were not colour blind. However, Norman, a free thinker, knew what he wanted – that was the feisty and bubbly Gemma, and his family had eventually come to accept their union after seven years of marriage. It could have something to do with the fact that with her talent and head for business Gemma had almost doubled Norman's fortune. Using a loan from Norman's family as capital, they had opened up three designer shops in affluent districts of London, Paris and New York and stocked them with Gemma's lines, which had been dubbed outdated by most of the fashion industry and the Press.

With a strong belief in her ability Gemma had reached out to a few patrons whom she knew thought a great deal of her designs. Most of those individuals happened to be wealthy fashion connoisseurs and socialites, to whom she donated one off designs. And with them wearing her creations, the word was automatically spread that she was still in business. Those high profile individuals had not only continued to patronise her shops, but had also attracted other well-to-do clients who were willing to pay well over the odds for her designs. Her hunch was spot on – just a handful of wealthy loyal clients had kept the business growing at an alarming rate and set the trend. And the Press had eaten their words and returned grovelling.

Within two years, the shops started to do incredibly well and Gemma decided to branch out. She employed mostly unknown new and innovative designers to create fresh lines which she sold alongside her own much loved exclusive pieces, taking her business to a whole new level of success which saw her expanding into South Africa and Abuja.

However, Gemma's success in the glamorous world of fashion design meant that the couple's affairs did not escape media scrutiny. The Press were unkind to Gemma over the years, defaming her as having been sexually pro-miscuous during her youth, going so far as to print a story that she carried the legacy of her wanton ways – childlessness brought about by a prevalent strain of a little known sexually transmitted disease that had robbed her of her womb and ovaries in her early twenties. The information had apparently been provided to the gutter Press by a one-time good friend of Gemma's, who had wished to remain nameless and faceless, and the informer had provided irref-utable documentary proof too. Ironically Gemma and Norman were childless which tended to lend credence to the story. To say she pampered her pouches would be an under-statement – those Chihuahuas were better dressed that some of the most famous television, film or music stars. I love my sister dearly and have never divulged to her the fact that I read that story when it was published. Gemma has never discussed the subject with anyone in the family.

If only my love for Gemma were requited. It may be partly due to her frustration at not being able to have children that she carries such venom within her heart for me. I have never done anything and would never knowingly do anything to hurt Gemma but she never misses an opportunity to deride me.

It is apparent that Gemma's derision of me also stems from the fact that I embrace my Christian faith – she seems to hate the fact that I have chosen a holy path in life, and she especially mouths me continuously about the fact that I have remained celibate and single. I cannot say why she has taken such exception to the fact that I want to "wait upon God to send me the right husband".

The ridicule had begun soon after she got married, first as one "off the cuff" remark or another, but had graduated over the years to sustained verbal onslaught. And over the past three years since I turned thirty-five, the pressure that Gemma has brought to bear upon me has increased to an alarming and almost unbearable level. It seems to have become something of a culture for her to insult me, but I try not to let her get to me and continue to love and pray for her without rancour, even when on occasions she has inveigled her husband to join in the verbal attacks.

"Don't you think Amelia looks frumpy in that dress, Norman", Gemma would say, and they would go on to discuss loudly the details of the garment that they found particularly offensive.

"Look at that neckline – its cut way too high", or "Look at the hemline – I wouldn't sell that dress to my worst enemy's grandma, Norm – just look at her", Gemma would critique, encouraging her husband, who would sometimes add his comments too. "No wonder she's still single", he would say in his best "old school tie" accent and would guffaw loudly.

Gemma used to bring me specially designed outfits or ones from her range. I would wear the more modest ones but donated the others to charity or good homes. Eventually she stopped giving me clothes when she realised that I was not wearing even 10% of them.

Although those verbal attacks have troubled me, I have never and will never retaliate – not because I am some kind of saint, but because of Jesus. I choose to let God's love flow through me, and not to be consumed by bitterness, although it has occurred to me on numerous occasions that I should retort that they are such an odd couple – he forty-nine with a deep tan that makes him look like a minstrel, and a weather beaten face that only family could love, and she thirty years old going on eighteen, and looking more like a friend of his daughter's (if he had one). And especially over the past year since she had taken to wearing the designs of her youngest employee and encouraged Norman to do likewise, they both looked as though they had totally lost the plot – but I would never tell them that, of course, unless it was in an effort to make them see sense, but so far I have resisted the urge to do so.

Gemma and Norman are seasoned travellers who flit from London to Rome to Lagos to New York to Kingston. They also own homes in all the exotic places of the world, from Ocho Rios to the South of France. I used to take them up on their numerous invitations to join them on their worldwide escapades and I have enjoyed many first class holiday breaks with them over past years. But although they continue to invite me away, I never accept their invitations anymore, because on the last two holidays they had tried to play matchmakers, pairing me off with some of their rich friends against my will.

I feel so sorry for Gemma – it's as though she is unable to stop herself from being nasty to me – sometimes I feel that her only real pleasure is derived from insulting and belittling me, and it saddens me that with all her possessions she apparently has no real peace. And although Gemma and Norman appear happy together, with all their wealth and privileges I get the distinct impression that they remain unfulfilled. On occasions in the past when I have tried to introduce them to the peace and love that stems from serving God, it has resulted in heated and outrageous arguments so now I simply pray for them.

Unfortunately Gemma and Norman comes visiting often. And since I still live at home with mum and dad, I see far more of them than I would like to. Over recent years, whenever they come around, I simply lock my door and remain in my room until they've gone. But even then I cannot escape the insults and snide remarks completely, because Gemma speaks deliberately loud so that I can hear her through the walls. For example, "Mum, you know Amelia should get out more". "Can't you set her up with one of the brothers at your church – even if it's an old one – she behaves like an old woman anyway", Gemma said once. Such remarks cut deeply and hurt and are not easily forgotten. So now I put on my headphones too when they visit, and listen to soothing worship songs which lull my soul and preserve my joy.

But occasionally, loving my sister as I still do, I venture out, to greet her or to sit with the family at dinner and at such times Gemma unleashes all the pent up evil words all at once. She seems oblivious to the hurt and pain she causes me. Hurt that has caused me to cry a lot when I remember her stinging words – but mostly I pray

"God please take away my shame – please send me the husband you promised you would and take away my shame".

Every day I say this prayer – I have done for years, and each time I feel hope arise within my heart as I am drawn back in my spirit to that revelation that I received from God in my early 20s. In the week before I received the revelation I had prayed and fasted intently for seven days asking God to send me one who would truly love and cherish me, one who would be faithful, one who would love me with an equal measure as my love for him, one I could respect and most importantly, one who would love God as much as I do. And on the seventh day I had received the revelation.

After prayer I had paused to mediate and drifted off into a trance – then

God had spoken in a vision conveying the divine message – my husband was on the way. I saw His hand reach through the sky. Then He opened his hand and sprinkled gold dust, coins and jewels and light upon a shadowy figure that stood upon the earth, and said the words *"this is my son – he pleases me with his …… and faithful ways"* – I cannot recall one of the words that He spoke. Then the person turned to face me for a fraction of a moment – I saw a flash of his handsome face which then disappeared. When I awoke I wracked my brain for hours and then I prayed but I just could not remember the exact message that had been spoken during the vision. But I was certain of one thing God's confirmation remained in my spirit – my love would be everything that I had prayed for. And I have clung to that promise through thick and through thin and in the face of Gemma's insults and others' disparaging remarks about my marital status.

What remained vividly imprinted in my mind was that my husband would be tall, strong and handsome – and in my spirit I knew that together we would take God's Word across the world and I wondered if he might be a Pastor.

It seemed that everywhere I went people were more concerned with my business than with their own. At work I often heard audible whispers from Monica, the office gossip. Monica was not concerned with the fact that I remained unmarried however because she did not believe in getting married. She lambasted me because I did not keep boyfriends or go on casual dates, even when she had gone out of her way to set me up, for Monica had once been my friend when I first began working at Pembleton District Council in the Child Welfare Department. But when she realised that I was truly saved, she had drifted away and since then had made it her business to spread it around the large Government building where I was employed as a PA to the Head of the Legal Section, that I was frigid and a weirdo.

Years ago I used to join in the social events at work but due to Monica's malicious gossiping, I now keep myself and my business to myself. If she will talk about me, I won't be the one to provide any information for her to manipulate and disperse. But unfortunately that doesn't stop her from making things up.

The only information about my life that I now share with my workmates is the fact that I am an avid churchgoer, and a gospel singer. I have invited them along to watch me sing on occasions, and some have honoured the invitation, following on from which news of the performances have been talked about non-stop throughout the office, many encouraging me to go on "Fame Game", a reality television talent show where many a star had been discovered. But such adulation would be relatively short-lived and Monica would work overtime to reinstate the negative mind-sets that several of my workmates had developed concerning me, which caused them to avoid me – some immature ones even sniggered when I walked by.

I found out from one colleague, Mavis, who was very nice to me, that Monica was also telling everyone that I am crazy for not using my singing talent to try and make it instead of working as a PA. If only Monica would say such things to my face, then I would let her know that I am not at all crazy, but that I am perfectly happy singing my Lord's praises – that I do not want to be a famous singer. But she only talks about me, not to me. In any case I would probably be wasting my breath – she would never understand my resolution to stay put and serve my Lord.

Chapter 4

There have been many men along the way – brothers who have approached Bishop Manning and asked for my hand in marriage, or those who have made it obvious that they were interested by smiling at me in that special way and others still who have approached me to make their intentions known. Once I had even courted for three whole months, when a very handsome eligible man called Rodney Snide had approached me to ask for my hand. But I had broken off the courtship, when Sister Rita (the all-seeing, all-knowing one at Born Again Church) had informed me that Rodney was not only Snide by name, but also snide by nature, and was in fact courting several other eligible young ladies in other churches within a 10 mile radius. I had not simply taken her word for it though – I had gone to visit one of the churches she had mentioned and had caught him in the act.

None of the other potential husbands had been right for me, either because I had discerned within my spirit that they were not the one, or because they were too super-spiritual and I could not get to know the real person, or because they did not approach me personally first rather than going straight to Bishop Manning. You see, no-one can choose a husband for me – I will make up my own mind. I will know when the right one comes along – God has promised to send him and I am expectantly waiting.

My mother has admonished me over the years and particularly in the last three years since I turned 35. She has reminded me often that I'm not getting any younger and advised me to seize one of the opportunities put before me in the form of eligible bachelors with promise, but I am holding out for my vision to manifest.

Bishop Manning has from time to time highly recommended one or other young man as a suitable marriage candidate, but I initially shared with him the revelation and the promise from God, and I have reminded him of that each time he has broached the subject of marriage. Bishop Manning has assured me that he understands, although he continues to advise me that I should fast and pray for acceleration of the promise and not simply dismiss potential mates without interceding first.

There are times when I become tired beyond measure, over tired of the gossiping, over tired of the cutting remarks and insults, over tired of waiting, and at such times doubt nibbles at the fringes of my mind. *"Did you ever really receive such a revelation?"* There are times when loneliness draws me close embracing me far too tightly, times when I feel like falling into depression's outstretched arms, times when I feel I am teetering on the proverbial edge – almost losing my mind – times when I have doubted my sanity – times when my own parents have declared that I have lost it. Like the time four years ago, when they learned that I had turned down a young man who had approached Bishop Manning for my hand – George Manning, a relative of Bishop's, whom he had highly recommended as a promising thirty-four year old doctor. George had resembled a suave and sophisticated Jamaican Prince – every woman's dream come true. And there had been an almighty uproar when my parents had found out that I turned down his proposal. They had begun to fast and pray for me in earnest, for God's mercy and grace to smile upon me once again. And I know that they had been terribly disappointed.

A few months after that, when I was approached by the next potential suitor, a handsome brother with his own computer business, who had smiled at me and said "hi, can I get to know you", I had been sorely tempted to throw in the towel, to smile back and give in to whatsoever transpired, to go through – all the way to the altar. But there had been only one date, and I had seen a side to the brother that no-one else could see apparently. Unaware that I had been totally put off by his evident self-centred nature, Bro Clifton had approached Bishop Manning for my hand, and once again I had declined, because try as I may I could not forget God's promise and He had not informed me that my husband would be an egotistic boar.

It did tug at my heart when I received updates from various sources about the suitors that I had passed up. My mother was the greatest source of such information. She would discuss the development of a certain brother's marriage with my father loud enough for me to hear on a regular basis. Her main protagonist was the handsome Dr George Manning. For over two years mum made sure that I received a blow-by-blow account on George. On an almost weekly basis I was made aware that he had married six months after I turned him down. Apparently his wife was a very beautiful sister from the Wolverhampton Church from a most respectable old Jamaican Christian family. He had installed her into a mansion and given her a wonderfully courteous child, who was now 2 but who behaved like a much older child in Sunday school. Quite how mother got her information I do not know, for Dr Manning lives over a hundred miles away with his family and has never attended our church since I turned him down.

Chapter 5

Many have attempted to prefix my name with some or other title of accolade or distinction, notably Bishop Manning who had once taken to calling me Prophetess Amelia, for he maintained that my choice of songs, the way I delivered them and the effect of my ministrations amounted to nothing short of the prophetic. And there was also the time when Sister Manning, Bishop's wife, had taken to calling me Evangelist Amelia, for she maintained, and does to this day, that I am a preacher of the Word in song and a winner of souls. Others still have sought to annex the prefix "Apostle" to my name, for they say that, like Jesus' first disciples, I have never been averse to going to wherever the Lord directs me to minister. I cannot deny that they are all right, for I have spread the Word in song in some of the most unexpected and forbidden places both in the inner Cities, the suburbs and in more remote areas. But, not wishing to take any credit for God's work in my life, I have always corrected them gently and, although reluctant to do so, most have acquiesced to my request and reverted to addressing me simply by my name, all except Bishop Manning, who still attaches a title of accolade when he introduces me from time to time.

A couple of years ago Bishop Manning was asked to comment upon my ministry by a certain well-known Christian journalist for an article which was later published in "The Covenant", a widely circulated church magazine. And he had said the following:

"When Prophetess Amelia sings she touches the depth of hearts, minds and spirits – she does not only sing but she ministers – she takes on the persona of an angel on assignment from heaven, and strains of heavily backing singers can be heard accompanying her – if you listen with your spirit. When Sister Amelia ministers, it so pleases God that he moves his hand to bless his people."

When I read those comments I felt so privileged to have been gifted by God in this amazing way – to be able to touch hearts and lives. And the suggestion that my ministration could actually provoke God's blessings upon others blew me away.

In another article, published in The Covenant a few months later the same journalist had written:

"It is Sister Amelia's gift of interpretation of a song and the anointing that her voice carries that draws listeners in and holds them transfixed at her command as she delivers each rendition".

The writer, Christine Giles, went on to say that she too had been smitten from the first time she heard me minister in song, and testified that for hours, days, weeks even months after she heard me minister, the songs would resound in her "mind's ear" and spirit, and that following each of her visits to Born Again she hungered for yet more and would be drawn back time and again to listen and to worship. She continued that she had visited Born Again more than 10 times over the past three years and referred to my voice as a remarkable miracle. She also wrote the following:

"It is not just the sound of Sister Amelia's voice that stirs sensation but a heavenly anointing appears to have attached itself to that earthen vessel and great miracles have taken place as Sister Amelia ministers. One notable miracle which I witnessed myself concerns a young man of 26 who was born deaf and dumb, who had attended the Born Again Church of God in the hope of receiving a miracle – he was seated in the pew directly in front of me. Moments after Sister Amelia began to sing, he started to gesticulate wildly with his hands, pointing to his ears and trying to talk. And as Sister Amelia ended her song, the young man had been led forward by his Aunt, who had invited him to church that day. She testified that her Nephew had never been able to hear anything or to speak since the day he was born. Her testimony was as follows:

"It was while Sister Amelia was singing that he started to point to his ears". "I asked him what was wrong with them and he just kept pointing to his ears". "At first I thought that he was in pain, but then he began to smile and then to grin and then to cry – tears of joy, and I knew then that he had been healed – glory be to God".

"The woman giving the testimony had then burst into tears of joy too".

"Minister Manning had tested the young man's hearing by clapping from behind him and getting him to repeat what he had heard and praises had rung out loud throughout the sanctuary when it was confirmed that the young man could now hear".

"There have been many such testimonies of miraculous healings and deliverances having taken place during Sister Amelia's ministration".

Chapter 6

It's truly amazing that I, Amelia Lanson could be so blessed of God. I am humbled by His favour upon my life and I strive to remain that way. Each time I read the articles I smile and thank God for using my life in this way. I gratefully accept that I am simply a vessel being used by God. And I give Him all the glory – sometimes I have to struggle with my ego but I always win. For I have vowed never to allow any of the praises and accolades heaped upon me following such divine occurrences to go to my head.

A few months after the healing of the deaf and dumb young man, Christine Giles had returned to Born Again and spoken to a few brethren, and solicited testimonies from many people who had been drawn into the Born Again Church of God just to hear me sing or to receive a miracle during my ministration in song. And with their permission she had published those testimonies. I was so in awe of God when I read them – they seemed unbelievable to me. I would never have believed them if those who testified were not personally known to me, and it brought great joy to my heart to think that my ministry was drawing souls to Jesus.

The first testimony was from Bro Steve.

"I have never been a church-going man but one Sunday in late September 2009 I was walking past the Born Again Church of God on Church Lane when I was stopped in my tracks, for I heard the most beautiful sound emanating from that sanctuary as I went by. The lady's voice nearly knocked me out for six – it wasn't just that she was a good singer, but there was something very special about her tone – it sounded like an angel singing and was more beautiful than any of the superstars who graced the world's most prestigious stages. I had never heard a sound quite like that before. It was so pure – as pure as driven snow and the minor inflections as it resonated only enhanced the rhapsody of the glorious noise. I cocked my ear towards the melody, then turned and walked into the cathedral as though entranced. As I entered the building I stood transfixed as I beheld and gazed upon the beautiful face of the angel with the miraculous voice. Her vocal chords strummed as though being skilfully plucked by a master musician and I thought of how immaculately crafted they must have been and this thought caused me to acknowledge the master craftsman himself – God Almighty. I searched my mind to find the value that I could place upon such a gift, but was stumped and settled that it was priceless, more so than the rarest and most exquisite of musical instruments."

"And as I was led to sit in a pew, I stumbled as I found my seat. I sat down and basked in the loveliness of the atmosphere as the angelic sound wafted throughout the sanctuary then embraced my spirit. I closed my eyes to savour more deeply the moment – the sound, but quickly opened them again because I also craved

to gaze upon the face of the delightful angel and the combination of her voice and her face caused my spirit to drift upwards, alternating between spiritual and soulful ecstasy. And I fell deeply in love with the gift and its bearer. Like an addict I was immediately smitten and I knew I would keep coming back, if only to listen again – to bathe my spirit and my soul – in that magnificent sound."

******

Steve Walters had become a regular attendee since that fateful Sunday morning having surrendered his life to Jesus Christ that very day. He was baptised two months after that first visit, when Bishop Manning had preached a sermon entitled "A New Creature" and had quoted the scripture, "If any man be in Christ he is a new creation – old things have passed away – behold all things have become new", and as the congregation listened, those invited by Bro Steve to witness his bold step, who knew him well and had known of his past operations, prayed a silent prayer that he had indeed been truly converted. Bro Steve too had listened intently, drinking in every word. It was as though Bishop Manning was speaking about him, if not directly to him. For he had given up a deeply sinful lifestyle that was far removed from his new found position as a born again Christian. Bro Steve had not given up everything though, for he had retained the benefits acquired from his past dealings, which he had vowed to put to good use in God's kingdom and he continued to enjoy a privileged lifestyle.

Having turned his back on his womanizing ways, Bro Steve intended to live clean. He needed a wife – he wanted a Christian companion to share his life and privileges with. And he already had someone in mind for that position – Sister Amelia. Steve had known that she was the one from the very first moment he laid eyes on her as he had unashamedly testified in the Covenant, and he had worked hard to be deserving of her righteous hand.

Chapter 7

It had not escaped Amelia's attention that the new convert Bro Steve was always trying to establish eye contact with her – she had become adept at avoiding his direct gaze. She first became aware of Bro Steve's romantic interest in her when at a singles seminar held four months after he joined the church, he had pursued her to within an inch of her life – everywhere she turned Bro Steve popped up and Amelia had gotten out of breath trying to avoid him because she was aware of Bro Steve's dubious past and did not wish to get involved with someone of that calibre, in spite of the fact that he had supposedly repented. She did not wish to be the one to find out that he had simply taken a dip in the baptismal pool. So Amelia had worked the room really quickly to stay ahead of Bro Steve who was hot on her trail, pursuing her at a pace that could rival Bolt's 100 metres world record.

Later that night as she lay awake reflecting, Amelia decided that she really did not wish to entertain Bro Steve's advances. Like so many potential suitors before him, she would write Steve off. It did occur to her that she had promised herself to stop writing suitors off too quickly, but the thought did not sway her from her decision. She searched her soul as to why she felt so strongly about having nothing to do with Bro Steve and concluded that it wasn't just because of his past, but she also hated the way he tried to commandeer her attention as though he already owned her and she surmised that surely it would be a constant reminder of the manner in which he had controlled the streets. She also disliked the way he leered at her and she was certain that the thoughts he was having about her were far from reverent. As far as Amelia was concerned Bro Steve's attention was definitely unwanted and she hoped that he had gotten the message that she had gone to pains to send loud and clear – that she had spoken in reply to his offer to get to know her better – she was simply not interested.

However, Amelia was soon to find out that Bro Steve did not seem to get the message. He managed to corner her after church a few Sundays later and started babbling on about getting married.

"Sister Amelia – you are such a beautiful lady – I have been looking for someone just like you to become my wife", Bro Steve spoke as though he had a hot potato in his mouth. He had to speak so fast, to prevent Amelia from getting away from him before he had said his piece.

"I really must run", Amelia had begun to say, then realising what she had just heard, she said, "I beg your pardon?" and stopped in her tracks, realising that Bro Steve had effectively just proposed to her.

Bro Steve felt happy that his message appeared to have gotten across and was ready with an answer.

"Yes, you heard me right Sister Amelia – I would dearly love to marry you", he replied affirmatively just as quickly as before.

Amelia was taken aback and for a split second she looked at Bro Steve with new eyes. For not many potential suitors in the church had ever had the guts to approach her directly in that way without going through Bishop Manning first. Most established Born Again Church people were aware of the Courting Protocol. She was intrigued – she cocked her head to one side, narrowed her eyes and pondered for a few seconds, then decided that she was not intrigued enough to entertain his offer and replied, "I'm not available, I'm afraid", her voice was calm but there was no disguising the sharp edge to it.

"How do you mean, I don't see any suitors around you", Steve blubbered before realising that he had said the wrong thing. He quickly tried to temper his stinging words by pleading, "You need to get to know me – I'm a good man – I will treat you the way a lady like you needs to be treated", but most of his plea was wasted on Amelia's back part as she walked away from him.

Steve was oblivious to Sister Rita's presence as she stood apparently innocuously close by, her all-hearing ears cocked and finely tuned. He stood looking dejectedly after Amelia as she marched away as though she were a bull who had just seen the flash of a red flag. Steve did not realise that he had just provided the latest Born Again news flash which would shortly be disseminated far and wide, or that his name would be devoured as though by vultures within that very hour for Sister Rita was not only the church's Senior Administrative Manager, who had the benefit of personal and business contact details of all the members and visitors at Born Again, but she also doubled as the Chief Church Gossip ("CCG").

Since the day that Bro Steve had mentioned marriage to her Amelia avoided him like the plague, while he continued to make every effort to accidentally bump into her. She did not attend any further singles conferences either, even though she had once been one of the staunchest supporters of that ministry, for she knew that Bro Steve would certainly be present.

On a number of occasions, Bro Steve had gotten lucky and accidentally bumped into Amelia after church. And each time he just happened to have a very expensive gift in his pocket which he had bought just for her and which he proffered by way of a peace offering. But over and again Amelia would decline his generosity, stating that she did not accept gifts from gentlemen she did not know. "Well why don't you get to know me then", Bro Steve muttered under his breath the seventh time.

"I beg your pardon", Amelia replied.

"Oh, nothing – I was just clearing my throat". Steve said. Amelia had made it clear that she did not believe him, by giving him "the look" and stomping off in a huff.

After each such encounter Amelia voluntarily thought about Bro Steve a lot. Although she had no romantic interest in him, she was impressed by his generous nature for she had learned through the grapevine that he was the church's secret benefactor who had made many gifts to several needy people and families since he joined the congregation. She wondered why she was not drawn to Bro Steve for she was also well aware of his incredibly handsome features – his oval face and pretty almond shaped light brown eyes, his full lips, naturally deep wavy hair and almost perfect small oblong nose with endearing slightly flared nostrils, complimented by a rich all-over creamy coffee complexion, all wrapped up in a six foot muscle toned package. But looks alone had never been enough to stir Amelia's emotions – she needed more, although she could not say what. But whatsoever the missing ingredient was Bro Steve did not have it. And Amelia just could not bring herself to accept his gifts or make her heart consider him as a suitor.

Confusingly, recalling details of the revelation that she had received from God, Amelia's head told her that Bro Steve should be the long-awaited suitor. But her heart told her otherwise. And she struggled to recall all the words that God had spoken to her during the revelation.

Initially not many brethren were aware of Brother Steve's interest in Amelia, but those with a discerning spirit and a few other interested parties were well clued up. Among them were Bishop Manning, Spiritual Mother Haines and the sisters who had zoomed in on Bro Steve with their quixotic lenses. Sister Rita was also very much aware of course – for all the wrong reasons. Being the church's font of eternal gossip nothing ever past her notice. But ahead of Rita by a nose was Sister Alice – she was super aware because not only was she Rita's Deputy Chief Church Gossip ("DCCG"), but she also had a personal interest in Bro Steve. And so strong was her romantic inclination towards the new convert that an ugly spectre of insane jealousy towards Amelia had taken up residence within Alice's heart and was growing more sinister every day. Her mind blinded by infatuated love, Alice now viewed the innocent Amelia as a deadly rival. And as the ogre grew within her heart she had begun to hate Amelia with a passion and hot sauce on top.

Amelia had become aware of Alice's evident dislike for her, but she could never guess the extent to which the deadly, unquenchable fire of jealousy raged within the heart of her sister.

Many a prayer of repentance had gone up from Alice's lips, as she begged God to forgive her for wishing to scratch Amelia's eyes out, or even worse. She often sat through whole services where the topic was healing, while willing Amelia to go blind by the end of the sermon and each time she listened to Amelia minister in song, she found herself wishing that her beautiful voice would crack up and be lost for good.

Many nights Alice would fall by her bed and cry out to God for his mercy and she would be led to read a particular scripture, and as she obeyed, her errant emotions would be subdued – but only temporarily until the next time she watched Bro Steve observe Sister Amelia, when the beast would escape from its leash and create havoc within her heart. Then Sister Alice would demonstrate hostility towards Amelia. For no apparent reason she would interject rudely when Amelia was in conversation with somebody else, speaking loudly to the other person but totally ignoring her perceived rival. This happened far too often to amount to mere coincidences, and Alice, who had hitherto been friendly towards Amelia, no longer greeted her and completely ignored any friendly gestures that Amelia made. And Alice also began to spread malicious gossip about Amelia, apparently.

Chapter 8

Many people spoke highly of Bro Steve, notably Amelia's mother Joyce, but no one really knew much about him. But as the Bible says …"the gift makes way for the giver", and some having received gifts from him, or having become aware that he made several anonymous gifts to members of Born Again Church of God, had become in awe of him, because of his evident wealth and generosity. Steve was also well-known for his humility. For when acknowledged by one or other donee of the gifts, who offered thanks with terms of accolade, Bro Steve would simply make light of his kind deeds, often changing the subject whilst continuing to smile. He did, however, appreciate the simple gestures of thanks heaped upon him, such as lavish home cooked meals each Sunday, prepared by the loving hands of one or other grateful sister or brother and their families.

Following days when one or other brethren had received much needed and desirable gifts from the benefactor, Amelia's mother would vocalise her admiration of the fine young eligible bachelor and she did so today on the way home from church. "Well that Bro Steve is such a wonderful young man", Joyce announced as Amelia set the car in motion. She ignored her mother, not wishing to get involved in yet another conversation where Steve Walters was the main topic. "It's hard to find young men of such calibre now-a-days – so kind and thoughtful", Joyce continued.

"Ummh", Amelia obliged, not wishing for her mother to think her insolent. This response however, provided Joyce with encouragement and she continued with more enthusiasm.

"Do you know that he gave Sister Beckton a top of the range professional food mixer and capital of £2,000 to start her own cake making business after she was laid off from her job. Apparently his heart was touched to make the gift when he found out that she would have no means of providing for her family because Bro Beckton had returned to full time study and had another year to go before he graduated as an Accountant. Sister Beckton had been the main breadwinner, you see – for the past 2 years", Joyce rattled on without pausing even to breathe properly.

"Really", Amelia replied, hoping that the topic would soon end.

"And apparently he was the secret donor who gave £3,600 to the Thomas's to pay up their mortgage debt and avoid losing their home", Joyce gushed, glancing over at Amelia to gauge effect. She was disappointed to be met with a simple non-committal half smile and half-hearted nod.

Amelia gripped the steering wheel tightly. She wished her mother would let the subject of Steve Walters drop. She was aware that Joyce was obviously trying to talk Steve into her head, but she remained unaffected by the reports of the gallant deeds of a young man whom her heart had rejected.

"I think that young man has shown how kind and considerate he can be
– someone with that sort of character would make good husband material",
Joyce offered. Amelia sighed, thinking that her mother was going too far.
"Well Amelia, what do you think? Joyce rattled on recklessly. "I know he likes
you – Sister Rita told me so and I have observed myself – it's obvious from the
way he looks at you, dear", Joyce gushed on. Her mind strayed briefly to the
"mother of the bride" dress that she had seen on her last shopping trip. She had
tried it on and now wondered whether she should have left a holding deposit.

Back to the present, Joyce turned to stare expectantly at Amelia, who
became aware of her mother's glare and shuffled uncomfortably in her seat
before casting her eyes up to the sky. She decided to ignore her mother and
returned to concentrating on the road ahead.

Amelia could feel her mother's eyes boring into the side of her face.
Mistaking her daughter's silence for coyness, Joyce took a deep breath and
continued in her quest, "I think I will invite Bro Steve for Sunday dinner in a
couple of weeks' time – so that we can get to know him better".

"I don't think that would be a good idea, mum", Amelia spoke decisively,
demonstrating that she was no more interested in Bro Steve than the last time
Joyce had attempted to stoke the flames of love.

"Look Amelia – good men are hard to find – don't you see how so many
of the sisters are giving Bro Steve the eye, most of them are much younger than you are", Joyce retorted realising she had gone too far when Amelia
slammed on the brakes, fuming.

"Look mother, may I remind you once again to leave my business alone –
I am capable of making my own decisions – I don't need your help – thanks
but no thanks". "Now please let the subject of Steve Walters drop for good,
will you – for your information I am not as impressed by his calibre as you
seem to be." Amelia said then she put the car back into gear and set off again
just as the drivers behind her had begun to hunk their horns.

So Joyce allowed the subject of Steve Walters to drop. But she was merely
biding her time and would certainly try again soon – she silently vowed not to
rest until she had succeeded. Joyce was on a quest to marry off her remaining
child, and had already pencilled Bro Steve in as her future Son-in-Law.

Later that afternoon Amelia apologised to her mother. She did not like
disagreements, particularly after church on Sundays. "I'm sorry but please try
and understand that I do not like Bro Steve in that way and I never will", she
said gently.

"But I don't see why not, dear – he's so right for you", Joyce replied.

"No mum, he is not right for me – God has not revealed so to me and I
trust Him implicitly with my future", Amelia submitted.

"God leaves decisions as to who to marry up to our own choice, my dear
– the only thing you should be concerned with is whether Bro Steve is a true
Christian or not and I believe he has demonstrated beyond doubt that he is",
Joyce replied.

"Yes, mum I have heard of his generosity too – I know that Bro Steve may be a good man, but is he my husband – I think not", Amelia said with an air of finality and Joyce knew better than to pursue the subject – for now.

Although Amelia had apparently written Steve off completely as a potential husband, only she knew that there remained a lacuna – "the God's will gap". She continued to pray asking God for His guidance – she would change her mind immediately if God revealed to her that it was His will. While waiting upon God Amelia concentrated on her spiritual life. She hungered to develop yet more spiritually and this desire saturated her thoughts, as did ponderings upon Bro Albert Cohen, who had unbeknown to him, become her spiritual mentor.

Chapter 9

Brother Albert Cohen had been a member of Born Again for just over three years and his testimony had also been featured in the same edition of The Covenant magazine as Steve Walters' – when he had documented his arrival at Born Again Church of God.

"One Sunday late in September 2008, I Albert Cohen (or "Al" as most people call me) was passing by the Born Again Church of God when I heard an angel singing, for surely only an angel's voice could resonate within the spirit so. I stood rooted to the spot – for a while, reluctant to advance into the sanctuary – I did not know what to expect – would I be welcomed wearing my full Jewish regalia? But I was unable to resist – it was as though my destiny depended upon me entering that holy place – I craved more of God's presence and also to look upon the face of His glorious angel whose voice had touched the depth of my spirit. So I followed the sound as though entranced and as I entered the sanctuary I beheld her there upon the altar, behind the pulpit and I believed that she was truly an angel, no less – on day release from heaven perhaps – but an angel of the highest order of that there was no doubt. For one possessing such a gift was surely God's own. And in the spirit I perceived a host of other angels that joined her in worship as she sang."

"An usher led me to a pew near the back of the large sanctuary, where I sat down. My mouth was agape and my mind was transfixed, as though I had been lulled into a somnambulant trance-like state. I allowed the righteous flood to wash over my spirit as I drank in the gentle power that charged the atmosphere as the angel sang, "I'm touching heaven on my knees", and as she continued to sing, my spirit soared higher than an eagle's and I touched heaven too."

****

Bro Al was almost 83 years old but if asked to guess his age, one would surmise that he was not a day over 70 – his still full head of hair was a distinguished full grey and his face having been spared the ravages of deep wrinkles normally associated with such seniority.

Born an orthodox Jew, Bro Al had upheld those traditions all his life. He had also encountered the teachings of the Bible many years earlier and was a born again Christian, having accepted that Jesus was indeed the long awaited Messiah.

That first Sunday of his arrival Bro Al had immediately fallen in love with the Born Again Church of God and all the brethren embraced the little man (he stood not a millimetre above 5 feet), into their congregation and extended to him unlimited charity which he accepted gratefully.

The church ran many programmes that cared for the elderly and needy and Bro Al was always the first in line to collect his dues. He loved the soups, curries, cakes and other goodies often on offer after the Sunday service and Bro Al was happiest when Sister Amelia had ministered in song during the service, and he had also collected a bag crammed full with goodies to take home with him which would sustain him throughout the following week.

After that first venture into the Born Again Church of God sanctuary Bro Al made his way to church every Sunday morning without fail. He soon took up membership and became known for his novel style of worship which integrated traditional Jewish styles with Pentecostal fervour. He loved the warmth of the brethren and he loved the Bishop but there was no doubt in his mind that the best thing about attending Born Again Church of God was to worship whilst being ministered to in song by Sister Amelia.

Unbeknown to Bro Al his admiration of Amelia was reciprocated, because there was a secret about him that Amelia kept buried deep within her heart, for from the first moment that she met him she had been inexplicably drawn to the older man. She loved the little Jewish man from the very depth of her spirit. Soon after their first meeting she had questioned God over and over again – who, what, how, where, when, she had asked. God had remained silent but the connection Amelia felt to Bro Al had only grown stronger. And she had continued to ask God for His direction and eventually received a re-confirmation within her spirit that God had spoken to her in the revelation so many years ago. Amelia knew that there was something in that vision that she had either missed or had forgotten and felt more confused than ever before. Of one thing she was certain though the man in the revelation was of a similar age to her and was much taller than her. And she mused that if only Bro Al were thirty years younger and almost a foot taller, he would be that man.

Each Sunday Bro Al was the first to arrive at church. He was always standing by the door when Pastor Gentles, the Assistant Pastor, came to open up the sanctuary. And he would kneel before the altar in the empty sanctuary and pray, inviting God's presence and committing the day's ministrations to the Holy Spirit. He bobbed his head back and forth in the same manner as Amelia had seen the Jews do when praying by the "wailing wall" during her visit to Jerusalem a few years previously. He sang the old Jewish worship songs as his devotion became more robust and he bobbed his head and danced about before the altar. Then he would become solemn and simply stand, his eyes upturned towards heaven as though he were looking directly into the face of God and he would smile. After a while he would speak words of endearment to the Lord as he continued to gaze toward the sky with his hands upon his heart.

Amelia liked to kneel at the altar, pray and meditate in the sanctuary before the service on Sundays when she ministered, inviting God's anointing and she had stumbled upon Bro Al during his worship ritual one Sunday morning soon after he had joined the church. On that first day she had remained at the rear of the sanctuary and so intrigued had she been that she had involuntarily abandoned her own worship and watched his, taken in by Bro Al's totally submissive veneration. And as she watched him she too had worshipped in her spirit and she had begun to learn from the worship master.

From that day onwards Amelia arrived early every Sunday morning and observed Bro Al's devotion. She would watch from her car parked across the street as Bro Al was let into the sanctuary. After 5 minutes or so, when she knew he would be preoccupied and would not notice her, she entered the sanctuary and sat quietly in the back pew. Then she sneaked out of the sanctuary when he was winding down and staring upward towards heaven because she did not want Bro Al to realise that he was being watched. Amelia knew that he was shy and she did not wish for him to become affected.

As Amelia watched Bro Al worship her spirit would rise as she joined him in spirit, whilst within her heart and under her breath she whispered words of love to Jesus. And she often fell to her knees in the pew and emulated Bro Al's bobbing style of worship, although in a gentler and less robust manner.

Sometimes Bro Al would bring a brightly coloured handkerchief and wave it as high as he could as he danced before the altar and Amelia began to emulate this form of worship too but in the privacy of her bedroom. She was fascinated by his show of devotion and reverence. And the effect of watching and learning from Bro Al took her worship and her ministry to a whole new level.

There was so much that intrigued Amelia about Bro Al. The fact that he was Jewish and more often than not would be fully adorned in his Judaic regalia yet did not feel out of place amongst the congregation, made up predominantly of Jamaicans, others of assorted Caribbean descent, a few Africans and a handful of Europeans and Asians. The fact that as a Jewish man he had accepted Jesus Christ as his Lord and had combined his Jewish style of worship with that of the Pentecostal Church style was amazing to her. And she found him even more mysterious because he did not speak much although he smiled a lot.

The two of them had spoken to each other only a few times in the years since Bro Al joined the church. Amelia recalled that once he had approached her to thank her personally for blessing his soul in song. "Thank you Sister – you are a great blessing", he had said in an accent that Amelia had found puzzling. Another time he had asked her to sing a particular song again "Hello, Sister Amelia – please would you sing "I'm touching heaven" again – it truly blesses my soul", once again leaving her intrigued as to where his accent might have originated from. She had been tempted on more than one occasion to ask him where he was from but had resisted, gathering that he was a private individual and Amelia was not one to pry into other people's business. However, she had learned from Rita Harris, who made it her life's work to pry into other people's affairs, that he was a Jerusalem born man who had lived in Africa and the Caribbean for many years. But even Rita had apparently not been able to elicit anything further from Bro Al even though she had taken to dropping him home to South Tottenham, where he lived alone in a small flat, hoping that he would one day invite her in and volunteer his life story. But Bro Al, having become aware of Rita's agenda had begun to avoid her, refusing to accept any further lifts, with the excuse that he preferred to take public transport as he liked to evangelise on his journey. Rita was not best pleased and she was unable to learn anything else about Bro Al from other sources, but Amelia was in no doubt that being the undisciplined professional gossiper that she was Rita was working over-time to find out more.

Each Sunday during the service Amelia sat two rows behind Bro Al, for she loved to watch him worshipping. So fervent were his reverential gestures that she found herself caught up in the rapture each time she beheld him. And observing Bro Al's devotion never failed to heighten her worship. She wondered whether Bro Al was indeed an Angel sent from God on assignment to demonstrate true worship. If so, God's act of kindness had been wasted on the likes of Bro Gerald and Sister Deeks, who constantly ridiculed Bro Al, laughing and commenting loudly to everyone who would listen, about what they considered were his nonsensical movements. "Im maddy maddy eeeh", Sister Deeks was heard to exclaim on several occasions whilst Bro Gerald would counter with "Poppy-show". Such disturbing utterances caused Bishop Manning to lower his spectacles and look directly at the perpetuators, which had the effect of silencing the negative voices – but never for long.

It mildly infuriated Amelia when she observed others ridicule her worship mentor, for she discerned in Bro Al a spiritual wisdom only detectable by one on a similar spiritual plane. She viewed him as one who was truly in touch with God – one not ashamed to worship in any way that he was led to by the Holy Spirit, whether by lifting up his hands the highest that they would go, often standing on tippy-toes as though seeking to reach heaven, or by singing at the top of his voice so heaven could hear him even though his ear was not finely tuned, or by lifting his eyes upward towards heaven as though staring directly into the face of God, or by falling prostrate in the aisles or before the alter, or by silently revering the Holy Spirit with tears streaming down his face – Bro Al knew how to worship and Amelia was certain that God appreciated and loved him – and she loved him too.

Yes, Amelia loved Bro Al, the rather unkempt little man. She guessed he was probably about 70 years old and must have been handsome in his youth. His eyes were brown, wise and kind, and although he spoke little, they betrayed that he had many experiences of which he could tell. Amelia loved his humble and simple ways and she revered him one of the most beautiful people that had ever worshipped at Born Again Church of God. She did not love Bro Al in a romantic sense, but in a spiritual sense – her spirit connected with his on a deep subconscious level. She loved him as a beautiful man of God, for she discerned that his soul was pure and lovely – a rare human being – more akin to a heavenly being.

When Amelia stood to minister she liked to look in Bro Al's direction. She would cast him furtive glances, for to watch him worship was a blessing in itself which heightened her ministration. She tried not to stare directly at him because she had once done so and it appeared that her gaze had so discomfited Bro Al that he had immediately pulled into his shell and for weeks after that he had not worshipped as demonstratively as before for fear, she believed, that she may be watching him.

Amelia was aware that Bro Al often cried as she ministered – as did many others, but the thought that Bro Al appreciated her ministration meant far more to Amelia than the approval from hundreds of others, although she would never admit so to anyone. To Amelia Bro Al was God's own PA on a brief holiday here on earth and she was in no doubt that he was close to God's own heart. And she thanked God for Bro Al's visitation – he had taught her the meaning of true worship for her spirit and her ministry had been enriched by his presence at Born Again Church of God.

Amelia appreciated Bro Al's smiles too – from them she gleaned strength – from them she gathered that he was praying for her; that he was thankful for her; that he loved her reciprocally. And she would smile back at him too but rarely spoke for she was so in awe of his presence. But her smile spoke a thousand words – that she was praying for him; that she appreciated him – his worship and his presence as a fellow believer – that she loved him reciprocally.

During the bleak winter of 2010, on the coldest Sunday of the year and the coldest day for the past 18 years, Amelia was sad to note that Bro Al's coat was inadequate against the harsh elements. So the next day she had withdrawn £100 from her meagre savings, taken it to Bishop Manning and asked that he pass it anonymously to Bro Al for him to buy himself a new warm coat. But Bishop Manning had refused to take her donation stating that "Bro Al has already been provided for, my dear".

"Oh really – what someone else has already donated money for him to buy himself a coat?" Amelia had questioned.

"Yes my dear the church's benefactor has stepped up again". "This morning I arrived at my office to find that an envelope containing £200 had been placed through the letter box with a message that it was to purchase a coat for Bro Al". "So you see my dear he has already been adequately provided for", Bishop Manning nodded as he spoke and smiled.

"Is it Bro Steve?" Amelia had questioned.

"Even if I knew for a fact who the secret benefactor was, I would not be at liberty to divulge such information, dear", Bishop Manning smiled.

That day Bro Steve arose in Amelia's estimation 100% and she appreciated that he was truly a good person for being so considerate towards one so in need. She was even tempted to make eye contact with him and smile at him, but resisted, not wishing to give him the wrong impression, for in spite of her feelings of gratitude, she still did not view Bro Steve as a potential husband.

Two weeks later Bishop Manning asked Amelia to attend a meeting where he informed her that someone had asked for her hand in marriage. He did not hesitate before confirming that the potential beau was Bro Steve. He encouraged Amelia to pray before rejecting the proposal. "I have every intention of doing so", Amelia had mumbled. "Pardon me", Bishop Manning had asked. "Oh, sorry, nothing Bishop Manning – I was just thinking aloud – I will of course pray about this proposal and ask God's guidance".

In earnest Amelia had prayed, asking God to show her if she was wrong about Bro Steve, questioning whether she should in fact give him a chance, but she had received no inclination in her spirit to entertain Bro Steve's proposal, and no vision of the night had instructed her to allow him into her life and though she listened intently, no still small voice had whispered words of wisdom to guide her. So when Bishop Manning approached her a week later Amelia was ready with her answer. "Bishop Manning, remember some time ago I told you that God had given me a revelation of what my husband would be like?" Amelia asked.

"Yes, my dear, I recall that", Bishop nodded as he spoke.

"Well that revelation did not indicate to me that it would be Bro Steve and, having prayed about it, God has not released me in my spirit to accept Bro Steve's proposal", Amelia said.

"Well no one can argue with God my dear", Bishop Manning replied and smiled – then said nothing more on the subject.

As she listened to Bishop Manning's reply, Amelia took a decision, she would try to speak to Bro Al – to get to know him better and she would make her move after church on Sunday. She knew he always stayed behind to socialise and she would do likewise and seek to engage him in conversation. Although he was an old man, she wanted to explore what the connection that she felt towards him truly was. Perhaps it was their love of worship and maybe their paths had crossed so that he could teach her about true worship, or perhaps the dream foretold that he would in some way connect her to her future husband. Either way Amelia needed to know.

Chapter 10

The following Sunday Amelia stood to minister. She had gotten caught in traffic on her way to church and had arrived later than usual – too late to observe Bro Al's worship ritual. She was unsettled in her spirit and needing to get into the right frame of mind she looked towards where Bro Al usually sat. He was not seated in his usual place and she scanned the whole sanctuary for his smiling humble face but he was nowhere. Amelia was shocked as it appeared that Bro Al was not present in church. She said "Hallelujah" a few times and scanned the sanctuary again but he was definitely not there so she proceeded to minister and closed her eyes in order to reach that special place of worship that beholding Bro Al's reverence usually channelled her spirit to. And she was a blessing.

When the announcements were made, Bro Al's name was amongst those needing prayer. Apparently he had taken ill and was in hospital. Amelia's heart sank as she imagined how alone he must be, for she was not aware that he had any family or close friends.

After church Amelia was among the first to approach Bishop Manning to enquire of Bro Al's wellbeing. "Bishop, do you know which hospital Bro Al is in – I would like to pay him a visit", she stated.

"No, my dear, I don't". "I had a call from a relative of his to ask for prayer, but stating that they did not wish for any visitors as Bro Al needed to rest". "Apparently he requested a recording of today's service which they will be collecting tomorrow – apart from that I have no other information", Bishop Manning said simply.

"Oh, so he does have some family then", Amelia said, relieved.

"Apparently so – I don't know an awful lot about him – but I am aware that Bro Al is a true man of God", Bishop Manning said before being distracted by another brethren.

Amelia smiled to herself, happy that Bro Al was not all alone in the world after all – then she said a silent prayer for the man of God whom she had grown to love dearly. And each day that week Amelia prayed for Bro Al's recovery. He was first and last on her prayer list in the morning and the first and last on her prayer list at night. And during the week she telephoned Bishop Manning to find out whether he had received any update on Bro Al's condition.

Arriving extra early for church the following Sunday, Amelia was unhappy to see that Bro Al was not back. She missed observing him in expressive prayer. After waiting for 15 minutes she got to her feet and walked towards the altar where she knelt and lifted her hands towards heaven as Bro Al was accustomed to doing. And emulating him she worshipped prayerfully, gentling bobbing back and forth as she focused her mind and heart upon the

Lord until her spirit soared, high and higher still. She was in a zone – oblivious to two sisters who entered the sanctuary and commented variously.

During the service Bishop Manning informed the congregation of an update he had received the day before about Bro Al's health and development and the whole flock was encouraged to pray for him as well as others who were absent through illness. And Amelia resolved to continue praying fervently for Bro Al, asking God to heal him and bring him back to fill the void in her heart for she missed her worship mentor so terribly.

It had not escaped the notice of her mother and other members of the congregation, including Bishop Manning, that Amelia had an unusual interest in Bro Al. Joyce commented to her daughter on numerous occasions that Bro Al was perhaps old enough to be her grandfather and Amelia assured her but failed to make her see that she had no romantic interest whatsoever in Bro Al, but simply loved him in a platonic spiritual sense. Bishop Manning understood where she was coming from though, and informed her that Sunday evening when she approached him to discuss Bro Al's condition, that he loved him too. "He is a true and pure man of God and the divinity in me connects with his spirit too Amelia – I know exactly where you're coming from – I love him just as much as you do". And that admission made Amelia smile as the joy of the Lord filled in her heart.

As expected Sister Rita and Sister Alice got wind of Amelia's feelings for Bro Al, and get the wrong end of the stick they did. Soon news scattered abroad about Amelia and Bro Al's courtship. One report was that Amelia had been camping out at Bro Al's bedside during his illness and was apparently nursing her beloved back to health. Another report was that Bro Al had asked for Amelia's hand and had challenged Bro Steve that he would make Amelia a far better husband.

"Sister Amelia – how is your beloved Bro Al doing", Rita asked Amelia that Sunday evening after church.

"Didn't you hear the announcement that Bishop Manning made this morning in church? Amelia asked – then she continued. "His condition remains serious but stable".

"Oh – I thought you would have more up to date news seen as how he is your beloved – that's all", Rita stressed the word beloved, looked knowingly at Alice and the two sniggered nastily.

"I would just like to know how an old and wrinkling man like that thinks he could possibly rival the young and strapping Bro Steve – not to mention in the looks department", Rita continued then sniggered but Alice was not amused. Amelia gasped.

"I beg your pardon?" shocked realisation that Rita was being rude and sarcastic hit home and Amelia promptly turned to walked off, deciding that it was best to ignore them.

"Well I just wish some people would stop playing about with the men in the church, that's all", Alice fired a passing shot loud enough for Amelia and everyone standing nearby to hear. Then the two back-biters sniggered, loud enough to invite further glances at Amelia and to question their distasteful behaviour, but they did not seem to care.

Such gossip did not tease Amelia to retaliate. Instead she drew from the Word that she had internalised, that reminded her to pray for those that spoke ill of her or hated her. And Amelia kept her joy. She later learned from her friend Jenny that upon hearing about Sister Alice and Sister Rita's disgraceful behaviour, Bishop Manning had admonished them about the evils of back-biting and the following Sunday he had devoted a whole sermon to the subject.

Perhaps as a result of the malicious gossip Amelia began to have a nightly recurring dream in which she saw herself and Bro Al getting married. So beautiful were the reveries that upon awakening from them, she would lay very still willing her mind to remain in dreamland, for there Bro Al was young, tall and handsome and truly her beloved. But his face was not that of the real Bro Al's but that of a figment of her imagination, the face that Amelia had daydreamed about for many years, as she hoped that her husband to might look. She tried to interpret the dream but could find no explanation for it. It did occur to her to share them with her mother who was gifted in the interpretation of dreams but Amelia decided not to do so since she fretted that her mother would judge her.

On Sunday 13 December 2011 Amelia set out for church bright and early. She was hopeful that Bro Al would be back in church today since the report about his health given last Sunday by Bishop Manning had been more favourable. Her heart sank as she arrived and did not find him before the altar worshipping in his usual manner. So Amelia emulated him once again and as her spirit soared she basked in God's glory, and she thanked the Almighty for the liberating gift of pure worship.

Later just after the service had begun, heads turned and eyes darted in the sanctuary to focus upon the pew where Bro Al usually sat as a carer brought him in a wheelchair and helped him out into his seat.

Many greeted Bro Al with wide smiles, and whispered "howdies", obviously happy to see him, but no one smiled wider than Amelia, demonstrating her joy at the return of her beloved brother Al – while Alice and Rita stared on and sniggered nastily. Bro Steve too had been affected by the gossiping, apparently, and was not best pleased to see Bro Al, whom he now regarded as a viable rival for Amelia's hand and seeing the look in her eyes. But Amelia knew that her love was without guile and untainted – she loved Bro Al with the pure love of God – if only they could experience such love they would not be so bitter – she was certain. Sadly, apparently the only person who understood that kind of love was Bishop Manning.

When the service ended Amelia made a beeline for the pew where Bro Al sat. As she approached him he smiled timidly yet fondly up at her – he looked pale and gaunt. Defiantly, Amelia stooped down and engaged Bro Al in a long embrace before saying, "It's good to have you back Bro Al, I've missed you so very much", as she drew back to look into his watery eyes.

"I'm glad to be in the house of God", Bro Al responded with some effort and Amelia could tell that he had a long way to go before he returned to full health and fitness.

"Thank you Sister Amelia for your beautiful rendition – I would like to say just how much I appreciate you using your talent to glorify the Lord – you are a real blessing. Please keep singing for God and to bring joy, peace and love to all who hears you", he spoke haltingly – then smiled weakly. It was the most that Bro Al had ever spoken to Amelia in the three years since his arrival at Born Again Church of God.

"Well thank you Bro Al for your wonderful compliment", Amelia countered, and continued "I give God all the glory for the gifts he has given to me and I am overjoyed to be used of Him", she continued "Thank you too Bro Al for demonstrating to me true worship – I have learned so very much from you", and then they both smiled widely at each other in reciprocal admiration.

The following Sunday morning Bro Al did not attend church – Amelia was saddened. Later, just before he brought the sermon Bishop Manning had an announcement to make. "I regret to announce that Bro Alfred Cohen passed away on Monday of last week", was the sad news that pierced Amelia's heart and she burst into an involuntary fit of sobs which was audible throughout the sanctuary. This outburst had the effect of moving Bishop Manning to tears also and he had to sit down and gather himself.

Joyce rushed to her daughter and helped her from the sanctuary. She was aware of the gossiping that had been circulated by Rita and Alice, which she had been uncertain held any substance, but seeing her daughter's reaction to this news, convinced Joyce that there may be fire that had created the smoke. But she loved her daughter and would defend her howsoever necessary. "Oh mum, I can't believe that Bro Al is gone", Amelia sobbed. "Mum, he was so special to me – I truly loved him, mum – he was a beautiful soul – a wonderful man of God", Amelia babbled, and her mother agreed but she did think her daughter was sorrowing for this man she hardly knew a little too much.

After Amelia had composed herself somewhat, they returned to the sanctuary just in time to observe the 1 minute silence that Bishop Manning asked for in honour of Bro Al's memory. "A wonderful man of God – we believe he is now at home with the Lord", Bishop Manning concluded the tribute. He then proceeded to announce that Bro Al had already been buried as it was the Jewish tradition to bury the dead within 24 hours' of death. The congregation, stirred by this revelation, demonstrated a new wave of sadness at not being able to attend a funeral to say goodbye to the eccentric Bro Al who had grown to be much loved by many if not most at Born Again Church of God. Bishop Manning then gave a tribute of thanks from Bro Al's family to the benefactor who had contributed substantially towards Bro Al's home-going formalities.

As Bishop spoke all eyes turned to regard Bro Steve and a loud cheer rang out throughout the sanctuary. Bro Steve tried to make light of his good deed as usual and Amelia's heart was once again touched by his kindness.

Rita Harris was the loudest complainant that the funeral had already taken place, but for all the wrong reasons – she had been relishing the thought of attending the funeral so that she could learn more about Bro Al and his family background. Others were genuinely sorry though.

Chapter 11

The following week passed in a haze of sadness and joy by day, for it was Christmas week, and a series of beautiful yet sad reveries during the night as Amelia moaned the passing of her brethren. During her waking hours she mused upon Bro Al's mannerisms and warmth and celebrated his life and salvation by emulating his ways of worship and reflected upon how he had influenced her life and ministry which had been catapulted to a far higher spiritual plane. And she thanked God continuously that she had encountered Bro Al, and for his lasting legacy of worship.

Something extraordinary happened on Christmas Eve, in the week after Bro Al passed away. On that Thursday night, as Amelia sat quietly reflecting in her room, her mother called up to her. "Amelia – telephone sweetie", she said in her customarily high pitched shrill.

"Who is it – tell them I'll call them back later", Amelia replied.

"It's Avarel – okay I'll tell her", Joyce replied.

"I'll take it", Amelia said immediately.

Amelia wanted to take the call – to satisfy herself that her mother was not pulling her leg. It had been so many years since she last received a call from Avarel who had cut ties completely with her long before Carly had also disappeared from her life.

"Hello – Avarel? She asked gingerly.

"Yeah, it's me girl – you're not dreaming – compliments of the season", Avarel replied in a gentle voice. She sounded as though she was concerned that Amelia would not want to speak to her.

"Happy Christmas to you too – hey girl – how are you?" Amelia gushed, continuing, "It's been a long, long time". She smiled broadly as she spoke and it must certainly have been discerned by Avarel on the other end of the 'phone line because she perked up.

"Girl, I owe you a big, big apology – sorry I haven't been in touch – I cannot provide a plausible explanation as to why ….. please forgive me", Avarel pleaded.

Amelia hesitated – she wanted to give her long lost friend a chance to get things off of her chest if she had a mind to do so.

"I will try and explain myself when I see you", Avarel went on.

"Okay – in your own time – but don't leave it too long", Amelia replied, and chuckled and as Avarel joined her in laughter, the ice was well and truly broken.

"Avarel must have something important on her mind to have called me at all yet alone at this time" Amelia thought, noting that it was past 11 pm.

"I've been meaning to call for a few months now – I cannot tell you how many times I have lifted the receiver, or started to dial your number, but had put off doing so – it has taken me so long to build up the courage but I finally did it today", Avarel sounded triumphant.

Then they talked – well Avarel talked mostly while Amelia listened. When the conversation ended Amelia mulled over their discussion in her mind

They had not talked about Brendon at all but Amelia recalled from information acquired about her friend over the years from news reports that Avarel and Brendon had divorced many years before – their divorce had been famous in its own right, only overshadowed by the one from her second husband, who Amelia recalled was an incredibly good looking male model or something. But she was not aware that Avarel had married for a third time, until her friend informed her – she referred to him as Simon, and her husband and her five year old son called Davy had been the dominant subjects during their conversation.

Avarel had spoken at length about her family and lifestyle. She stressed her privileges, as if Amelia wasn't already aware that she had done extremely well for herself – it came across as if Avarel was showing off in fact, but Amelia didn't mind. She recalled how poverty stricken Avarel's family had been when they were growing up and realised that her friend's success had surpassed her wildest dreams, so she could tolerate her showing off a little. But as Avarel spoke about her husband and son, Amelia gathered that all was not well with her personal life.

When Avarel asked about Amelia's current marital status – she replied "I'm still waiting on God girl", and an awkward silence had ensued, which was broken by Avarel.

"Girl, I just can't believe those brothers have let you alone for all these years – are they blind – look how beautiful you are – are they crazy?" she said, which teased a little chuckle out of Amelia.

Then Amelia had steered the conversation around to spiritual things and had immediately sensed a great spiritual hunger in Avarel.

"Church has changed so much since we were teenagers" Amelia had reported.

"Church – church – I feel so far removed from my life in church now", Avarel sounded pensive.

"Oh you mean Born Again – yeah – what church do you attend nowadays?" Amelia had asked curiously.

"To tell you the truth I haven't been to a church in years", Avarel confessed.

"Wow", was all Amelia said.

"I really messed up with God, Amelia", Avarel continued – she sounded close to tears.

"Well you know that He is always there for you Avarel – just reach out to Him and he will reach right back to you", Amelia reassured.

"Yeah – I would, if I could only remember how", Avarel said candidly.

"Has it gotten so bad that you have forgotten how to pray?" Amelia asked, trying to imagine what such a state might feel like.

"I'm trying to find my way back, though", Avarel said, "Please pray for me Amelia". "I will come and visit Born Again soon – now that I have mustered up the courage to call you, it won't be so hard to take the next step.

"Sure, that would be wonderful", Amelia gushed excitedly.

"I'll let you know when – well I've got to go now – by the way, do you see Carly – I heard that she has a big family now", Avarel said.

"Yes, she has 6 children now but no I haven't seen her for many years – I see some of her children at church sometimes though – they are absolutely beautiful". "I send her greetings through them from time to time but she has never gotten in touch – I get the impression she just wants to leave her past behind her", Amelia replied, recalling her last conversation with Carly many years before.

"Really", Avarel replied.

"Yeah – it would be great to hear from her though", memories of God's Three Little Angels flitted across Amelia's mind as she spoke.

"Yeah – that would be wonderful, wouldn't it", Avarel replied and continued. "I will call you soon to arrange a visit to Born Again".

"Okay – anytime", Amelia replied, not knowing whether to believe her friend or not.

"Okay – I'll speak to you soon – Amelia, thank you for taking my call and speaking with me after all this time", Avarel sounded genuinely grateful.

"No problem – it was great to hear from you again", Amelia said and smiled widely.

"Bye then", and Avarel was gone before Amelia replied "Bye".

Avarel's promise sounded genuine and Amelia lay awake that night into the early hours, relishing the thought of seeing her childhood friend again. And the joy that she felt at this prospect overshadowed the sadness at the death of her beloved worship mentor.

Chapter 1

The New Year arrived and Amelia looked forward to the promise of new beginnings. Time passed quickly and uneventfully after the Christmas and New Year celebrations, Bro Al's demise and Avarel's telephone call. Bro Steve continued in his efforts to woo her and by March, having received no encouragement, he stepped up his labour of love to an even higher level, going so far as to offer her a brand new car. The offer came via Bishop Manning at a prearranged meeting.

"Prophetess Amelia – God has smiled upon you today", Bishop Manning announced beaming. He was wearing an ear to ear smile that told Amelia he had good tidings to bring. "I know you are aware of the fact that this congregation has a secret benefactor", Bishop paused to gauge her response. She nodded and he continued, "Well, you have come into favour Sister Amelia – the benefactor has singled you out to receive a brand new car", Bishop Manning said – once again he paused for effect. Amelia was not sure how she should react to such news. The natural and automatic reaction should be to praise God, to get excited, holler and shout jubilantly, but she didn't feel like doing anything like that. The only thought that occurred to her was that Bro Steve was trying to buy some love.

"The car has already been purchased – all you have to do is call into Samson's Car Sales, collect the keys and drive it home".

It occurred to Amelia that she could certainly do with a new car, since the one she now drove she had purchased over 8 years ago, and was second-hand by 4 years when she had bought it. It was getting rickety with age and she was sorely tempted to accept the gift. But when she thought again about the strings that Bro Steve was trying to attach to her, she replied, "Bishop, I'm sorry please tell the benefactor that I cannot accept his gift", which response rendered Bishop Manning speechless for a beat. When he found his tongue again he tried to encourage her to take the car, stating that he believed that it was being offered in good faith. But, since Amelia was uncertain of Bro Steve's integrity or how he had made his money in the first place, she remained disinclined to accept anything from his hand – she did not want Steve getting the wrong impression that she could be bought – so she stuck to her guns without even asking of the car's make or model.

Although the benefactor always attached a condition of confidentiality, forbidding the receivers of gifts from discussing their good fortune with others, Amelia learned through the grapevine (i.e. her mother who was one of the First Lady's closest friends in whom she confided), that Bishop Manning had also received many expensive gifts from the hand of the secret benefactor. Notably, he had received not one, but two motor vehicles. The first he had received in the week following Bro Steve's baptism – a brand new 7 series BMW, and the latest was a brand new top specification MXLX Saloon Sport, which he had accepted unreservedly, handing down the first gifted motor to his wife. And he had testified to the congregation that those gifts were a great blessing from God. Amelia could overlook the first gift, but she thought the second was unnecessary and excessive – in her opinion Bishop Manning should have refused to accept it. And it was the first time since meeting Bishop Manning, who had been the Head of Born Again for more than 14 years, that Amelia had ever had cause to question his integrity. But even as she sought to condemn the man of God, her mind rationalised that there was no good reason for him not to accept those gifts, because Bro Steve had now changed his ways. But Amelia just could not get past the criminal tag.

Amelia's viewpoint was at odds with that of her mother and father's, who fully supported Bishop Manning's decision to accept gifts from the benefactor's hand and they defended their pontiff's corner vehemently when Amelia finally verbalised her concerns. After their debate on the subject Amelia felt mildly ashamed and asked God to forgive her as she searched the depth of her heart and realised that her stance was due to her innate and irrational mistrust of Steve Walters. But she could not shake the base of her feelings towards the man. She surmised that such strong feelings were either a warning from God himself or a hindrance from the devil which opened up a whole new chain of reasoning.

Chapter 2

The presence of a secret benefactor at Born Again Pentecostal was seen by many as a unique attraction. In the two years since the coming of the benefactor, it was apparent that several new members had joined Born Again Church of God, most of who had defected from neighbouring congregations and it was noised abroad that many had been enticed by the news of the lucrative gifts being distributed by the church's secret benefactor.

Each week many gifts were recorded amongst the brethren of the Born Again congregation. And forbidden testimonies of thankfulness and joy rang out week after week as brethren gratefully gave thanks for their windfalls and blessings. Many well-meaning brethren who had not received gifts rejoiced with those who had been blessed, while no doubt whispering a prayer in their hearts that their turn would come around soon. But there was a minority who had not received, that became sour or bitter (depending on your taste), with jealousy. Such green brethren had become so incensed that they stopped speaking to those who had been blessed and also resorted to treating Bro Steve less favourably than they had done before, blaming him for having apparently overlooked them.

The loudest grumbler was Rita Harris, who became the voice of those aggrieved and led the cavalry which culminated in an exodus of ten or so brethren who left Born Again as they *"could not continue to worship with such materialistic individuals"*. Their main contention was with those who now treated Bro Steve as something of a local hero. Curiously though, Rita did not resign her paid employment as the Senior Administrative Manager of Born Again, or as the CCG for she continued to man operations through the DCCG and others who still attended services at Born Again, and also by listening through doors and walls of Bishop Manning's office, and what she didn't know she made up.

Just before the departure of the aggrieved, a rumour began to circulate that the secret benefactor was in fact Bishop Manning himself and not Steve Walters after all. This virulent rumour went further in alleging that Bishop Manning was stealing money from the offering pot to buy himself luxurious items and that, to cover up his misdeeds, he was also giving his favoured brethren presents out of the church funds. No-one knew how this poisonous rumour had originated.

As soon as he heard the rumours, Bishop Manning immediately called a church conference to address what he referred to as "the lies of satan". However, this step only served to empower the maligners who surmised that he was only trying to cover his misdeeds and although most of the church's financial affairs were laid bare at the conference and checked out except for a couple of thousand pounds, the irrational accusing fingers still pointed towards Bishop Manning.

Of course no right thinking brethren believed the malicious lie but there were others, particularly new converts, who were persuaded – and some left the church soon after Rita and the initial defectors due to the fact that this gossip stunted their spiritual development. But there was no question in Amelia's mind that the allegation was baseless and she guessed that Rita and Alice were at the root of the lie.

Chapter 3

In mid-May, a month or so after Rita and her cronies left the church Bishop Manning handed Amelia a letter after Sunday service which he said was from the secret benefactor. She placed the envelope inside her handbag intending to read it when she got home. She was so curious to know the content of the letter that upon arriving home from church she immediately ran to her room and ripped the envelope open while at the same time she flopped upon her bed – and she began to read:

> *"Dear Sister Amelia,*
>
> *I have learned from Bishop Manning that you refused to accept the motor car that was gifted to you and I am writing to implore you, to rethink the position that you have taken.*
>
> *May I point out that this gift is given without any reservation or obligation whatsoever – it has been made to you following the leading of the Holy Spirit. Through revelation from God it became known that this gift will meet a need in your life. God wants to reward you for all your labour over the years and your wonderful song ministry which you have wholeheartedly given which has blessed and liberated so many people from sin, sicknesses and oppression.*
>
> *The keys for the motor vehicle are now with Bishop Manning and it would give great joy if you would accept them.*
>
> *However, if you would perhaps prefer to receive a monetary gift in place of the motor car, please let Bishop Manning know.*
>
> *Yours truly,*
> *Your Secret Benefactor*

Amelia folded the letter and put it back into its envelope. She pondered – it certainly sounded well-meaning. And she said a silent prayer for guidance. As she ended her plea, it immediately occurred to her that perhaps she was being a little hard on Bro Steve. Amelia wondered whether God was putting this thought to her and she resolved to pray some more to be certain. So she prayed in earnest all that week. By the end of the week she felt that she might accept the gift. But she could not follow through with this because the feeling that it was inappropriate for her to accept the car due to Bro Steve's obvious romantic interest in her was a stronger compulsion and she made up her mind to tell Bishop Manning so.

The following Sunday after church Amelia waited for the chance to speak with Bishop Manning. After he had seen most of the brethren off he ushered her into his office and gestured to her to take a seat as he spoke.

"Well Sister Amelia – have you made up your mind about the motor vehicle", Bishop got straight to the point.

"Bishop Manning – I don't think I should accept the car at this time", Amelia replied. Bishop Manning nodded. He said nothing further causing her to feel ill at ease and before she knew it she had blurted out, "I need to pray about it some more".

"Okay – I'll leave it with you then, but I must have an answer by Friday of this week – the garage cannot hold the car indefinitely". "If it is not accepted by then, the gift must be reallocated, I'm afraid", Bishop replied. Amelia got the distinct impression that Bishop Manning wanted her to accept the gift. As she arose to leave, she was just about to say goodbye to him when he looked up at her, engaged her eyes and said, "Amelia, you trust me, don't you dear?"

"But of course Bishop Manning – I do trust you – I believe you are God's true servant", Amelia replied immediately and smiled.

"Well, let me provide you with some guidance – I believe that your benefactor has genuine philanthropic ways – I would advise that you accept the motor car", he said.

"Thank you very much Bishop Manning – I will let you know as soon as I have prayed about it some more", Amelia replied and she bade him goodbye – as she did so she experienced a "de ja vu" moment and wondered where she had heard the term "philanthropic ways" before.

Amelia did not know why she was procrastinating, but by Friday evening she still had not made up her mind to either accept or reject the car. She switched her mobile to voicemail not wishing to receive a call from Bishop. On her return from an evening out with Jenny, her mother informed her that Bishop Manning had telephoned her and asked that she call him back before 10 pm. However, she did not do so and retired to bed informing her mother that she was very tired and needed to sleep. An hour later she overheard her mother saying "Sorry Bishop – Amelia is asleep". Bishop Manning left a message on her voicemail the next day but she still did not respond. He must have gotten the message and never called again. Amelia was relieved because she was still not ready to give him an answer. "If the benefactor wants to give the gift to someone else – so be it", Amelia verbalised her thoughts as she acknowledged a deep peace within her spirit.

The following day Amelia attended church as usual but in order to avoid Bishop Manning, she sneaked out the back entrance after the service. When her parents arrived home Amelia was in the kitchen putting the final touches to Sunday lunch. As they entered the house they began to shout jubilant praises to God. She rushed towards them. "What's going on – has something happened", Amelia asked.

"Praise be to God, Amelia – God is good – he has touched Bro Steve's heart to offer us a brand new motor car", Joyce enthused.

"Praise the Lord – a top of the range Mercedes no less", Patrick shouted in affirmation.

"That's …. great", Amelia said a little hesitantly – she imagined it was the same gift that she had rejected but said nothing to her parents.

Joyce and Patrick went on to inform Amelia that they were due to collect the car from the garage the following day and further informed that they had been so overcome with joy that they had invited Bro Steve to Sunday lunch in two weeks' time in order to express their gratitude.

"Great", Amelia mumbled and smiled widely as Joyce gave her a questioning glance.

Although she tried to put up a joyful front, Amelia was far from happy that her parents had accepted the car, and she began to dread the dinner in two weeks' time – she felt anger rising within her at what she saw as Bro Steve's intrusion into her family's home by buying his way in and it grated on her least sensitive nerve that her parents now held him in the highest esteem. It occurred to her that she could make alternative plans for dinner that Sunday. However, her mother later informed her that she had invited all her other siblings and their spouses to join them that day and celebrate with them. Joyce went on to tell Amelia that they all wanted to meet Bro Steve for themselves, and Amelia realised that it would seem disrespectful if she were to be absent, especially since she lived in the same house. So she decided she would have to face the music.

Chapter 4

On Sunday 6 June 2012 Bro Steve came to dinner. He looked dapper, wearing a fetching three piece suit with an engaging smile fixed in place. In order to avoid him and Gemma's venomous tongue Amelia stayed in her room for most of the afternoon, having previously arranged to do some homework. She had already assisted her mother to prepare lunch that morning before church so that there was no obligation placed upon her to be downstairs helping out.

Although she stayed in her room with the door firmly shut, she could still hear clearly her mother's best hosting voice downstairs. Amelia heard Joyce's exaggerated jovial laughter clearly and knew that her mother would be doing all that she could to put Bro Steve at ease, "Yuk – mum is such a groveler", Amelia verbalised her thoughts. When her siblings and their families arrived one by one Amelia heard the greetings being exchanged and was tempted to rush down and embrace them but did not give in to her natural inclination. Alison and her husband were the last to arrive with their daughters and her nieces immediately came in search of her. "Aunty Amelia, Aunty Amelia – can we come in", Peaches called out to her favourite aunt. Hungry for their love Amelia rushed to let them in and hugged and loved them up before freshening up and being led by each hand down to dinner.

The girls insisted that Amelia sit with them at the additional table that Patrick had set up in the conservatory for the children and Amelia was glad, because not only was she out of the way of Gemma's venomous tongue lashing, she also got to avoid the inevitable match making attempts of her mother. But she could still clearly make out the conversation taking place in the dining room.

"Bro Steve I thank you for your thoughtfulness – it's so rare to find someone so generous – may God continue to bless you and don't change from your philanthropic ways", Joyce said. She had paid similar compliments three times in the last half an hour.

"Oh – it's no problem", Steve said humbly.

The words that her mother had just used to compliment Steve caused Amelia to ponder – "philanthropic ways" – Bishop Manning had used those same words during their meeting only the week before when he had spoken of the benefactor, but she had heard them before that, only she couldn't quite recall where. Amelia wondered whether God was trying to tell her something and mused for a moment, searching her heart deeply, but her heart had not changed towards Steve Walters.

Gemma spoke in the loudest voice possible and as expected Amelia's unmarried status was her favourite topic. "I don't see a wedding ring on your finger, Bro Steve, may I confirm that you are indeed still single", Gemma asked shamelessly. "Yes, I am, but I can assure you that it is not through choice", Steve replied, then continued, "I'm available – if only the right woman would say yes to my proposal and make an honest man of me".

"Amelia is a nice young lady – a little bit old fashioned though", Gemma replied.

"Yes, Sister Amelia certainly is a lovely young lady", Steve replied with a wink and a smile in his voice, adding "if only she would give me the time".

"Amelia is a little shy – that's all", Amelia heard her mother join the matchmaking and cast her eyes upwards with a sigh.

"She will make some man a wonderful wife someday", she added, causing Amelia to fume silently – she could die of embarrassment as her mother began to stir the matchmaking pot.

At that point Bro Kirk, who was well aware of Gemma's penchant to deride Amelia and their mother's mischievous tongue, interjected into the conversation before Joyce or Gemma had the opportunity to say anymore.

"God has certainly been good to us all, Bro Steve, and we are grateful for his manifold mercies", Kirk veered the conversation onto a more spiritual plain and Amelia breathed a sigh of relief. Alison's husband took up the thread from Kirk.

"Yes God is so good – it is wonderful that we have all come together at this time and it's not Christmas", he said to chuckles all around.

"We have so much to be thankful for – we are all healthy and happy", Alison chirped in. And so the dinner party went on.

The children kept Amelia well entertained and she did not feel she was missing out as the only adult seated with them. They enthralled her as they recounted stories of school and Sunday school adventures, achievements, ambitions, and as they played together and cemented family bonds.

When Joyce requested that she help serve dessert Amelia dutifully obliged although she would have preferred not to. As she did so her mother seized the chance and switched the conversation back to the question of marriage. "Bro Steve you are such a wonderful man – the kind of man that would make very good husband material", Joyce chuckled jovially and was joined by Steve, Gemma and Norman. Then Joyce nudged her husband under the table and Patrick took up the thread as previously instructed by his wife – they were on a mission to marry off their one remaining child and both agreed that Bro Steve was an excellent prospect. "Yes, Bro Steve will no doubt make some woman a great husband someday, don't you think Amelia?" Patrick asked.

"Great now mum has got dad on side as well", Amelia thought – she said nothing but simply smiled sweetly. After a beat she addressed Steve, "So what exactly do you do for a living, Bro Steve?" Amelia asked. She hoped he would have no plausible answer so he would be somewhat discredited.

"Oh, a little bit of this and a little bit of that – you know wherever there is money to be made I'm down", Bro Steve said.

"Well that told me absolutely nothing about what you do for a living", Amelia thought.

"Like what for example?" she pressed.

"He's a wheeler/dealer, darling", Joyce interjected.

"Ummh", Patrick agreed.

"Yes, that's me – I wheel and I deal", Bro Steve said, and if Amelia wasn't mistaken he breathed out carefully as though seeking to disguise a sigh of relief.

"For example", Amelia repeated, refusing to let him off the hook.

"I buy and sell – import and export – wherever there is money to be made in the world – I'm there", Bro Steve said smiling smugly. Before Amelia could press him further he changed the subject. "Sister Joyce this fruit crumble is the best I have ever tasted – so delicate, ummh". "Do you think I could have another helping?" he said and all chuckled.

"Oh yes – but of course", Joyce replied then she continued, "Oh Amelia made the fruit crumble – isn't she a great cook?"

"She's going to make someone a great wife someday", Patrick chipped in like a scratched disc, and both parents looked at each other and smiled knowingly. And Bro Steve looked at Amelia and smiled too then said "I only wish that that lucky fellow could be me".

"Well is that a proposal, Bro Steve", Gemma said eagerly.

"Ummph – I'll say it is", Patrick said then laughed heartily as all eyes turned to stare in Amelia's direction.

"Sorry, I've got some work to finish", Amelia blurted out and immediately headed upstairs to her bedroom. As she left, Peaches and Opal tried to follow her but were scolded by their father, Harry, "No, you can't go yet – you must sit down and finish your food first", and they did as they were told.

Sitting alone in her bedroom, Amelia stared blankly at the front page of the folder of papers that she was supposed to be working on. She could hear Gemma continue to drive the conversation downstairs, suggesting to Steve how he might go about wooing her. She noted with some consolation that her sister was not referring to her in derogatory terms – but she still sounded ever so desperate to marry her off, which only had the effect of strengthening Amelia's resolve never to give Steve Walters the time of day. And she did not venture out of her room again until it was time to return to evening service.

Chapter 5

Having gotten wind of the fact that Bro Steve had visited Amelia's home for Sunday lunch, Sister Alice had turned dark green with envy and rage. She always got what she wanted and she wanted Steve Walters with a burning passion and scotch bonnet sauce on top. From the moment she had laid eyes on him, digested his good looks and learned that he had a few million pounds to splash around, the compulsion to have him had sprouted and grown stronger day after day. She had employed every weapon in her feminine arsenal to get him and Alice was annoyed that Bro Steve had so far not been persuaded. She had no further tricks – she had used all the ones that she knew to try and hook him, from telling Steve in no uncertain terms that she was romantically interested in him, to turning up uninvited at his home wearing skimpy outfits that had probably reserved a place in hell for her – on more than one occasion. The most she had gotten from him was an admission that he loved her like a little sister, but she was a woman and wanted to be his woman, not his friend or charge. Alice was now desperately confused. She could not understand why Steve had apparently chosen Amelia Lanson, who was nearly 40, over her, a young woman of 26 – nearly half her age.

Every day Alice looked into the mirror and noted that God had not spared on beauty when she was created. With big bright eyes, beautiful lips, an unobjectionable nose, a delicious mid honey complexion and radiant smile, she had all that most men found irresistible. She was tall enough and had the perfect hourglass figure with child bearing hips that men desired and to cap it all she had been well trained by her mother to be the perfect wife and mother. Young, energetic and vibrant, she was surely better than the older woman – but none of that seemed to make any difference whatsoever to Steve. His eyes were unwaveringly fixed upon Amelia Lanson – everyone could see that.

By far the most upsetting thing for Alice was the fact that Steve had never given her any gifts as he had done to so many other brethren at Born Again. She became aware that he had given Amelia's parents a brand new car and Alice wanted one too. When she asked Steve why he had never favoured her, he replied, "I don't choose who to bless – God does", and refused to say anymore on the subject. She let it drop, but she was far from happy that Steve had overlooked her and her family and rancour simmered upon the back burner of Alice's heart. She hoped that Steve would soon wake up to the fact that she was the best thing for him, but she was becoming fed up to the back tooth of not having so far received the reward for which she had toiled and her frustration stirred up the hatred that she had for Amelia.

With deadly malice stirring within her heart Alice took the decision to have a word with Amelia the next Sunday evening – she needed to find out whether there was any truth in the latest news from Rita that Steve and she were dating.

So after service Alice made her approach. "Sister Amelia, can I have a word please", Alice pulled at Amelia's arm gently, then more forcefully, drawing her aside. "I heard that you and Bro Steve are an item now – is that true?" Alice got straight to the point as she stared intently into Amelia's disbelieving eyes.

"I beg your pardon", Amelia responded immediately.

"Bro Steve and you – are you seeing each other?" Alice said brusquely. "I'm sorry young lady – where did you get that idea from?" a grave expression crossed Amelia's face.

Alice appeared stumped to come up with an answer then she replied, "Well everyone is talking about it".

"Talking about it – talking about what exactly?" Amelia laughed – a dry mirthless chuckle. She also shook her head from side to side in disbelief – "Bro Steve – you actually think there is something between him and me?" Amelia placed an over exaggerated emphasis on "me".

"What are you laughing at?" Alice said insolently, discomfited.

"I'm laughing because that concept is so absurd – I'm laughing because I cannot believe how fertile people's imaginations can be – the stories that they make up – I'm laughing because, well, because Bro Steve is certainly not my type – he is evidentially more your type Alice", Amelia said, then she became serious. "But seriously though – you obviously have some sort of crush on Bro Steve – am I correct?" Amelia asked.

"Crush – nnnoooo – of course not", Alice said way too casually, belying her obvious passion for Steve.

"Yes you do…." Amelia surmised, unchallenged, "….and believe me Alice – you have absolutely nothing to worry about where I am concerned", she continued. "God bless you Sister Alice", and with that Amelia smiled and walked away leaving Alice feeling more confused than ever.

Throughout the following week Amelia prayed for Alice whom she suspected may have lost her mind, if not her virtue. She prayed lovingly, not from a self-righteous perspective, but as she did so, Amelia found herself wondering why it was that everyone but she thought the world of Bro Steve.

Chapter 6

In the weeks that followed Bro Steve stepped up his efforts to win Amelia's heart yet more, emboldened from the conversations he had had with her family at the dinner party. Apart from following her around and his endeavours to lock eyes with hers, he also approached her on three occasions to ask her out to dinner. The third time he asked and received a negative response from Amelia, Bro Steve hissed air through his teeth, and commented "I really don't know why you keep on refusing me – it's not as if you have people queuing up to ask you out", causing Amelia to see red.

"Look, I'm not interested, get it? Why don't you try Sister Alice – I'm sure she would be only too happy to oblige".

With a scowl on his face Bro Steve walked away. As Amelia watched him go, she made a decision – she needed to have a word with Bishop Manning about the way in which he was behaving. Despite the fact that she had made it clear that she was not interested, Steve had persisted in approaching her. Amelia could not understand why because he could have his pick of up to six younger and more beautiful women who would jump at the chance to marry him. And it annoyed her that she was being constantly observed by Sister Alice who spied ubiquitously upon her at every turn, especially when Bro Steve was close by.

On Wednesday afternoon Amelia made her way to Bishop Manning's office. She paused before entering the rear entrance of the church and said a word of prayer before proceeding. She hoped their meeting would be productive.

"Hello, Sister Amelia – so lovely to see you", Bishop Manning greeted her heartily as she entered his newly refurbished opulent office.

"Good to see you Bishop, Amelia countered, as she smiled widely", she looked around approvingly, as she made her way to the seat opposite Bishop Manning. "I love your new office, Bishop – it's really beautiful", Amelia commented.

"Oh thank you my dear Sister and praise be to God".

After exchanging further pleasantries Amelia announced the purpose of her visit. "Bishop please would you mind having a word with Bro Steve – you know he approached you before to ask about marrying me and I said "no", well he has not allowed the matter to drop and has been pestering me to go on dates with him", she paused to breathe, then continued. "I am simply not interest in Bro Steve in any romantic sense, Bishop and I just wish he would leave me alone. "Now he has also started to display hostility towards me for declining his advances". "That is why I thought it best to draw the matter to your attention – could you please have a word with him?" Amelia complained. Then she sat and eyed the Bishop expectantly.

Bishop Manning did not speak – he just nodded his understanding, prompting Amelia to continue pouring her heart out to him. "The fact is that there are many other sisters in the church that would be happy to entertain Bro Steve". "But I am simply not interested and never will be". "Please would you speak to Bro Steve and make him understand that", Amelia rested her case.

"Sister Amelia, I am not at all happy to hear what you are telling me – no not at all happy – no not at all happy", Bishop Manning repeated the end of the sentence as he was accustomed to doing when he felt strongly about something. His voice was a monotone, bereft of emotion but his frown demonstrated his displeasure.

"I thought that since the time when you informed me that you were not interested, a response which I relayed to Bro Steve – I thought he had gotten the message – I really did not realise that he had taken to pestering you – I really did not realise – no, I really didn't realise at all, at all, at all", Bishop Manning said. "So I am very happy that you have brought this to my attention – yes, I will speak to him without delay – leave it with me, my dear, leave it with me – just leave it with me", Bishop Manning promised and closed the chapter.

"So Sister Amelia, would you please prepare to minister next Sunday – the message that God has laid upon my heart is "Anointed and appointed to serve", and I think an appropriate rendition would be the song entitled "Let me be a servant, Lord", Amelia nodded her approval as Bishop spoke, then commented, "Yes – that is a difficult song to sing so please pray for me Bishop", then they both laughed. Neither realised that Rita was listening to their laughter and interpreting their mirth from a completely warped perspective.

After praying together Amelia said goodbye to Bishop Manning and made her way home oblivious to the fact that someone was at that very moment using her name to sow seeds of discord amongst her brethren.

Chapter 1

The following Sunday morning 21 August 2011 Amelia arrived for church early and ran through the usual worship ritual before anyone else arrived in the sanctuary. She had to focus her devotional worship particularly this morning because she was preparing to minister in song. She knelt at the altar and began to chant praises and as her worship heightened she began to bob her head gently back and forth as she had learned to do from observing Bro Al. Amelia sensed in her spirit that God was well pleased as she felt his Spirit draw near. Suddenly she received a revelation to minister an incomplete song that she had begun to write. The melody and lyrics arose strongly in her spirit and she savoured them and began to hum quietly. Amelia could not understand why but she had only been able to write what sounded to her to be the bridge and chorus of the song despite having employed strenuous efforts to write a verse. And she wondered why God was leading her to minister the incomplete song today. But she knew she would be obedient as she began to sing the words quietly to herself. It dawned upon her that the lyrics fitted Bishop Manning's theme perfectly.

I said I'd be a servant but you made me a Queen.
I bowed down before you and you lifted my head up high.
With your mighty hand Lord – so powerful I have seen
You created a palace for me
I'm glad to be home – so glad to be home
Never will I wonder from the comfort of your bosom
Never will I roam, to drink of pleasures that could never satisfy my soul
I'm where I want to be – your love embraces me – here at home.
I'm where I want to be – where you can use me – here at home
And I'll always be your servant – here at home.
For you lifted me high – made me a queen – here
I'm where I want to be – your arms protect me – here at home.

As Amelia stood to minister in song, she scanned the sanctuary for those whose worship was visual, upon whom she liked to focus during her ministrations. As led by the Holy Spirit she began to sing the unfinished song and her eyes settled upon a gentleman whose countenance embodied pure worship. She had never seen the stranger in church before but he seemed oddly familiar. In spite of the fact that she was worshipping, Amelia could not help noticing how incredibly handsome and unusual looking the stranger was. In a fleeting moment she surmised that he appeared tall although he was sitting down. His eyes were slightly bulbous, like those of an ancient Egyptian, and his nose classically straight. His cheekbones were chiselled and his lips were half-full, smooth and perfectly shaped and outlined. He looked exotic with his slicked back wavy hair, (whether natural or chemically enhanced Amelia could not tell). His complexion shone out luminescent like hot molasses, and as he opened his eyes briefly she could just make out the colour as light brown which seemed odd against his dark hue.

As Amelia sang the chorus of the incomplete self-composed song, she looked upon the stranger as he closed his eyes again in worship. There it was again – the flash of recognition – then it dawned upon her where she might have seen before – but she could not be certain.

Amelia continued to watch the stranger worshipping, but she suddenly realised that the sight of him was having an undesirable effect upon her emotions. She was losing control of her focus which was being drawn toward the handsome stranger's visual beauty and away from the spiritual. An inner struggle then ensued as Amelia wanted to continue looking at the stranger and drawing spiritual strength from his evident fervency, but she also wanted to drink in the exquisite contours of his face, and as her palms began to sweat and her heart started to pound, Amelia looked away and cast her eyes towards heaven.

The presence of the Holy Spirit was palpable in the atmosphere as Amelia repeated the refrain "so glad to be home" over and over again. The worship singers found their places behind her and joined in at her behest and their mingled voices created a crescendo of pure veneration as spirits in the sanctuary soared in worship and thankful praise.

When the service ended Amelia looked over towards where the stranger was. He was still seated there but was now deep in conversation with the person sitting next to him, whom Amelia was surprised to notice for the first time was in fact Avarel. Happiness surged throughout her being as she pressed through the crowd to reach her old friend. When she got to where Avarel was standing, she gushed "Avarel – oh gosh, you came – oh it's so good to see you", Amelia placed an emphasis on "soooo". Avarel smiled beamingly and arose to hug her childhood friend enthusiastically. Their hug was long and hungry accompanied by mutual pats upon backs and exchanged "Happy Birthday" wishes. When they broke apart Avarel introduced Amelia to the beautiful stranger.

"This is Yan – Yan Kennelly, my darling friend", she held the stranger's hand firmly and looked meaningfully into his eyes as she made the introduction. And everyone standing around including Amelia could tell that they were more than just good friends.

"I'm pleased to meet you Yan", Amelia said smiling at the stranger, as an elderly woman who recognised Avarel seized upon her, drew her aside and engaged her in conversation.

Amelia proffered her hand to Yan who shook it heartily. He smiled back "I am very pleased to meet you, Sister Amelia", he said emphatically, he spoke with a strong yet endearing Jamaican twang, and Amelia wasn't mistaken – he gave her a longer than expected searching look – she had encountered such a look many times before in her lifetime, but never before had her body responded in this way, for her cheeks burnt red hot, she began to perspire profusely all over and her heart beat loudly and fast. "*Most peculiar – how odd*", Amelia thought and she was intrigued to know what Yan might be thinking. The way he continued to regard her led Amelia to conclude that he was obviously a big flirt.

Taking a deep breath, Amelia's heart galloped and leapt several beats as she appreciated the nearness of Yan. She managed to maintain a fixed smile though. Yan adopted a military stance (legs apart). As he rubbed his smooth chin, he looked at Amelia with smiling eyes and then around the sanctuary before returning his gaze to her. Amelia struggled to normalize her thinking – she needed to say something – anything. So taking another deep breath she managed to say, "So Bro Yan – did you enjoy the service". Yan shuffled from side to side as though trying to digest the question, then his smile widened and he replied, "Oh yes, Sis Amelia – I was truly blessed – that was a very beautiful song – such a wonderful inspiration", he said then gave her another long searching look.

"Yes it is a beautiful inspiration – but it is unfinished you know – did you notice", Amelia asked, genuinely curious to know what he thought.

"I must admit I did notice that it began and ended rather abruptly but apart from that it was a beautiful song – it will be even better when it's finished", he said in complimentary terms.

"Thank you very much", Amelia smiled

"I have been privileged to worship at Born Again this morning", Yan continued – he spoke with real enthusiasm as Avarel returned and grasped his hand possessively.

"Yes, your rendition was highly anointed Sister Amelia – I was greatly blessed", Yan said. He looked ill at ease with Avarel's open show of affection within the sanctuary but did not pull his hand free.

"Aaah wasn't it beautiful?", Avarel commented and continued, "Amelia you have surely grown as a singer – and that song – we need to talk about that song – it sounds like something I have written myself – like the part of my unfinished song that I have been trying to write", Avarel said thoughtfully.

"Really – I was struggling to write the rest of that song too – strange", Amelia said. "Perhaps we should put the two parts together", Avarel replied and they all laughed.

"Yes – your ministration was truly anointed", Yan repeated.

"I am merely an instrument in God's hand – I give Him all the glory", Amelia said and smiled humbly.

"Wonderful", Yan said and smiled at Amelia as he searched for her eyes again.

Amelia avoided eye contact. She felt so attracted to Yan that she was finding it difficult to breathe normally so close to him and if she looked into his eyes, she felt she might just hyper-ventilate. Instead she looked at Avarel and if she wasn't mistaken she detected a hint of jealousy in her old friend's eyes and demeanour.

"I believe I saw Carly earlier", Avarel changed the subject.

"I don't think so – Carly doesn't come to church anymore – she hasn't been to church for well over 18 years now", Amelia replied.

"I am certain it was her though – she was sitting over there", Avarel pointed towards the far right hand side of the large sanctuary but no-one resembling their old friend was anywhere to be seen.

"It would be an absolute miracle if you both returned to church on the same day", Amelia said, continuing to scan the sanctuary.

"Well, we have to rush off now Amelia", Avarel announced suddenly.

"Oh – so soon", Amelia said.

"Why so soon", Yan echoed.

"I've got an important interview in less than two hours and Yan there is something I need to discuss with you so come, let's go", Avarel commanded.

So they said their goodbyes and Avarel and Yan promised to return to Born Again in the not too distant future.

Chapter 2

Avarel was right – Carly had been in church. She had crept out as soon as the benediction was said and was now well on her way home, glad that she had driven her own car and not travelled to church with her father, who enjoyed working the sanctuary after church. The older children had also stayed behind to fool around with their friends after Sunday service in the same way that she used to do when she was a teenager – Carly smiled at the memory. Carly contemplated how light she felt – as though a burden had been lifted from off of her shoulders. And she wondered why she had stayed away from church for so many years.

Upon arrival at home Carly busied herself preparing Sunday lunch. When Rufus and the older children arrived home she delegated the finishing touches to them and retreated to her bedroom with an order not to be disturbed during her afternoon nap. But Carly could not sleep – instead she sat reminiscing, reflecting upon the great blessing she had received at church, the highlight of which had been her old friend Amelia's ministration in song.

Carly wondered what her life might have been if she had stayed with the Angels – if she had not met Dwight and allowed him to inveigle her into leaving the church. Might she now be as spiritually mature as Amelia was? Might she now occupy the same high and lofty place as her childhood friend, whom everyone revered as Church of God royalty? Carly cast her mind back into the distant past when she was one of God's Three Little Angels – a strong and whole Christian youth with a bright and certain future and stars in her eyes. Then she thought about where she was now – a strong yet broken woman – a single parent of six approaching middle age who was happy in part but not whole. Dwight had reconciled with his wife (not that she would have ever had him back in her life in any case), and it was unlikely that she would every meet a man who would marry her and take on her ready-made family. So Carly had resigned herself to the fate of a single mother for life – never married and never to be married. As she contemplated her circumstances, tears began to form in the corners of her eyes and she allowed them to flow, to smudge her make-up, transforming the flawless perfection of her Sunday morning face into a grotesque mess. As she cried the bitterness, sadness, hurt and pain that she had internalised flowed out of her as she thought of Dwight's repeated betrayals, of her unfulfilled marital destiny and the burdens he had heaped upon her to carry through life. And for many minutes she remained in that place.

Then an overwhelming feeling of guilt came over her – Carly loved her children so much – each one with an equal 100% measure and she began to beat herself up for allowing the thought that they were a burden to creep into her mind? She repented in her heart and began to count her blessings as the bitter tears subsided and gave way to new tears – sweet tears of joy as hope for a brighter future flowed into her – and Carly smiled through those tears, happy in the knowledge that she had found her way home.

Chapter 3

On the journey home from church Amelia shared the good news with her mother, "Did you see Avarel in church today, mum?"

"Avarel – you mean God's Three Little Angels Avarel?" Joyce enthused. "Someone told me that they saw Carly as well", Joyce continued in the high pitched squeal that her voice defaulted to when she was excited. "It is marvellous that they planned to return to church on the same day – simply wonderful."

"No mum, they didn't plan it – it's an absolute miracle", Amelia beamed, and added, "They haven't been in touch with one another for donkeys' years".

"That is simply amazing", Joyce said, "simply amazing".

After lunch Amelia retired to her room for a nap – she lay across her bed staring blankly up at the ceiling – only her mind was active. Since meeting Yan, his face and person had remained emblazoned upon the front page of her mind. Several conscious attempts to erect a mental barrier and block it out had failed because as soon as she lowered her guard he returned as vividly as before.

So Amelia let go and allowed her memory a free rein to replay images of Yan – his smile and the curious look on his face – the sound of his voice – the effect of his nearness. She slowly drifted off to sleep as she thought of him and a sweet reverie ensued in which Yan played the leading man and she the damsel in distress.

When Amelia awoke she remained in a dream and was still there as her father drove them home from church that evening, She closed her eyes and dissociated herself from the conversation between her parents as she thought of Yan, recalling each contour of his face, his towering physique and his mannerisms – but what delighted her most was the way he had looked at her and as she recalled the effect of his gaze she smiled and her spirit drifted upwards.

As they entered the house Amelia made her excuses and went straight to her room – she wanted to be alone – to pray fervently, for something peculiar was happening to her, something she did not understand.

Falling to her knees, Amelia began a dialogue with God, "Lord, what is happening to me?" "Help – please", she said then fell silent as though awaiting His reply. She felt like a wanton woman for having allowed her emotions to roam, having gone so far as to imagine how it might feel to be caught up in a lover's embrace with Yan – and further still – she had imagined a kiss, not just a friendly peck on the cheek but a KISS with tongues, like she had seen in forbidden sultry love films that she had sneaked away to watch with her peers as a mildly rebellious teenager. And knowing that Yan belonged to someone else, not least her long lost and dear friend Avarel caused Amelia great sadness and confusion. "God please forgive me and help me to overcome my fleshly desires", she petitioned.

Amelia had never felt this way before – this feeling that she might die if she never met Yan again, or ever saw his face again, or listen to him speak or watch him walk away until he was out of view again. The emotion was too strong – overpowering her will. These feelings were threatening to take complete control of her mind and she was not sure how she should deal with them.

As Amelia knelt in prayer her mobile began to buzz. After a few seconds it stopped but almost immediately it started to vibrate again. She ignored it but it did not go away – it vibrated incessantly and relentlessly for many minutes. Sighing in exasperation, she grabbed the offending gadget from the bedside cabinet and checked to see who could not wait – it was Avarel and it occurred to her that that was the last person she wanted to speak to at the moment.

Her mind was in turmoil and Amelia struggled between the desire to be faithful to her long lost friend and her need for Yan. Her head dictated that Yan was no more than a stranger but her heart yearned for him as though he had been her love for many years – for a brief moment she felt that she might die if she did not marry Yan, and her inborn life preservation instinct took over, suggesting to her mind that Avarel was, in fact, no longer a friend but an adversary who would keep her from realising her heart's desire. But reining in her rebellious thoughts, Amelia took a deep breath and defiantly pressed the answer button on her mobile.

"Hello girl – how are you?" Avarel sounded nauseatingly bubbly to Amelia's ears.

"Hi – I'm good and how are you?" she feigned enthusiasm.

"Oh girl sorry I had to rush off so soon this afternoon – I had some very important business to attend to, Avarel said.

Now that she had made her first step by going back to church that morning Avarel wanted to stay in close contact with Amelia, whom she knew was stable in her Christianity and could hopefully guide her back to the place where she needed to be with the Lord. She could feel already God's love all around and an unspeakable joy that she knew came only from being in His presence and she never wanted to lose that feeling again.

Avarel talked and Amelia listened for more than an hour. She spoke of having recently become disillusioned with life in the public eye, for the first time confessing to Amelia her failures as a mother. Then she spoke candidly about her chequered love life (understating the details, in order not to shock her morally untainted friend too much). She admitted that it was her unacceptable behaviour that had led to the breakdown of her third marriage and intimated that Simon had been the one to instigate divorce proceedings, even though she had been willing to continue the fight to save their marriage. She confided about her son Davy's evident happiness at now being a part of a true family and of the pain she felt when he spoke favourable about his new step-mother and step-sister.

"But I am moving forward now – learning from my mistakes and picking up the pieces of my life and running with them". "I am so happy that I connected with Yan again – I have always wondered what it would be like for us – we have always shared something special". "He and I first met over 9 years ago when Simon and I had been married for just over a year". "We got together then, you know, and it was special, but because I was married we couldn't take our feelings any further at that time", Avarel yapped on, oblivious to the fire of anxiety that she had ignited and was stoking within Amelia's heart. "But now that my husband has gone I am free and I am sooo glad Yan and I are together again – God is so good to me". "I just can't wait now for my divorce to be finalised so that I can be free to marry him – I don't intend to waste any time at all – and when I get married this time it will be for life – trust me, Amelia – trust me". "After all my experiences, I have learnt my lesson now – husband number four will be my very last – I will work so hard – I won't ever let Yan out of my sight for one moment", Avarel said then chuckled.

"Okay", Amelia replied. The word almost stuck in her throat. She tried to sound upbeat but her mood was dark. She was thinking of how unkind life could be, for after all the years of waiting patiently upon God, she had finally met a man that caused her heart to dance, and he happened to belong to her friend who was about to add him to her collection of husbands as number four – life seemed so grossly unfair to Amelia. And she almost gave in to the desire to cry as she contemplated the circumstances.

Taking a deep breath Amelia attempted to change the subject, "So, how did your meeting go then?"

"It was productive", Avarel replied then went on to tell Amelia what the meeting was all about – her new album on which she would start working shortly.

"I would love you to duet with me on the album, Amelia – your voice has become so absolutely beautiful – I want it on "Nectarous", Avarel enthused, then went on to explain that that was the name of the album. "I have just the song for you and I to duet on", Avarel sounded as if she was about to make Amelia's wildest dreams come true. Fifteen years ago Amelia might have been in awe of such a proposition with someone of Avarel's musical calibre, but now she was a Song Minister and no other genre was of interest to her. Her mind was set – she and her talents were God's property and would be used only for His honour.

"Is it a Christian song?" Amelia asked, already aware of what the answer would be because she knew that Avarel had never in her career performed any Christian material. A few seconds' pause followed then Avarel replied, "Well not exactly Christian but it is very positive".

"Uh – I'm not sure Avarel – I would have to hear it before making a decision – I would like to pray about it too – I pray for God's guidance in everything", Amelia stated, sounding ultra-spiritual to Avarel's ears.

"I sing only Christian material as a rule – it is a promise that I made some years ago – to myself and to the Lord – I dedicated my life – body, my mind, my spirit and my voice to His service, so I'm not at liberty to simply do what I want", Amelia informed.

"Aw really? Avarel asked, thinking *"steady on girlfriend"*, but sounding curious, then added, "Waw – we'll have to arrange to get you down to the studio to listen to the track then, and modifications can be made if necessary in any case".

After having just listened to Avarel confess about all the wantonness and debauchery that she had incorporated into her lifestyle since leaving church, and recalling the news reports that she had read about her friend over the years, Amelia was not inclined to want to duet or be associated musically with her at the present time. But she did not want to tell her that and silently hoped that Avarel would forget the idea of the duet – she would certainly not be reminding her.

When Avarel returned to the subject of Yan, this time going into more detail about her innermost, unholy desires, Amelia found it unbearable and abruptly ended the conversation by stating that she had a very early start the next morning. She promised to call her back later that week.

Their conversation at an end, Amelia dropped to her knees again in intercessory prayer for her friend, and for herself.

That night Amelia slept fitfully. She was awoken at least three times during the night, each time by a bad dream. Each dream had begun beautifully – of Yan in various romantic roles – then they had suddenly turned sinister as the threat of never getting close to Yan played out in Amelia's subconscious. In the final dream/nightmare Avarel was the nemesis who was relentless in her quest to separate them. Amelia awoke in a cold sweat and close to tears – it had all seemed so real and she struggled to get any restful sleep after that, waking up tired on Monday morning. At work she almost fell asleep at her desk while day-dreaming about Yan. Monday night followed the same pattern as Sunday. By Tuesday night the nightmares had disappeared but the dreams remained. They came one after the other, varied reveries filled with romance entertained Amelia each time she closed her eyes in sleep. But when she awoke the sadness of reality overwhelmed and Amelia often cried.

As the week progressed Amelia sought more and more to be in her own company, shunning family and colleagues to escape into daydream land. Apart from the excitement that her imagination provided, the week progressed uneventfully until Thursday evening when Bishop Manning telephoned. Joyce answered the landline and received the news – the church had been burgled last Sunday night and the offering, which was secreted away in his office waiting to be banked on Monday, had all gone together with various artefacts such as the one hundred piece set of golden communion goblets and two antique lead crystal and gold decanters – even the silver name plaques had been chiselled from the stone wall into which they had been inlaid at the rear of the sanctuary.

"Bishop Manning – that is terrible". "Who could have done such an awful thing?" Joyce exclaimed, her brow creased and she stared angrily at Patrick as though he were the culprit. He had come to stand close by, eagerly awaiting full details of the conversation, having overhead Joyce's reaction and realised that something terrible had taken place.

"I have no idea, Sister Joyce, but whoever it is better not think that they will get away with it – they will soon realise that God has seen them and He will certainly defend His house", Bishop Manning replied.

"That's just terrible", Joyce commiserated.

When the call ended Joyce informed Patrick of the news in full and the couple discussed the development in indignant tones which drew Amelia from her room to investigate the reason for the furore.

"I have been saying it for a long time that the church needs more security", Patrick stated angrily. "But they have been ignoring my warning and now look at what has happened". "Those artefacts are priceless and now they have gone for good – they are irreplaceable" he moaned.

"It is just terrible", Joyce repeated.

"What is it mum?"

"Somebody broke into the church last night", Patrick answered

"What – oh my Lord – what is this world coming to?" "People can just walk into a church and steal from God's house like that?" Amelia joined in the ruminations.

"It's terrible – simply terrible", Joyce could think of nothing else to say.

Chapter 4

Avarel contemplated her circumstances – she had made up her mind to change her lifestyle – to get closer to God – she knew there would be drastic changes to be made to her everyday routine and she set about tidying up straight away. For one, she no longer wished to sing material that was sexually explicit, which had always been her signature. So realising that she might be hammering the first nail into the coffin of her comeback she swallowed the bitter pill and called her Manager. She was ready to face whatsoever transpired from her decision. From now on she intended to perform only material that had a high moral content – songs that would benefit the world in some way, not ones that inveigled men to cheat on their wives or girlfriends or vice-verse or which advocated lust and immorality.

Having requested that her Manager seek to renegotiate the terms of her contract involving lawyers if necessary, Avarel set out on a shopping trip – she went to buy a Bible. That afternoon she sat alone leafing through the Holy book and felt the beginning of her spiritual healing – she had a long way to go but she had taken the first baby steps and felt full of hope of becoming stronger. But on Friday morning she learned that she could not attend church on Sunday due to the fact that a full day's recording had been scheduled. This followed her express instruction that she did not wish to work on Sundays in future and she was furious.

"Jimmy, why have you booked me up for Sunday?" "When you asked me on Monday about recording on Sundays, I specifically told you that I did not want to work on Sundays in future, didn't I?" Avarel breathed deeply in an attempt to control her temper. Jimmy Reynolds was a good Manager, but they did not always see eye to eye – he liked doing things his own way which was often at odds with her own perspective.

"Avarel – we need to do this – we need the extra time in the studio". "We should consider ourselves lucky – they don't usually open on Sundays but I managed to persuade them to and we got a super deal which means that we can stay within budget".

"Okay but just this Sunday, right".

"I booked every Sunday for the next 12 weeks at the special rate of less than half the price".

"What?" Avarel shouted.

"It makes sense – no other artiste works at Summerose Studios on Sundays, so we'll have the whole place to ourselves – no distractions", Jimmy said.

"But I specifically asked you NOT to book me on Sundays in future", Avarel reminded him.

"What's the deal Avarel – you have never minded working on Sundays before – this was a chance not to be missed". "I cancelled Fridays – you hated working on Fridays so I didn't think you would mind", Jimmy said and Avarel could understand where he was coming from – the Studio was over-patronized on Fridays. The arrangement would be great if she hadn't decided to turn a new page and go to church on Sundays. If she was still at the pinnacle of her career she would have stomped her feet and insisted that he cancel the Sunday bookings but the truth was that she was lucky that Jimmy had stuck with her – she didn't want to "rock the boat" – she needed his guidance on "Nectarous" to get her back into the charts. It occurred to her that she ought to put God first, but she shooed the thought aside and promised to make a large donation next time she attended church which quietened her conscience.

With a half-heavy heart Avarel telephoned Amelia next day.

"Hello Amelia".

"Hi there Avarel – how are you?"

"I'm good, but I can't make church tomorrow as planned".

"Really – why is that?"

"Work, work, work – just can't get away from work – say a word for me please Amelia", Avarel sounded sad.

"Yes sure will do", Amelia replied sincerely.

"Yan told me he will be there though", Avarel said. She did not detect the sudden intake of breath from Amelia as she gasped involuntarily at the mention of Yan's name.

"Amelia – are you still there?"

"Yeaah, yeah…. I'm here".

"If you happen to see him please look after him for me – won't you?"

"Yeeeaah – aaa I'll do that", Amelia stuttered.

"Well – I'll see you then".

"Yes – see you then".

The revelation that Yan was going to be in church the next day stunned Amelia. She began to fidget, fuss and fret about what she was going to wear. She customarily washed and set her tresses on rollers every Saturday night – tonight she took extra care to deep condition her locks, adding more than twice the measure of setting lotion, for she would not risk a hair being out of place this Sunday morning.

An over-excited Amelia arrived for church half an hour before the doors were opened up. She sat in her car praying and reading her Bible as she awaited Assistant Pastor Gentles' arrival. After her usual morning devotion she took a seat near to where Yan had sat the previous week – she wanted to observe him at close range. However, he didn't turn up or if he did attend church today, he must have sat in another section of the large auditorium.

After the service Amelia scanned the bustling congregation for Yan. She was disappointed that he was nowhere to be seen and surmised that he had not turned up after all. But her spirits were lifted by the sight of Carly making a dash for the door. Amelia fought her way towards her friend and managed to catch up just before she escaped. "Carly – oh how wonderful to see you", as she spoke Amelia moved to engage her friend in a hug. But Carly shifted uncomfortably as the memory of how terribly she had treated her friend at their last encounter popped to the forefront of her mind.

"Hi Amelia – it's wonderful to see you – thank you very much for acknowledging me", she said with a weak smile.

"What do you mean – of course I acknowledge you – I am overjoyed to see you back at Born Again after all these years, Carly – how long has it been?" Amelia was beaming and Carly perked up. Her children gathered around her like chickens around a mother hen, each gazing with innocent curiosity at their mother as she renewed acquaintance with Sister Amelia, whom they revered as Born Again royalty.

The ladies talked for a good while before exchanging numbers, promising to "catch up" during the week. Then Carly walked to her car, with part of her brood in tow. Before they were out of earshot Amelia heard the children firing questions at their mother as to how she had come to know the renowned Sister Amelia so well. "I'll tell you all about it later", Amelia heard Carly say as she walked back towards the sanctuary.

"Hello Sister Amelia – I've been looking around for you", Amelia thought she was dreaming as she heard Yan's voice. She whirled around and stared into the brown eyes that she had seen over and again in her dreams during the past week.

"Yan", was all that she could say then lost the will to speak.

"I looked everywhere for you", Yan repeated as Amelia smiled stupidly. It was all that she could do as no words formulated in her mind. She regarded Yan with a warm smile, hoping that he would carry the conversation by himself – he obliged. "It has been another blessed service even though I wished you had ministered – Born Again is a wonderful church", Yan went on to tell what he had enjoyed about the service. And Amelia just kept on smiling.

They were standing in the outer foyer of the church and as many brethren crowded into it on the way out, their combined voices drown out Yan's, so Amelia motioned him back inside where it was now quieter. She was oblivious to the scrutiny of beady eyes that watched her every move. Eyes of the resident gossip mongers, who used Sunday morning fellowshipping as their hunting ground. Like ravenous beasts the gossip mongers scavenged for fresh meat to devour in long conversations where even the veritable angelic would be torn to shreds, demonized and defamed by their venomous tongues. Rita Harris, the CCG had been absent from Born Again since the exodus but Alice the DCCG had been well trained and deputised efficiently. And there were various other apprentice gossips who had studied under Rita Harris also lurking about.

By far the most inquisitive pair of eyes that followed Amelia and Yan though was Bro Steve's. As he watched them the pain of denial became unbearable, but he could not stop staring at them and wishing that Amelia would look at him in that way – even once.

As Bro Steve followed the couple surreptitiously, he was in turn being stalked by his own predator – Sister Alice who was multi-tasking, deputising for Rita and also looking out for her own personal interest. Rita's apprentices dispersed throughout the sanctuary studied the developments too. Later they would report dutifully back to their coordinator.

Sister Manning who had received an anonymous report that Amelia was messing with her husband Bishop Manning also showed some interest in her movements. She was still "on the fence" as to whether she believed the report, because having known Amelia and her family for over 14 years, she knew the young woman to be virtuous. And as she studied the way that Amelia was looking at the handsome young man Sister Manning made the decision to dismiss the report as one borne out of malice. She wondered who could want to hurt Amelia's reputation by spreading such gossip and decided that she would discuss the matter with her husband with the aim of getting to the bottom of it.

The negative charge of jealousy, rage, suspicion, sadness and facetiousness combined and fought to overpower the holy anointing that had fallen in the sanctuary during the service but grace abounded and holiness prevailed.

"I need to discuss something with you Amelia – something very important", Yan said way too loudly.

"What's that?" Amelia found her tongue.

"It's about your ministry – I will tell you all about it when we meet", Yan said and smiled warmly. His smile put Amelia at ease and she proceeded to give her telephone number to him.

"I'll call you in the week, he promised.

"Okay".

Chapter 5

On Monday Amelia wafted on a very high and fluffy cloud nine. And when Yan telephoned her on Tuesday evening to arrange for them to meet up at Wednesday lunchtime, she hit cloud ten – for just a moment. Then reality gave her a little tap on the shoulders as she recalled that Yan belonged to Avarel.

"Isn't this something that we can discuss over the telephone?" Amelia asked.

"We could but it wouldn't seem right to do that – it's best that we meet up face to face", Yan replied, leaving Amelia wondering what an earth he could want to discuss with her. She thought perhaps that he might want to ask her to minister somewhere and wondered why he didn't just come out and say so – but she said nothing. The thought also occurred to her that Yan was more than likely a player. Yes – she was certain of that but she was powerless to resist him and before she could say anything else, Yan had finalised the plan for them to meet the next day. He would take her to lunch at the popular venue the Parque Café near her workplace.

"Okay, I'll see you tomorrow then".

"Okay, I'll see you then", Amelia heard herself reply meekly.

It immediately occurred to Amelia that she should tell Avarel about the planned meeting with her boyfriend. So she dialled her friend's number straight away – the call went to voicemail and she left a message asking for a call back.

Amelia hardly slept a wink that night and the next day she was a full bag of nerves. Unable to concentrate on her work she watched the clock constantly dreading the arrival of one o'clock yet praying for that hour to come. And as she made her way to the meeting place her legs barely provided support as her knees wobbled like jelly.

As she entered the bustling Parque Café, Amelia reminded herself to be on guard. She anticipated that Yan would show his true colours as the player that she strongly suspected he might be. He was nowhere to be seen at the entrance of the establishment where they had planned to meet – Amelia looked around full circle but still no sight of Yan. The venue was incredibly busy and she wondered at how popular it had become since her last visit a few months earlier when she recollected the place had been practically empty. Looking around again she caught sight of the sign "Under New Management", and marvelled at the difference it had made.

"Hi – I thought it best to get us some seats", Amelia was startled at the sound of Yan's voice as he approached from the right – a beaming smile lightened his face.

"Oh hi there – good idea", Amelia replied and smiled back.

"You can face the window or the crowd – take your pick", Yan said as they arrived at the table he had reserved by placing his umbrella across it.

"I really hate people looking at me when I eat, so you can take the crowd", Amelia chuckled, beginning to relax.

"Okay Lady Amelia – there you go" Yan pulled out the chair invitingly and Amelia moved to take her seat, still smiling. She indeed felt like a royal lady in the presence of this prince.

They perused menus and Yan went to put in their orders of coffee and secret recipe toasted sandwiches. On his return he took his seat and wasted no time in announcing the reason for their meeting. "Lady Amelia – I thank you for taking the time to meet with me today".

"Oh – that's okay" Amelia had never felt so happy before in her life.

"You are so beautiful and talented and the world needs to know it", Yan searched for eye contact as he spoke. He soon found them as Amelia looked at him questioningly.

Amelia was amazed at Yan's boldness – he was evidently coming on to her. She wondered whether she should make her excuses and leave then, but found that she was rooted to her chair and her tongue was too heavy to form the necessary words.

"Don't look so surprised Lady Amelia – you are indeed beautiful and talented", Yan's smile went into hiding, demonstrating the seriousness of his statement.

"Well – thank you very much", Amelia found her tongue involuntarily.

"I work with a company called "Astral Ventures International". "We are a large public company and have our fingers in numerous pies – I work for the Head of the music production arm, who relies on me to find and develop new talent", Yan spoke and Amelia listened intently as her opinion of him changed rapidly. This indeed sounded like serious business.

"We are always on the lookout for fresh talent and Amelia when I heard you minister last Sunday, you absolutely blew me away", Yan moved his head up and down and side to side for emphasis as he spoke.

"Thanks a lot – God has blessed me", Amelia said modestly, as she visibly relaxed.

"Yes – God has certainly blessed you Lady Amelia", Yan said simply.

"Why do you keep calling me "Lady" Amelia?"

"Because that is what you are a completely beautiful lady", Yan sought her eyes again and found them as they locked in a moment of spontaneous intimacy.

"Do you mind me calling you that – I'll stop if you do", he continued.

"No, no – call me anything you like", Amelia chuckled.

"Okay my Lady", Yan said, causing Amelia to blush as she thought how wonderful it would be to be truly his lady.

"The long and the short of it is that Astral Ventures International would like to offer you a recording deal – the world needs to hear your voice – to experience the anointing and to see your beauty", Yan said, then paused for a response.

"Are you serious?" Amelia asked and Yan nodded. "Hitherto Astral Ventures have not signed any uncompromisingly Christian artistes, so Lady Amelia you will be the first major Christian signing but you will definitely not be the last because we want to move more in that direction musically. I'm assuming that you will agree to move forward with Astral that is", Yan said as Amelia continued to search the depth of his eyes for sincerity.

"Since it will be the very first Christian venture for Astral – I want this album to send out a strong Christian message", Yan's eyes met and locked in Amelia's.

"So you are definitely the right candidate for this project, Lady Amelia", Yan said and continued. "To be perfectly honest doing a Christian album would have been unheard of for me a few years ago but three years ago I accepted the Lord Jesus and this new direction is way overdue", Yan said soberly. Astral Ventures will go with anything I recommend and that's you, Lady Amelia – so what do you say?"

"I have no recording experience – I've never even been in studio before", Amelia sounded fretful.

"That's nothing to worry about – we all had a first time", Yan said as though speaking from experience.

"So you are a singer too?"

"Yes – I have been known to croon a little – just BVs though", Yan chuckled.

"What's BVs?

"Oh backing vocals", Yan smiled.

"Wow" Amelia stared into her coffee as she stirred it.

The waiter interrupted their discussion to place their sandwich orders on the table.

"So what do you say – will you come on board or do you need time to think about it?" Yan asked then took a large bite out of his sandwich.

"It sounds like a wonderful offer – I would like to minister to the world", Amelia felt as though she was in a dream.

"So is that a yes then", Yan pressed her.

"I suppose so – but I will be praying for revelation of God's will though".

"Okay, wonderful – so I will arrange to get you down to see the studio, meet some people that you will be working with and I will also arrange to have the necessary paperwork drawn up", Yan said excitedly.

"You can instruct your own lawyer if you so wish, Lady Amelia", he continued.

"Lawyer?" Amelia questioned.

"You know – to go over the paperwork – ensure that your best interest is represented", Yan explained.

"Wow", Amelia exclaimed.

"I think it best if you do instruct a lawyer to look after your interest", Yan said then continued. "I'll send you a link to a list of entertainment law firms when I return to the office if you send me a text of your e-mail address", then he took another chunk out of his sandwich.

"Wow", Amelia repeated as she nibbled on the best BLT sandwich she had ever tasted.

They polished off lunch with cinnamon pretzels before Amelia had to rush back to work. Before they left they arranged to meet again at the Pentagon Studios the following Saturday afternoon and then Yan walked Amelia back to her workplace.

That evening, having heard nothing from Avarel, Amelia tried to telephone her again. Once more she was put straight through to voicemail. She left a further message. "Hi Avarel – I hope you are well – bell me back when you get a chance", Amelia really needed to speak to Avarel – she would feel a lot better if she knew that she had her blessings to deal with her fiancé.

Chapter 6

It was Sunday afternoon – Amelia had just finished having lunch and was relaxing in the living room. She contemplated why she had not received any return call from Avarel for over two weeks despite leaving numerous voice-mails. Suddenly, her telephone buzzed – she had a text message. She picked it up and read.

"Hi there, sorry I have not called you back – really busy at the moment, working on Nectarous but hopefully in a few weeks I will get a break – will give you a call then". "Avarel"

Amelia read the text over a second time then tapped out a reply.

"Hey girl – good to hear from you – hope the album is going well". "I just wanted to discuss with you my project with Yan's company – I guess he must have told you all about it already." "I'll speak to you soon then". "Amelia".

Amelia smiled as she pressed "send". She imagined her friend's smiling face as she received and read her message the other end. Moments after she had sent the text her 'phone began to buzz. Amelia picked up and was happy to hear Carly's voice. "Hi Amelia"

"Hi Carly – I caught a glimpse of you in church this morning but before I could reach to where you were you had disappeared – I wanted to say hi – give you a hug – how come you never hang around after church?", Amelia asked and chuckled.

"Oh, as you can see I have my hands very full, Amelia", Carly replied, a big smile evident in her voice.

"Uhmm, I can see that – you're blessed with all those beautiful children", Amelia said, conscious that she was speaking life into her friend. She was fully aware that Carly thought less of herself for being a single parent to six children and having never been married, and she wanted to build her morale.

"Oh, thank you Amelia – they are beautiful aren't them", Carly replied and continued "I love them all so very much".

"Yes you are truly blessed, Carly – do you want to give me one of them?" Amelia joked and chuckled.

"You can take three of them if you like", Carly replied breaking into Jamaican dialect. The friends both laughed loudly – long and hard.

"Amelia – I am getting baptized", Carly announced when the laughter had subsided.

"Wow – that's awesome news – what at the next baptism in three months' time?

"Yes – on 1st January – straight after Watch Night Service – I am starting the New Year as a new creature – I am leaving old things behind in 2011". "And this time I am not going back AGAIN", Carly placed great emphasis upon the last word of her sentence and the two chuckled infectiously.

"I would like you to sing a song with me for my baptism", Carly said when the urge to laugh out loud had become less infectious. "It is a little chorus with which I was inspired when I decided it was time to come back to church". "I know this will sound odd, but it fits perfectly with that song you ministered a few weeks back on the first day that I returned to church". "You know the one that says, *So glad to be home*". "Well my chorus goes "I want to come home", but it's exactly the same melody". "Believe it or not, I wrote it before I heard your song".

"Wow – God is awesome – Avarel told me something similar happened to her, but she only wrote a verse", Amelia said.

"That is really mysterious, because I could only write a chorus – nothing else – I tried so hard but I couldn't get past the chorus", Carly said, adding, "God is doing something here".

"Yes indeed", Amelia concurred, and they both laughed out loud once again.

Rehearsal was arranged for the following Tuesday evening, and as they ended the call each marvelled at how quickly they had re-bonded. As she clicked the "end call" button and reclined upon the sofa Amelia breathed a prayer of "thank you" to God for bringing her friends home. Her thoughts were interrupted by the 'phone – it was Avarel.

"Hi Amelia – what's up – what's this about your project with Yan", Avarel announced her reason for calling.

"Oh, hi Avarel – didn't Yan tell you then?" "His company Astral Ventures has offered me a recording deal", Amelia said excitedly.

"Really?"

"Yes – isn't that wonderful – I am so happy – it's really great – I'm doing all my own material – 100% Christian", Amelia gushed. "Yan must have mentioned something to you", Amelia said, although judging by her friend's silence, she already knew that Avarel was hearing about the deal for the first time.

"He doesn't discuss his business with me", Avarel snapped, then tempered her manner. "That's great for you", she sounded artificially enthusiastic. Amelia sensed that Avarel wasn't that thrilled by the revelation. She could not guess why Avarel would not be happy for her but surmised that there could be any number of reasons for her reaction.

"Is everything okay with you?" Amelia wanted Avarel to talk to her if there was something on her mind that she needed to offload.

"Fine – no problem whatsoever", Avarel chuckled.

"I was just speaking to Carly – she's getting baptized at Watch Night service".

"Wow – that's great – I might just join her", Avarel sounded pensive.

"That would be awesome", Amelia enthused.

The conversation never really took off from there on and after a few moments Avarel had to go as she was in the middle of a rehearsal when she called.

Amelia was concerned about her friend. Since Avarel's visit to church with Yan she had never returned. It had proven difficult to keep in contact with her too in order to provide encouragement, because she never returned calls. Amelia was aware that Avarel was incredibly busy, and empathized to a certain extent, in light of her own gruelling schedule, but she felt Avarel could make more of an effort. And Amelia wondered whether her friend had been really serious about rekindling her relationship with God.

Chapter 7

Time passed swiftly as Amelia's every moment was taken up with rehearsals, recording, ministry and the day job. Soon Christmas beckoned again and with festive shopping added to her agenda, she operated at manic pace.

Due to the nature of their work Amelia and Yan were thrown together more often than was comfortable for her. For two months she saw him nearly every day. As time passed she found it increasingly difficult to work alongside him. Her feelings were becoming stronger and eventually Amelia began to lose complete control of her unruly thoughts. However, she persevered with the recording project because she was enjoying it and, being fully aware that such an opportunity to take her ministry to the world was one not to be passed up, she struggled on with her emotions, praying earnestly each day for strength.

Amelia avoided Yan as much as possible and in particular tried not to be alone with him. A strong invisible force came into play whenever she was close to him because she could not avoid him completely. And an irrational fear gripped her heart whenever she was alone with him, a dread of giving in to the emotional pull that willed her to try and engage his attention or to come clean about her feelings regardless of the consequences. Even when he wasn't around her, Yan haunted her psyche and memories of him replayed over and again, especially in her dreams. It didn't help matters that he never missed attending Sunday services at Born Again and made a point of seeking Amelia out in order to fellowship with her. Amelia endeavoured to get others involved in their conversations and she had become adept at leaving him to talk with one or other brethren whilst making a hasty retreat.

****

Bro Steve appeared to have gotten the message at last and had stopped pursuing her and Amelia became vaguely aware that he and Alice seemed to be getting closer. Quite bizarrely though, now that he was no longer chasing after her, it often occurred to Amelia that she may have made a mistake in not giving him a chance – but such thoughts were fleeting and quickly dismissed.

****

The album was due for release in January 2012, and all efforts were being employed to meet the recording deadline of 30 November 2011. Amelia had to take two weeks off work, one without pay in order to facilitate the recording schedule. Almost all her colleagues were very understanding, many voicing their opinions that it was about time she took her singing seriously. And her superiors too were generally happy for her and provided her with limitless encouragement.

Although Astral Ventures Limited had offered her a lucrative deal with an advance of several thousand pounds, Amelia had declined to take any money up front. For her this was about ministry, not money. She was aware that just the production and release of the album alone would go to thousands of pounds and all would be chalked up as credit. Astral had given her a most generous 60/40 deal and had added a clause that they would bear all losses, so Amelia had little to worry about, but she fretted that should the album flop, Astral and Yan would take the hit. If the album actually made any money, she would be a good steward and pay her tithes and offering and only then would she take any benefit from the project – if God released her to do so. Amelia was not a materialistic soul – Bishop Manning could testify to that fact. He had released the motor vehicle back to the benefactor who had reassigned the gift due to the fact that Amelia had not accepted it, although he had exhausted all efforts to get her to do so. This attitude had re-affirmed Bishop Manning's opinion of Amelia that she had a selfless heart, that of a true woman of God, and when his wife had shared with him that someone had sought to malign her by suggesting that there was something going between them, righteous indignation had stirred within him and he had prayed, asking God to reveal to him the source of the rumour.

******

When they had finished the recordings everyone was overjoyed at the accomplishment and were more than happy with the end result. Yan had planned a celebratory dinner for everyone involved with the project, on the evening of 2 December. Amelia really wanted to go and celebrate with the others, but she did not because Yan was going to be there. Her excuse that she had to catch up with work from her day job was pretty weak and everyone was disappointed that she could not make it. By far the most disenchanted by Amelia's absence was Yan who had planned a big surprise, for he had intended to announce the title of the album tonight "Lady Amelia Lanson – I'm Touching Heaven". He was also concerned, having become aware of Amelia's lack of engagement with him, that she had developed a dislike of him for reasons that were not apparent to him, for he had gone out of his way to be more than nice to her and in spite of the repeated rebuttals, continued to extend the clean hand of friendship. It saddened him a lot because he enjoyed her company – her personality and general demeanour had impressed him from their first encounter. He had seen the depth of her heart, had recognised in her someone he could talk to about just about anything and he was not one to give up easily upon someone so genuine, well aware of the value of having such a person in your corner. He desired her lifelong friendship, to become another sister to him or the mother he had lost in his youth – one he could trust with his life.

Yan planned to get Amelia alone – he wanted to discuss with her the reasons for the sudden change in her behaviour towards him, because he was not mistaken, they had hit it off when they first met. But the promise of a good friendship had disintegrated into nothing due entirely to a lack of engagement from Amelia.

Chapter 8

It was with great relief that Amelia looked forward to resuming her normal work/church/home routine now that the recordings had been completed. She was exhausted, physically as well as emotionally and almost mentally depleted too. She needed a real break and was happy that Christmas was just two weeks away. She was unprepared for the reactions of her colleagues when she returned to work. Upon entering the office she was greeted by wide smiles and optimistic countenances, and everyone in the large building seemed aware of her "success" in having been offered a recording contract. By Monday evening she was even more exhausted than she had been before, having had to recount over and again details of the venture.

That evening Amelia telephoned Avarel and they spoke briefly, mostly about the recording of Nectarous which was still on-going.

"It's taking such a long time to complete Nectarous", Amelia commented, never one to wonder about something and not ask.

"Yes, but if you want the best you have to go that extra mile – being a superstar means that the public expects a high degree of professionalism", Avarel replied then continued. "I wish I could go into the studio and finish an album in less than 4 months but unfortunately only amateurs can get away with that – the Press would have a field day", when she had finished speaking Amelia felt suitably cut down to size. She wondered whether Avarel realised how small she had made her feel. During the rest of the conversation Amelia was not happy with the manner in which Avarel addressed her – she was curt, if not rude and lacking in warmth, if not cold. Avarel had started to behave in that manner since finding out about her recording project with Astral Ventures and Amelia surmised that she was not happy that she had been working with her significant other. When their conversation ended Amelia contemplated the circumstances. Then she breathed a sigh of relief, glad that her day to day contact with Yan was now at an end so that she could begin to repair any breach in her friendship with Avarel.

On Tuesday things more or less returned to normal in the workplace and Amelia was glad. However, the sight of Yan standing outside her workplace that evening caused her heart to skip a beat with excitement and anxiety at the same time.

"Hey Amelia", Yan said in his usual jovial manner.

"Hiiii Yan" Amelia's stuttered. There was a pause as the will to speak deserted her and she began to fumble with her handbag. Words formulated in her mind but her brain could not send them to her tongue. Yan spoke again.

"Amelia – can we go for a coffee – I need to discuss something with you", he said far louder than was necessary, telling of the efforts he had employed in making the request.

"No…. ii…. I must get home …" Amelia suddenly found her voice.

"Please Amelia – just one coffee – just half an hour of your time", Yan pleaded as though his life depended on it. There was a further pause as he anticipated Amelia's reply.

"Okay – just one tea then – I don't drink coffee, remember", Amelia smiled. And Yan breathed out heavily.

They returned to the Parque Café where they had had their first meeting and sat in the same seats. The familiarity of having "been there and done that" provided some charm and they were catapulted back to the ambiance of that first meeting. "Amelia – I would like us to be friends, yet you keep on avoiding me – is there any reason for that?" Yan asked directly after settling back into his seat, having returned from placing their orders at the counter.

"Friends – but we are friends though", Amelia replied, side-lining the real issue.

"Amelia – I would like us to be real friends – not merely acquaintances at a distance", Yan said.

"Oh I see" was all that Amelia could muster. She was becoming overwhelmed by his nearness and his words caused her breath to catch in her throat.

"I like you a lot Amelia and I need a friend like you", Yan said and paused before blurting out. "No – let me confess that I want you in my life forever", he said and sought Amelia's eyes. He eventually found them when he said "Amelia, please look at me", and as she did so, he continued, "Amelia I'm in love with you – I have loved you from the first moment I met you". "In fact I loved you even before I met you, because I have seen you in my dreams before that – many times".

Amelia listened as Yan spoke and she felt as though she was dreaming. *"This is a dream"*, her mind suggested. She shook her head from side to side to refocus and then accepted that she was wide awake – this was no dream. She was dumbfounded and could not speak so she stared at Yan, her bottom lip dropping slightly open.

"I wasn't going to say this tonight, but my heart is leading me to – Amelia, my interest in you goes way beyond friendship – I would like us to contemplate marriage", Yan said then fell silent. He breathed out heavily as though he had just completed a humongous task

After a thirty second pause Amelia exclaimed, "Are you mad?", then continued, "No – let me rephrase that – Are you c-r-a-z-y?" she stretched out the word "crazy" for emphasis.

"No – I am perfectly sane Amelia – I have been searching for you all my life – you are the one I want to marry", Yan affirmed.

"What about my friend – what about Avarel?" Amelia's mind and her tongue had suddenly reconnected and the words flowed from her lips effortlessly.

"What do you mean?" Yan asked.

"How dare you think that I would be a party to your philandering ways", Amelia was furious now.

"Philandering – I am not a philanderer, Amelia – I am very serious about you".

"Like you are serious about Avarel, right?" Amelia was on her feet now – her eyes flashed dangerously.

"Avarel and I are friends – no more than that", Yan replied.

"Do you propose marriage to all your friends then Yan – is that your modus operandi?" Amelia said and moved to walk away.

"Please sit down Amelia – you are drawing attention to us", Yan pleaded.

"No Yan, I will not sit down – our little discussion is over – I am leaving now", Amelia said then walked out – Yan ran after her.

"Amelia, Amelia – Avarel and I are friends simply that – I have never asked her to marry me" Yan stated.

"So you are telling me that my friend is a liar then – that she made up the story that you two are an item and are planning to get married" Amelia said as she marched.

"Amelia I have never proposed marriage to Avarel – that is the honest truth", Yan stated as he walked at breakneck pace to keep abreast with Amelia.

"Well if that is the truth, perhaps you had better tell Avarel, but knowing men like you I know that my friend is not mistaken", Amelia said as they arrived at the bus stop.

"I am not one of those "men like you" people", Yan replied, before realising that he must sound deranged to those in the large rush hour queue gathered at the bus stop.

"Don't you ever dare bring such a subject to me again – you – you player – you philanderer – WOMANIZER", Amelia gave her parting shot as her bus arrived and she jumped straight on ahead of those who had been queuing before her – some muttered their discontent.

"I'LL HAVE TO SPEAK TO AVAREL ABOUT THIS", Yan shouted back, then suddenly becoming conscious of tens of eyes looking at him, no doubt questioning his sanity, he turned on his heels held his head high and walked off in search of his car.

Amelia was furious. She mumbled under her breath as she travelled home on the bus. "What a liberty?" and she contemplated upon Yan's arbitrary act in attending at her place of work. "How dare this riff raff put such a question to me", she moaned as the people sitting nearby cast her worried side glances. "What on earth does he take me for?" She was still fuming when she neared her stop and pushed through the crowd towards the exit door.

Chapter 9

Arriving at home, Amelia was glad to find no one at home. She made her way straight to her room where she fell to her knees as soon as she closed the door behind her. She hobbled on her knees over to the side of her bed and buried her head in the billowing folds of bedclothes then she began to sob loudly. "God why, why God – God why?" Amelia questioned, "Why are you letting me go through all this?" "I'm not strong enough for this Lord, please – I can't take any more". Then she fell silent and began to ponder. She felt helpless, out of control, for she could not deny the way she was really feeling. Raging within her heart was the fire of unquenchable love, an emotion so strong as to threaten her sanity. And Amelia questioned why God had put her in such a position to fall in love with her friend's fiancé. She felt ashamed. She felt confused. She felt unbelievably sad. She felt hopeless. She wanted to praise through the situation and tried to do so, but failed, for the only words that she uttered composed questions beginning with "why, what and how?"

After a full hour Amelia crawled into bed and fell asleep. She was awoken by the slamming of the front door and her mother's voice, "Amelia – are you at home?"

"Yes mum – I'm sleeping" she replied and nestled back into the covers for comfort. She forced her tortured mind to relax by breathing deeply and thinking about something positive. But before long her thoughts relinquished control to her heart and Yan's face returned to the front page of her psyche – haunting, taunting, teasing, and testing. Amelia felt helpless as she involuntarily recalled her conversation with the desirable man. He had said that he dreamed about her and had done so even before they met. He had said that he wanted them to contemplate marriage – that she was the woman he wanted to spend the rest of his life with – that he was being honest – so why didn't she believe him. How could she believe him when her friend had confided in her that they were an item and were planning to get married? How could she have allowed herself to fall for this cad – this global player – who was obviously so adept at his game that he thought he could string two close friends along at the same time?

The questions seemed never ending as Amelia sought for answers that did not come. And then the biggest question of all presented itself in her mind – how would she tell Avarel about this – for surely her friend needed to know – she wanted to warn her about the devil that she was dating – a player for whom she herself had developed undeniably strong feelings. Would she be a hypocrite for telling her friend about this episode? Would she be a hypocrite for not telling her friend? And if she didn't tell her could she watch Avarel go through with marrying this cad, knowing that he would surely break her heart someday soon?

When her mobile began to ring, Amelia ignored it, but it refused to go away. So after a full three minutes she reluctantly picked up.

"Hello"

"Hello – Amelia, I cannot believe that you are so sneaky, so malicious as to wheedle your way in between me and Yan". "After I confided in you how I felt – how much I loved this man – how much he means to me – about my wedding plans, all you could do was try and steal him away from me – how could you Amelia", Avarel launched in.

"Avarel – it's not true – I…I never led Yan on …I"

"Oh yes you did – playing little miss innocent – you led him on alright". "I knew it in my heart – I knew you were attracted to him from that first day I introduced you to him – I could just tell by the way you were looking at him – you sneaky fool".

Avarel spoke in a malicious and vindictive tongue that was foreign to Amelia's ears. She did not recognise this person who had suddenly turned from her friend into her accuser.

"Avarel are you drunk?" Amelia dared to ask.

"Shut you mout – how dare you – you betta mind I don't come round you house and bash you face in" Avarel's speech was slurred as she lambasted Amelia, calling her every negative name under the sun, including two beginning with "S" and one with "W" that describes women of ill repute and one beginning with "B" that describes one of a malevolent ilk or a female dog. Amelia listened passively as her friend poured out her wrath upon her. She tried feebly to defend herself. "Avarel, you are wrong – I have never led Yan on in any way – there has never been anything between us", Amelia pleaded, but her pleas served only to invite a fresh deluge of insults.

"Listen you Christian tart – just shut up and listen – you keep away from my man – you hear me?" "Just make sure you keep away from Yan, right – he's mine", Avarel spat the words out like a snake does its venom. And then she hung up on Amelia, leaving her more sad and confused than ever.

"Lord, why is this happen to me when all I have ever done is try to behave myself – Lord you know that despite my feelings for Yan, I have never encouraged him in the least because I knew about Avarel's feelings". "What have I done to deserve this, Lord – why did you make me have feelings for Yan in the first place in any case?" "Why?" "Have I not prayed and fasted enough?" "I have been praying and fasting and asking you for all these years to bless me with a husband and the only man that I have ever met for whom I have deep feelings happens to belong to my friend – how cruel is that Lord?" "Lord WHY?" And anger began to arise in Amelia's heart – anger at God – for surely He could have averted this tragedy. And she became convinced that God did not love her after all.

"God why do you hate me so – after all I have sacrificed to remain within your will?" "Why Lord?" Amelia asked over and again, and the thought that God had brought her together with the only man who had ever moved her, who had now proposed marriage to her, whose proposal she would have happily accepted under normal circumstances, but who happened to belong to another – no less her long lost friend, dug a wound deep within Amelia's heart. She had a brief momentary vision of Him looking down and having a big laugh at her expense and she withdrew her trust in God and began to backslide within her heart.

As the week passed Amelia became angrier at God but as Sunday dawned, being a creature of habit, she was up and dressed for church in the usual way. But Amelia did not worship with her signature fervency and love today instead she went through the motions, lifting up hands, lifting up her voice, but not her heart or her spirit. And for the first time in her life she knew what it might feel like to be a sceptic in the company of believers.

When the service came to an end she made a beeline for the door – she wanted only to escape, to return to the solace of her bedroom where she could once more wallow in self-pity and continue practising her backward spiritual slide.

"Aunty Amelia, hi", she felt a light tap on her right shoulder and whirled around to see Dwightene, Carly's daughter who took her hand and led her back into the sanctuary. "Mummy wants to see you".

A glowing Carly embraced her with all the love a friend could muster. And Amelia felt better for a while.

"You didn't come to rehearsal on Tuesday as I expected – and is there something wrong with your phone – it has been switching straight to voice-mail", Carly enquired and continued. "And you haven't returned my calls".

"No, I've just been very busy this week – sorry", Amelia said, telling herself that it wasn't a lie – she had been very busy – busy dealing with her emotions.

"Will we be rehearsing on Tuesday?" Carly smiled and added. "We need to you know".

"Yes, I'll be there on Tuesday", Amelia promised. Then she hugged her friend and the little ones and renewed her efforts to escape.

"Amelia – please can we talk", Yan's voice surprised Amelia as she exited the sanctuary for the second time – she was surprised because she did not realise he was in church today. But her response was immediate.

"There is nothing to talk about, Yan", she replied through gritted teeth.

They stood within earshot of Bishop Manning. The man of God was surprised because he had never heard Amelia being rude to anyone before. He was aware that she and the young man who had been visiting the church over recent months were working on a recording project together and had personally thanked God for that development in Sister Amelia's ministry because he had always known that her ministry was an international one. Bishop Manning had also taken a liking to Yan whom he found to be courteous, so he could not understand why they had apparently fallen out. He glanced over at the couple as Amelia turned and walked out the door and Yan followed her. However Bishop Manning did not go after them – he decided against intervening in the altercation, fearing that to do so might blow it out of proportion. But he made a mental note to find out later from Sister Amelia if everything was okay.

Amelia walked briskly from the sanctuary into the freezing cold December afternoon. Yan was on her heels, followed by Bro Steve, who during his usual observation of Sister Amelia had also become aware of the altercation.

"Please Amelia, please – we need to talk", Yan pleaded.

"Look, will you please leave me alone – I repeat, there is nothing for us to talk about", her eyes flashed fire.

"Amelia – is everything okay?" Bro Steve interjected as both Amelia and Yan turned to look behind them.

"Oh Bro Steve – how are you?" Amelia asked as she walked back towards Steve and linked arms with him. She smiled, then motioned and they walked away together, "Bro Steve – how are you getting home – did you drive today or can I give you a lift", Yan heard Amelia say, words that sounded like music to Bro Steve's ears who immediately jettisoned his memory, and forgot that his car was parked just around the corner. Without answering Amelia's question, he smiled and they walked away together. Yan stood watching after them – as did Sister Alice who stood at the mouth of the sanctuary. And she was fuming.

"Steve you cannot humiliate me like this and get away with it", Alice mumbled. *"I will teach you a big lesson"*, she vowed within her heart. "I swear I will", she double-vowed in a whisper. She was on the 'phone to Sister Rita within a minute of arriving at home and within half an hour the news flash was disseminated far and wide.

As soon as Amelia had set her car into motion she began to regret her actions. Now alone with Steve she felt caged – she wanted to escape as he began to reveal his heart and Amelia suddenly realised why she was so put off by him – he was just too full on.

"So Sister Amelia – would you like to come to dinner with me on Friday night – I know this lovely little Caribbean restaurant over at Riverside Quay – it's just been opened and a friend of mine who visited it said the food is to die for", Bro Steve visibly salivated as he spoke.

Amelia smiled but made no immediate reply. After a beat she smiled again and said "Friday…. Friday – you know what Friday is not a good evening for me", and hoped Bro Steve would drop the subject.

"Well how about Saturday then?" Bro Steve replied immediately, annoyingly.

"Saturday is even worse", Amelia replied, speaking a little too loudly. She tried to temper her harsh reply with a feigned smile. "I'm going to be really busy over the next few weeks – until well into the New Year in fact, sorry Bro Steve". Then thinking quickly she added, "Why don't you ask Sister Alice to accompany you – I am sure she would love to go".

Steve squirmed visibly then replied "Oh Alice is not for me, Amelia – my heart belongs elsewhere", Amelia felt uncomfortable as she felt Steve's eyes boring through the side of her face. She was happy when he unexpectedly changed the subject.

"So tell me Sister Amelia – why have you never accepted that motor car?" Steve was prompted to ask when Amelia drove over a hump and the old rickety car sounded as if it might expire. Amelia contemplated how she might reply as Steve eyed her in anticipation.

"Bro Steve – I don't like anything that comes too easily – I like to work hard for whatever I own", Amelia said pointedly, making reference to his easy-gotten wealth and his persistent availability.

"Oh – I see", Bro Steve said and smiled thoughtfully. "Intriguing", he continued, "You see that is why I love you so much – you've got class", Steve said and looked at Amelia with puppy dog eyes as he attempted to stroke her left hand where it rested on the gear lever.

"Don't do that"

"Oh sorry – I just wanted to get closer to you – that's all – I don't mean any harm", Steve sounded desperate.

Amelia felt most uncomfortable now and began to beat herself up mentally. *What on earth were you thinking, Amelia Lanson?"* Then she floored the accelerator as she drove along the duel carriageway in haste – she could not wait to reach Bro Steve's destination in an affluent part of London and discharge her offensive cargo.

Steve Walters did not like reckless driving – he felt as though his heart would pound out of his chest as Amelia made her little car bob and weave through the traffic. This was a new side to her that he had never seen before and his attention was fully taken by her rally road racer antics, so that he did not utter another word until they had exited the dual carriageway and were just around the corner from his home. "So, Sister Amelia – I didn't realise that you were such an ahm… confident driver", Bro Steve breathed out heavily as he spoke.

"Oh – I've been driving for many years Bro Steve – it has taken a long time for me to become such an accomplished driver", Amelia replied, her mind was preoccupied with getting Bro Steve home as quickly as possible.

"So Sister Amelia – would you care to come inside for a coffee", Bro Steve solicited as Amelia drew up in front of his block. Amelia was curious to see Steve's flat because she wondered how opulent it might be inside – she had driven through this part of London often but had only ever seen the inside of the homes on TV or in magazines, "Bro Steve I only wish I could", she replied and continued, "I have got a lot of work at home waiting for me and I want to go back to evening service", but Steve did not easily take "no" for an answer.

"Oh go on – just one cup", but Amelia was resolute and she brusquely dismissed Steve and breathed a sigh when he gave up and stepped out of her vehicle. He closed the car door and was about to lean back through the half open window when Amelia set the car in gear and drove off at speed, leaving him staring after her with a look of surprise on his face.

"What on earth were you thinking Amelia Lanson – dumb move", Amelia verbalised her thoughts then she breathed in and out deeply in an effort to relax.

Arriving at home Amelia retreated to the solace of her room and closing the door behind her, she began to weep again. She was not sure whether she was crying because of the on-going episode with Yan or because she had gone back on her vow never to give Steve the time of day, or because of her separation from God who had always been her source of joy and strength. But Amelia could not stop the tears from falling. When she finally pulled herself together over an hour later, she reached for her 'phone and changed the setting from mute, which she had forgotten to do so after church. She noticed that there were five missed calls from Yan and began to weep all over again. As she wept it occurred to her what Monica might think if she could see her in that state, and heard her ex-friend's voice quip in her mind's ear "pathetic creature", a favoured term that she used to deride Amelia.

"Amelia dinner is served", Joyce called.

"Not hungry mum", Amelia replied. She deliberately used few words, not wishing her mother to detect that she had been crying.

"Are you alright dear?" Joyce sounded concerned.

"Yes", Amelia said. She wanted to add a request to be left alone but bit her tongue. The thought crossed her mind that she should look at moving to her own home and she resolved to begin searching for a flat the next day.

Amelia did not return to evening service, the candlelight carol service. This was totally out of character for her – she had never missed it before. In fact she was noted for always ministering a solo at the annual event but tonight she feigned a virus and asked her mother to extend an apology to Bishop Manning and the other organisers. Joyce's enjoyment of the service was curtailed due to worry that something was seriously amiss with her daughter. Afterwards, she was fellowshipping half-heartedly when the young man with whom Amelia had been working on her recent musical project approached her.

"Hello Sister Joyce – God bless you", Yan said timidly.

"God bless you too – Yan is it?" Joyce replied and smiled.

"Yes – that's right".

"We've never really spoken before but I know you have been working with Amelia on her album". "Thank you for allowing God to use you – it was way overdue for Amelia's talent to reach out to the wider world", Joyce rabbit on as Yan listened. He had intended to ask for a meeting with her, so that they could have a serious discussion about Amelia, but all too soon Joyce was snatched away by another brethren and the opportunity was lost.

As Yan was about to leave the sanctuary, Bishop Manning approached him and questioned, "Are you okay, son – you know if you ever need to talk about anything you can make an appointment to see me during the week – I am always available", Bishop Manning sounded as though he knew more than he was letting on.

"You know, Bishop, I might just do that", Yan replied, nodding his head as he shook the Pontiff's hand. Then he pulled up his collar and launched out into the bitter cold of the night.

Bro Steve watched Yan leave and cast several daggers at his back and if looks could kill, Yan would have died. Then he also went in search of Amelia's mother as Sister Alice watched him passively biding her time.

Chapter 10

The following week passed quickly for Amelia. Her time was taken up with preparations for the Christmas celebration amongst other things. She continued to avoid Yan's calls, but she knew that she would have to speak to him eventually – there were creases to be ironed out in readiness for the album launch on January 14th. But for now she kept on putting off the inevitable. She had changed her hours of work – going in at 7 am and leaving by 3 pm, so as to avoid Yan if he came to meet her at work again. She was allowed to do this under the flexible working provision in her employment contract. And to make doubly sure she came and went by a side entrance and got on and off of the bus at a different bus stop, even though she had a longer walk.

Tuesday and Thursday evenings had been reserved for rehearsals with Carly to "polish up" their rendition. They also planned one final rehearsal – a dress rehearsal – on Saturday 31 December 2011. The old flame of friendship had been fully rekindled and it felt just like old times. Carly's dormant gift for playing the piano had also been re-awakened, and when they sang together the unmistakable anointing of the Angels was resurrected in part. Rufus and the children were enthralled each time they ran through the beautiful song. The older children expressed amazement that their mother was so talented and had immediately enrolled in various music classes at school. Following initial lessons, they had received positive comments from their teachers about their natural aptitude, which suggested that they had inherited their mother's and grandfather's musical talent, for Rufus too was an accomplished musician – the bass guitar being his instrument of choice.

On Sunday 18 December 2011, Amelia did not attend church – once again she feigned illness. Joyce was beside herself with worry at her daughter's evident spiritual decline and requested prayers from Bishop Manning and other brethren. She and Patrick also fasted and prayed in earnest for their daughter's deliverance, for it was the very first time that Amelia had ever missed church without being truly poorly, and it was obvious that her physical health was not impaired since she continued to go about her daily routine.

Joyce had tried to talk to Amelia about the real reason for her not attending church but she had simply shrugged and refused to discuss it. The fact that both Bro Steve and the new young Man, Yan, had each been asking after her daughter suggested to Joyce that Amelia's truancy had something to do with her personal circumstances, so she directed her prayers accordingly.

****

Yan had approached Joyce after morning service. "God bless you, Sister Joyce – how are you today?"

"Oh God is Good Bro Yan – I am very well, thank you – and you?", Joyce smiled jovially as she spoke, her chubby rouged cheeks reminding him of a black female Santa.

"I'm very well thank you Mother Joyce – and how is Sister Amelia – I see she is not in church today?"

"Oh she is a little under the weather – nothing serious though", Joyce replied.

"I've been trying to call her but can't seem to get through to her – is there another number that I could get her on?" he continued.

"No, not really but if you give me a message I will pass it on"

"Please would you ask her to call me – say it's very important", Yan requested.

"Ok – I'll do that".

When Joyce left church she had three messages to pass on to Amelia. The second was from Bro Steve and the third from Bishop Manning, asking Amelia to come in and see him.

As Amelia sat on the bus towards home on the day before Christmas Eve she was thoughtful. She wanted to try and speak to Avarel again – to set the record straight – to say that she was not guilty of having led Yan on in any way. She had tried many times to telephone her friend but Avarel was not taking her calls and she had not so far plucked up the courage to leave a message.

The bus crawled along in the Christmas rush hour traffic and by the time Amelia arrived home it was after 3 pm and she felt exasperated – all the staff had been allowed to leave at 1 pm today, but the bus journey that usually took no more than 40 minutes had taken over two hours. She soon calmed down though, glad to find that the house was empty – she needed to be alone with her thoughts. Amelia knew that she would most likely have the house to herself for the next two or three hours, as her mother dragged her father around the shops, picking up essential items without which Christmas would not arrive. Most of such items invariably turned out to be grossly surplus to requirement and ended up in the bin, a fact that caused Joyce to repent each year but a lesson was never truly learnt as she would repeat the same mistake year after year.

A loud sigh escaped from Amelia's lips as she sat down and allowed her body to slump into the sumptuous leather armchair. She hit the recliner switch and relaxed every bone. For more than an hour she remained in that position and thought about the rift between her and Avarel – she prayed too then she fell asleep and dreamed that Avarel and Yan were getting married, and as she and the rest of the wedding guests looked on, the officiating Minister took Yan's right hand and placed it upon Avarel's right hand and said "What God has appointed, no man can disappoint".

The words of the Minister echoed clearly in Amelia's mind as she awoke from sleep and she knew that God was speaking to her. She interpreted the dream to mean that Avarel and Yan were meant to be together. "But I have never done anything to lead Yan on – have I Lord"? Amelia asked God as though he were standing in front of her. "Please forgive me if I have inadvertently done so", she continued. Then she fished into her bag for her mobile and dialled Avarel's number once again. As she anticipated her call was put straight through to voicemail. Amelia took a deep, deep breath and launched into the spiel that she had rehearsed in her mind for days.

"Hi Avarel – it's Amelia – I've been trying to call you for over two weeks now but I guess you've been avoiding my calls". "I can't say I blame you though", Amelia gasped another, deeper breath then continued, "I want to apologise for leading Yan on. I must have subconsciously sent him the wrong signals because, to be honest Avarel, you are right I was attracted to Yan from the moment you first introduced us", Amelia paused, took another gulp of air and continued, "So I guess I did encourage him without really meaning to". "I'm very, very sorry – I really am – I didn't mean to hurt you, honestly". "I shouldn't have undertaken that recording project with him in the first place seeing the way that I felt". "But I can promise you one thing Avarel, you have absolutely nothing to worry about in future because the infatuation is gone for good now – I no longer have any feelings for Yan", as the words left her lips Amelia knew she was not being truthful. She paused once more then continued. "I really value our friendship Avarel and I hope we can get past this", then another pause before she ended her message, "Love you girl – let's not make a man come between us – I wish you the best, bye". Then Amelia hung up and headed to her room as she involuntarily burst into tears. On the other end of the line, Avarel listened to her friend speak her heart and a solitary tear formed in the corner of her right eye.

Amelia's anger towards God increased with each teardrop as she blamed Him for the situation. "God why is it that other people's love lives just seems to fall into place but not mine – God why?" "Look at this mess that is my life – why don't you do something to change this situation – you are God and you can do anything". "All I have ever done is to be faithful to you – to keep myself pure in order to please you – I have made so many sacrifices and this is my reward". "Look at what you have allowed to happen to me". "You know what God, I don't trust you anymore – you obviously don't really care for me – if you did you would not allow this to happen – you are God – so why don't you do something?" Amelia had a one-sided argument with the Almighty where she shouted but did not listen and as her anger increased yet more she allowed negativity to saturate her soul and sank deeper into the mire, and overcome by the surge her dissent was quickened yet more when she silently vowed never to trust God ever again.

When her parents got home Amelia informed them that she just wanted to be left alone, and went to her room where she remained all evening wallowing in self-pity. Christmas Eve followed a similar pattern. As she embraced anger and bitterness, the two emotions joined forces and began a more fiery rebellion against God, which rose up from deep within her heart. Amelia did not discourage the foolish thoughts that suggested she should change sides –

terminate her allegiance to God for good, but instead embraced them, and as she did so a void crept into her soul – a wider separation between herself and the Father who had always been her mainstay. And the chasm grew wider with each passing moment as Amelia's soul entered a free-fall – but she did not care that she was falling fast, that she was committing spiritual suicide.

Late on Christmas Eve night Amelia's anger reached an apex. The emotion that suggested she should reject and curse God was so strong, yet another power kept her from doing so. The two forces wrestled for total control of her mind and drained her spiritually, mentally and physical and she fell into a fitful slumber. And as she slept something miraculous happened – she had a vision. It was as though Bro Al actually appeared to her in person. He was dressed like an angel in baby blue swaddling robes and he beckoned to her. "Come my dear, come". Amelia was surprised to see him and the joy at his presence overpowered every other emotion.

"Bro Al – it's wonderful to see you but …. I don't understand you are supposed to be dead – how come you're here?" she asked.

"I am here because you need my help, my dear – you need to find your way back", Al replied. She followed as he led her along a winding path that led to a beautiful altar where he began to worship and encouraged her to join him.

Amelia watched as Bro Al worshipped in his usual spirited and haphazard style – he beckoned and she joined him and as she worshipped the bitterness began to flow out of her soul and she drew close to God again. Bro Al began to sing a song as he worshipped.

"Trust God my dear, trust God. Trust God, trust God", he sang, and Amelia found that she knew the harmony to the song and joined him. "He will never fail – his ways are not our ways – he will never fail – trust God", she was still singing the sweet refrain when she awoke.

Jumping out of bed Amelia looked around fully expecting to see Bro Al, but it soon dawned upon her that she had been having a dream. "What a beautiful dream", Amelia spoke her thoughts. And as she revised the vision in her mind tears filled her eyes as she felt the love of God embrace her again. She rolled out of bed, found her knees and continued to worship, and the Holy Spirit assumed full control of her mind again as she asked God's forgiveness for failing to trust him. "O God I am so sorry for not trusting you – and thank you so much for sending an Angel in the form of Bro Al to rescue me, by reminding me of how beautiful and faithful you are". And Amelia's relationship with God was fully restored.

On Christmas morning, Joyce and Patrick were overjoyed to find that their daughter was her old self again, for Amelia was the first one up and ready for church. On arrival at church she was greeted enthusiastically by all who had missed her presence the week before. During the service Bishop Manning made a special mention that he was glad to see that she was feeling better now and the congregation cheered loudly. Amelia felt much loved as she sat in a pew towards the front of the sanctuary.

Evidentially one of those happiest to see her was Bro Steve who was ushering and came to stand nearby. He kept on glancing over at her which Amelia found disconcerting. Everyone in the sanctuary became aware of his avid interest in Amelia, if they were not previously so aware. And Sister Alice became more furious than ever before. She regretted the fact that she had just spent most of Christmas Eve with Bro Steve at his flat, when she had prepared a most sumptuous turkey dinner for him and his brother and his brother's girlfriend. Steve had been full of compliments about her making someone a good wife very soon and Alice had taken the compliments to mean that progress was being made in her quest to get Bro Steve to propose to her, but seeing the way that he was eyeing Sister Amelia, she realised that she was fighting a losing battle and felt more scorned than ever before.

Amelia involuntarily scanned the sanctuary in search of Yan but did not see him and a tinge of sadness crept into her soul which she struggled to shake off.

That afternoon just as he was locking up the sanctuary, Assistant Pastor Gentles took a telephone call from an anonymous caller, and the revelation it brought was a shocking one. From the information provided by the caller Pastor Gentles knew immediately that there was some truth to the revelation and as soon as he replaced the receiver, he picked it up again and dialled the Police.

This Christmas was as festive as ever before. The Lanson household was brimming with family, food, fun and frolics and caught up in the jovial atmosphere Amelia shook off any remaining sadness and joined in fully with the festivities. The unhappiness of the past two weeks forgotten, she basked in newfound hope and reclaimed joy. So intent was she on turning a new page that she even took Yan's call, among the many others that telephoned with greetings and best wishes. "Hi Yan – Happy Christmas to you".

"Happy Christmas Sister Amelia – sounds like you are enjoying the festivities", Yan said, relieved that she had finally decided to talk to him.

"Yes, I love Christmas – it's my favourite time of the year".

"I saw you at church this morning but you disappeared before I had a chance to greet you personally", Yan's words caused Amelia's heart to leap.

"Oh – I didn't see you in church".

"Yes I was there" Yan replied, and then he continued in a more serious tone. "Amelia I need to talk to you".

"What, about the launch?"

"Well yes – but we need to discuss us too", Yan replied.

"Look Yan, its Christmas day, please don't spoil my mood – I've told you before that we have nothing to talk about unless it is the recording project", Amelia was firm.

Yan reluctantly conformed to Amelia's request and they discussed the up-coming launch of the album due the second week in January. He could have talked to her all night but she abruptly brought their conversation to an

end after 30 minutes, "Okay, so I think all sounds in order with the launch
– Yan, thanks for everything – I must go now – I'm neglecting my family",
Amelia said and quickly hung up.

After their call ended Amelia's mind would not rest – the feelings towards
Yan that she had convinced herself she had buried came rushing to the surface
of her psyche and her heart began to ache. She tried but failed to pull herself
together, so she retired to her room at 9 pm. There she allowed her heart to
dictate to her head and her heart led her head to think of nothing other than
Yan Kennelly. She wondered why he sounded to be alone on Christmas day –
why wasn't he with Avarel? Why wasn't he with his family? Amelia had been
tempted to ask him during their conversation but had decided not to – she
did not wishing to send mixed signals. She had made a promise to Avarel and
would keep her word – she only hoped that in time her heart would give her
a break.

Part VII – The Home-coming

Chapter 1

The Old Year was almost at an end as the heaving congregation gathered in the sanctuary at Born Again Church of God. Each year the turn out for Watch Night Service was over-subscribed and this year beat all records with "once a year" attendees making up the larger part of the congregation. Due to fire regulations, no further bodies were being let into the main sanctuary. Late comers had already filled up the overflow room and unauthorised bodies were now crammed into the foyer and spilled out of the front door. Those outside the church who had unsanctified hearts did not want to understand that the fire regulations prohibited anyone else from being let into the large building, and argued amongst them as they watched proceedings being projected on a large screen in the foyer that was visible from as far as the front gate of the sanctuary. Such miscreants cited favouritism as the real reason for being denied entry, without there being any evidence to support that argument. Some uttered swear words and inappropriate sentences, accompanied by unholy gestures as they forgot that they were standing on holy ground. This largely unholy bunch stood fast, however, their antics juxtapose against those taking place inside the holy sanctuary, where hands and voices where lifted up in praise and worship. They dared not move because tradition dictated that it would be taboo for them to be found between destinations when the clock struck in the New Year.

Due to the fact that his flight from Canada had been delayed Yan had also arrived late for the service and now stood outside amongst the throng clutching his coat collar about his neck while shuffling his feet to try and keep warm. He had come straight from the airport, having just arrived back from visiting family. As the temperature gradually dipped significantly, Yan's glances at his watch increased in frequency, as he prayed for 12 o'clock to strike, for he knew from experience that minutes, if not seconds after the ushering in of the New Year most of the "once a year" attendees would head off to parties or night clubs where they would continue to celebrate, believing that because they had seen the New Year in at church, they would have God's covering for the rest of the year.

If it had not been necessary for him to return so soon, Yan would have remained in Canada for a few more days, but he had come back early to witness the baptism of Arthur Minder, a new convert whom he had met at the men's fellowship evening, who had requested him to be present tonight to witness his bold step.

Wading through the sea of departing bodies, Yan made his way into the sanctuary and took his seat on a side pew half way to the front of the building. He looked towards the baptismal candidates seated in the front row of the church and caught sight of Arthur who was also scouring the sanctuary for his "support network" – those he had invited. Arthur did not have much family, his mother and father having passed away many years before, his only Sister had emigrated to Jamaica with her husband and could not make it tonight, although she had assured him that she would be praying for and thinking of him. He had also invited his only brother but did not hold out much hope of him turning up because he was a rebel who lived an alternative lifestyle. Arthur had himself been one of a rebellious ilk prior to his encounter with the Lord Jesus, so he did not expect the friends that he had invited to turn up either. So he was very happy to see that his newly found Christian friend was present to support him and his wide smile upon catching sight of Yan demonstrated his joy.

The candidates were introduced one at a time and gave their various speeches and testimonies – some sang songs whilst others recited self-penned poetry – others still just praised, following which each was led into the water to be immersed by Bishop Manning and Assistant Pastor Gentles.

When it was Arthur's turn, he spoke of his prior misgivings at taking the bold step to declare his faith in Jesus Christ – he gave thanks to God that he had overcome them and for salvation and deliverance. He also mentioned that Bro Yan had been a great encouragement to him. Yan was surprised – he had not realised that the simple conversations he had had with Arthur were of such great encouragement to the baptismal candidate and he spoke a silent "thank you", to God that he had been used by Him in such a subtle way.

Then it was Carly's turn to grace the pulpit. As she did so, instead of speaking, unable to contain her tears, she began to sob. Amelia left the congregation, made her way to her side and placed a supporting arm around Carly's shoulders. At the same time she proffered a tissue and encouraged her to dry her tears. Carly composed herself, then she spoke, "For my testimony tonight, I have written half a song", and seeing the look of surprise that crossed many faces, she continued. "Let me explain what I mean – you see this song has two parts – Sister Amelia composed the other part". "God gave me only a part of the song when I was in adversity". "And He also gave Sister Amelia her part of the same song while she was in security – for Sister Amelia has never left home". "Many of you will know that I was once a church girl but then I walked away from God – I left home and went on a distant journey". Carly paused as the congregation waited silently for her to continue. "But I made it back home again". A loud cheer suddenly rang throughout the sanctuary drowning out Carly's voice so she stopped speaking again for a while. When the furore died down she continued. "I asked Sister Amelia to sing her part of the song first and as she does so, please bear in mind that her story should be mine and I declare that from today – from now on it will be in Jesus' Name".

"I thank God, yes I praise God that he has brought me home and given me another chance". "My part of the song was prayer my when I was a long way away from home – a prayer that God has now answered". "Please listen to Sister Amelia sing her part and then I will also sing my part as my testimony". As the congregation cheered loudly Carly walked over to the piano and began to play. And Amelia began to sing.

> I said I'd be a servant but you made me a Queen
> I bowed down before you and you lifted my head up high
> With your mighty hands Lord – so powerful I have seen
> You created a palace for me.
> I'm glad to be home
> So glad to be home
> Never will I wonder from the comfort of your bosom
> Never will I roam to drink of pleasures that can never satisfy my soul
> I'm where I want to be – your love embraces me here at home.

There then followed a musical interlude as Carly played skilfully and touched the congregation and "hallelujahs" and "praise the Lords" rang throughout the sanctuary. She was just about to launch into her part – the chorus that God had inspired to her, when they heard another voice – one singing loudly from the aisle. It was the voice of Avarel.

> I walked through far desert places unknown
> Squandering wealth I'd not sown
> Just like the Prodigal son
> So unworthy of your grace and love I am
> Yet I see you standing in the distance bidding me to come
> To return into your loving arms' embrace
> To the place of holiness where I was safe
> Just like the Prodigal Son,
> Lord I'm your Prodigal Daughter
> Just like the Prodigal Son
> I'm your Prodigal Daughter

Amelia and Carly were surprised that what Avarel sang fitted perfectly with the melody and chord sequences. One of the sound ministers ran to her with a mike and as Avarel sang the congregation whispered "hallelujahs" and many a tear was dabbed away as the words touched hearts. She made her way towards the altar where she knelt and repeated her part more prayerfully, which then flowed naturally into Carly's part – the Chorus – and Carly sang.

> I want to come home
> I want to come home

Too long I have wondered from the succour of your bosom
Too long I have roamed drinking of pleasures that could never satisfy
my soul
I'm so much wiser now – Father this prodigal daughter wants to
come home

Then Avarel joined Carly and Amelia in harmony as they sang the chorus together again. As they sang many "once a year" attendees made their way to the front of the sanctuary and fell before the altar – some were weeping as they surrendered all to Jesus.

After they had ended the somewhat impromptu rendition Carly went to be baptised and Avarel indicated to an usher that she too wanted to take the bold step that night and was led away to be prepared. And 5 others new converts decided to be baptized too.

It had taken great effort on Avarel's part to make it to church tonight. Usually on New Year's Eve night she would have honoured one or two of several much sought after party invitations – and some would kill for the invites that she had turned down or ignored to be in the sanctuary tonight. But Avarel had never felt better about a decision. Her soul was at perfect peace with getting baptized this New Year's Dawn.

After all the pre-arranged candidates had been baptized Avarel, the first of the 6 impromptu baptismal candidates graced the stage to give her testimony – just a short sentence. "Thank God for bringing me home" and she raised her hands and voice in rapturous praise. Amelia and Carly joined their friend on the altar and together they sang again

So glad to be home
So good to be home
No more will I wonder from the comfort of your bosom
No more will I roam to drink of pleasures that can never satisfy my soul
I'm where I want to be
Your grace embraces me – here at home.
Then Carly and Avarel took it in turns to sing the following lines.
So much wiser now Father – your Prodigal Daughter has come home

When the service ended it was 5 am but no one seemed tired or ready to go home. Voices could be heard speaking about the blessing that had descended upon the house this New Year's Dawn and the anointing of God's spirit hovered and rested freely in the Born Again Church of God sanctuary.

Yan stood in conversation with his friend Arthur – he was just about to bid him goodbye when Avarel approached them and asked to speak to him in private. Yan bade Arthur goodnight and followed her obediently as she led him towards the rear of the sanctuary. "Congratulations on your bold step tonight", he said.

"Praise the Lord, you know Yan I am so glad I did it – I feel so light right now – as though a weight has been lifted from off of my shoulders", Avarel gushed excitedly. Then she continued, "Wait for me here a minute – I've just got to get something from the sanctuary", she said as they reached the rear corridor. Yan obeyed and stood humming the catchy chorus of Prodigal Daughter as he waited.

Minutes later Avarel returned, but she was not alone. She was holding Amelia by the hand as she approached Yan. Heartbeats were almost audible as Amelia and Yan looked at each other in great surprise. They then turned to look at Avarel who grabbed hold of both their right hands, placed Yan's upon Amelia's and said, "What God has appointed, no man can disappoint", and she then burst into tears again. "Amelia, Yan, I am soooo very sorry", she blubbered. "I have gotten so used to getting my own way – buying anything I want – seducing any man I fancied", Avarel confessed. "When I introduced you too, I felt the spark that ignited and I determined then to try and manipulate the situation by elaborating my relationship with Yan because I wanted him for myself, but in reality I was the outsider looking in". Avarel turned and looked Amelia in the eye as she spoke. "I am so sorry my dear friend – I was out of order in the things I said to you – please forgive me – I was consumed with irrational jealousy and was being controlled by my sinful nature" "Yan – I'm so sorry". Both Amelia and Yan nodded their forgiveness. They each hugged Avarel warmly and verbalised their forgiveness.

Then Avarel replaced their hands together before walking of swiftly, back into the sanctuary, leaving Yan and Amelia mutually stunned and ecstatically happy. Avarel did not tell them of the dream she had had the previous night, well more of a vision than a dream. In the vision she was standing in between them and a voice from heaven had warned her "Move because what God has appointed, no man can disappoint".

Amelia wanted to pinch herself to see that she as not dreaming, for Avarel had said the exact words that she had heard the Minister say in her dream. Her happiness knew no bounds – she felt free – she felt vibrant and alive. She wanted to shout out her joy but instead she just said "I don't think Bishop Manning would approve of us holding hands in the sanctuary", while her smile sent the message loud and clear to Yan that she was ready to answer his proposal.

Chapter 2

Bro Steve was upset. Returning home from the Watch Night baptismal service at 6.00 am he sat alone in the darkness thinking until morning turned to day. He was thinking about Amelia and Yan and he was in pain for it was obvious that something had transpired between them tonight. Steve had watched as Avarel took Amelia's hand and led her into the back corridor of the church and he had also seen Amelia and Yan emerge from that place together moments later. He had observed how they looked at each other and in particular how Amelia had regarded Yan. And his heart had been pierced, for he had dreamt a thousand dreams of her looking at him in that way. And he had drawn close enough to hear the promise Yan had made on saying goodbye, "I'll call you later", and those words had resonated in his psyche over and again, causing him to get more and more upset. He thought until he became tired and irritable and fell into a fitful sleep. But before he fell asleep he had prayed a silent prayer that God would open Amelia's eyes to see that he was the only man for her and not Yan Kennelly.

Yan could not sleep after returning home from the Watch Night service. He had been sorely tempted to call Amelia right away but knowing it was best to wait, he had wrestled with the urge to do so for a few hours. But he was finding the waiting hard and by 10 am he reached for his phone and dialled her number.

Upon returning from the Watch Night service at 6.00 am Amelia gave God a glorious praise, so enthusiastic was her eulogy that her parents had been prompted to enquire whether she was okay. And having reassured them, Amelia had toned down her prayers, following which she had fallen into bed and experienced the most restful sleep that she had had in weeks. She dreamt of her wedding day over and over again – she was at the gates of the sanctuary with her bridal party when the bells began to toll. Amelia was surprised to hear the bells because she was not aware that there were any bells at the church and as she walked towards the door of the edifice the bells tolled yet louder and more insistently. So insistent was the tolling of the bells that they awoke her from sleep and she realised that her phone was ringing. Reaching for it she answered and heard the sweetest sound – Yan's voice.

"Hello Amelia – or can I say darling?" Yan said, now assured that the response from Amelia would be reciprocal.

"Hello Yan – darling", Amelia replied and giggled loudly – still half asleep.

"Sorry I woke you up, but I couldn't sleep – I needed to hear your voice", Yan confessed.

"Oooh so sweet", Amelia replied, now focused.

"Can we meet up later today?" He asked.

"Yes, of course", came the anticipated reply. And they planned to meet that evening at 6.00 pm at the Star Apple Restaurant just off the Strand.

The Star Apple was already busy when they arrived at 6.25 pm. The venue was bustling with New Year revelry but there was very little conversation between Yan and Amelia during the early part of the evening. Their smiles and amorous glances spoke loudly one to the other. The richness of their love was evident to all around them as they basked in the glow of each other's presence. Later, as they waited for dessert to be served, Yan began to talk about his relationship with Avarel – he instinctively knew that Amelia would want to know the truth.

"Avarel and I met around 10 years ago when we were introduced by a mutual friend". "I was drawn by her beauty and asked her to be my girlfriend, but she turned me down and confessed that she was married although she did not wear her wedding ring". "A few months later we met again by chance". "One thing led to another and we ended up spending that night together". "We kept in touch and met up from time to time".

I wanted to take things further, even suggesting to Avarel that she should get a divorce, but she did not want to – she was happy with things as they were, so I backtracked". "But our paths crossed several times in the following years and we dabbled a little here and there".

Yan looked Amelia in the eyes as he spoke, "I changed the intimate nature of our relationship just over two years ago when I became a born again Christian, although we remained platonic friends". "The next time that we met after I got baptized was at a music industry awards event". "Avarel told me that her marriage was in trouble and hinted that she wanted to be with me". "She intimated that she was ready to divorce her husband and marry me but I made it clear that I was no longer the man I used to be – that I did not believe in divorce and could not encourage her to leave her husband". "I also spelt out the fact that I was celibate and would remain so until I got married". "I witnessed to her about the Lord Jesus and encouraged her to change her adulterous and sinful lifestyle – I recall that she had laughed at me". Yan raised his eyebrows as he cast his mind back in time. "I never heard from her again".

Amelia listened quietly as Yan spoke. It was her turn to raise eyebrows – his last sentence did not seem to make much sense, but as he continued to speak all became clear.

"When I ran into her outside the church that first Sunday that I visited, I was more than surprised".

"So you two did not arrive together then?" Amelia sounded surprised.

"No – we arrived separately"

"Did you know she was coming?"

"No, I didn't know she was coming – we met by chance just outside the church", Yan confirmed – then he continued. "That afternoon after we left church Avarel asked me if we could pick up where we had left off". "She explained to me that her husband had left her for someone else and that in those circumstances she was free to marry me, but I had moved on by then and had also matured as a Christian and if anything I wanted a wife that would be on the same spiritual plane, so I told her so.", Yan took a sip of his sour sap juice then continued. "The truth is that having met you, my heart was with you from that moment on".

"So you mean you and Avarel were not engaged then?"

"No – we were not – I think Avarel was hoping that we could pick up where we had left off, but my heart was elsewhere", Yan looked deeply into Amelia's eyes and saw that she understood.

"I understand", Amelia said simply and smiled as their dessert arrived.

Now that the situation had been clarified and they had Avarel's blessings, the two began to look forward to their future together. They agreed that they would get married at the end of June, when the weather was warmer – they also agreed to make Bishop Manning aware of their courtship right away. Yan promised to telephone him the following day to relay the good news. And they planned to meet again the next day to visit the jewellers in search of a suitable engagement token.

When Amelia arrived home she was bursting to tell her parents the good news and as soon as she opened the front door she wasted no time in shouting, "I'm getting married". Joyce and Patrick rushed to their daughter's side, thinking she must have lost her mind but were soon aware that she was simply ecstatic. So they celebrated with her, caught up in the rapture of her joy. Their joy was untold, having learned that their long unmarried daughter was finally to be plucked from the top shelf.

"What a wonderful way to begin the New Year, Joyce quipped, and they all agreed that they had never before celebrated such a joyous occasion on the very first day of a New Year.

Chapter 3

Amelia was wafting on clouds of joy – she had to keep pinching herself to see that she wasn't dreaming and on Sunday morning as she prepared for church special effort was put into her appearance – today was the day that she had dreamed of for many years – the day that her engagement would be announced. She met Yan in front of the church and they entered together as Bro Steve burnt red under his creamy coffee hue. He paced about relentlessly like a Tasmanian devil, as he muttered a prayer, "Lord, please open Amelia's eyes to see that I am the right one for her – please do something, Jesus".

When Bishop Manning made the announcement, the whole church erupted in joy – some danced in the aisles while others shouted praises. Yan and Amelia were made to stand in front of the altar and many well-wishing brethren left their seats to walk to the front of the sanctuary and congratulate them personally with hugs, kisses and handshakes. Such greetings were impromptu and when 5 minutes had passed without abatement, Bishop Manning had to call order by asking everyone to return to their seats, thereby reinstating etiquette. Amelia was overwhelmed by the demonstration of love from the brethren. But not everyone celebrated their joy – Bro Steve was sad.

After the service Bro Steve watched as Bishop Manning and other brethren thronged the happy couple to convey love and best wishes to them, and a solitary tear sprung up in his right eye as the thought "It should have been me", presented itself in his mind.

Conversely Amelia was riding on the crest of a joyful wave – she felt like s veritable superstar as they were literally mobbed. After about half an hour she and Yan could move freely again and made their way towards the exit. As they stood at the top of the stairs at the front of the church, two Police officers approached them. The attention of all the brethren was immediately drawn to the Police as people wondered what their business might be.

"We're looking for Yan Kennelly", the first officer announced brusquely.

"Me?" "Why are you looking for me?" Yan asked immediately.

"Would you kindly accompany us to the station – we need to speak to you about a particular matter", the second officer announced.

"Me – what do you want to speak to me about?" Yan enquired, as a look of abject surprise crossed his face.

"We will explain when we get to the station", the first Policeman stated.

"No, explain now, please", Yan replied.

"We will explain later", repeated the first Policeman louder than was necessary.

"And what if I refuse to go with you?" Yan asked – his irritation was evident.

"We don't want to cause an ugly scene in front of the house of God, now do we, Mr Kennelly?" the first officer replied suggestively threatening.

"Yan – what's going on?" Amelia asked as her cheeks began to sting with embarrassment.

"I have no idea what this is all about", he replied then addressed the Police, "I want to see my Lawyer".

"We can talk about that at the station", the second officer replied then the first officer grabbed him. Yan remonstrated, "I've done nothing wrong – you can't just arrest me like that for nothing", he said.

"We have enough evidence and yes we can arrest you – you can come quietly or not", the first Officer said gruffly and began to drag Yan away.

"Yan – what is this all about?" Amelia shouted after them.

"I don't know Amelia", Yan replied as he was dragged away.

Amelia wanted to go with Yan but was restrained by Bro Steve who came and placed his arm about her shoulders. He spoke words intended to console her but which only had the effect of upsetting her more. "Don't worry my dear – let him go – you are too good for the likes of him", Steve said.

"What do you mean?" Amelia asked, tears welling up in her eyes.

"Well, my dear – it was only a matter of time before everyone found out who he really is", Steve announced so loudly for all to hear including Amelia's parents who came and whisked her away home.

Later that afternoon Joyce received two telephone calls – the first and briefest was from Sister Manning, and the second was from Sister Mona, an old established member of Born Again.

"Sister Joyce, I hope you don't mind me calling you – I asked Sister Manning for your number".

"I don't mind you calling – Sister Manning called me to say that you would be telephoning me". "She also told me that you knew the young man Yan and had some information that would be of interest to us".

From upstairs in her bedroom Mona overheard the mention of Yan's name and immediately came down the stairs to stand by her mother who was seated on the single chair in the hall.

"I love your daughter, Sister Joyce – I love her like she was my very own child – she always blesses my soul with her ministry", Mona's voice was sincere as she spoke as though with urgency. She launched on. "Well, when I saw what happened at church earlier today, I called Sister Manning as soon as I got home because I wanted to speak with you – to let you know that the boy that your daughter is engaged to marry is a common criminal", Joyce gasped loudly at this information. She beckoned to Amelia to draw closer as she pressed the speaker button on the 'phone.

"A criminal – how do you mean?

"I can't hear you too good", Mona replied.

"Oh – I have just put the 'phone on "intercom" so that Amelia can hear what you are saying – carry on, I will speak louder", Joyce shouted.

"Oh, I see", Mona replied then continued. "Yes, that young man is from Wash House Estate". "That is where I grew up and I know all his family –

well I don't know them personally exactly but I know of them – everybody around Wash House knows about the notorious Kennelly family". "They are infamous". "They control all the drugs and organised crime in the area". "They rule Wash House Estate and the surrounding areas with an iron fist". Mona barely paused to breathe as she delivered her message. "The whole of them – the father was Harold Kennelly and the mother was Martha". "There are 7 sons and 1 daughter and plenty grandchildren – all of them are now also involved in crime".

"Oh my goodness", Joyce exclaimed upon the mention of Martha Kennelly's name. She recalled stories as a young girl about "Mafia Martha", who was known for prostitution, all immorality and was especially renowned for fighting and lawlessness – taking on and beating men twice her size. She also recalled the big news story when both Martha and Harold had been gunned down in their own homes some years earlier. It was thought to have been a gangland slaying and to this day no murderer or weapon had ever been found.

"As soon as I set eyes on the young man, I recognised him – and when Bishop Manning announced his name I knew for certain that I was not mistaken". "I wondered what your daughter was doing with such a lowlife – he is one of the worst of them all – he a "Prison Bud" *(bird)*" – he lives in prison – he is never out for too long". "I saw him the first day he stepped into the church and I recognised him then". "So when I got home I called my son who knew the Kennelly boys from school, to ask him about him – I think his real name is John". "My son Justin told me that he had just been released from a three-year sentence for armed robbery", Mona spoke quickly as though a hot potato was upon her tongue – she could not get the words out fast enough.

"Oh my goodness", Joyce said again as tears of indignation began to form at the back of Amelia's eyes.

"I have it on good authority that he is guilty of the church burglaries – and I believe he is guilty", Mona adjudged – she took a deep breath before continuing.

At that point Amelia turned and walked towards the stairs – she had heard enough. She did not reach the privacy of her room before the tears poured from her eyes and her heart began to break anew. She could hear her mother continue the conversation as she sobbed, "It can't be true – no, it cannot be true", and she shook her head from side to side in denial.

Carrying the steaming hot cup of tea that she had lovingly brewed for her daughter, Joyce reached the top of the stairs and tapped lightly at Amelia's bedroom door. She waited patiently before tapping again and asking "Amelia – are you alright dear?" Still no reply so she added. "I've made you a nice of cup of tea dear – open the door and tek it no", Joyce lapsed into her endearing Jamaican lingo.

Amelia opened the door but hid her face behind it. She reached out and took the hot mug, "Please mum – I just need to be left alone", she said and pushed the door gently as though to shut it.

"Yes – okay dear", Joyce replied dutifully, closed the door and went into her own bedroom where she fell to her knees.

Absent-mindedly Amelia sipped the hot brew and accidentally scalded her tongue. "Ouch ooooh" she exclaimed. The pain provided an excuse and she began to sob all over again. When she stopped crying she began to reflect and it dawned on her that she did not know much about the man she had agreed to marry after all. She had not bothered to dig deeply into his background – not really. He had told her that he was an orphan and that he had several siblings scattered across the globe, most of whom he was apparently not close to, but she had not troubled to ask him anything more about his background, satisfied that he was a Christian, she had just taken him at face value, thinking that she would learn more about him as time passed. Now she wondered about the ostentation, the glamorous job – was it all a farce? Where did all the money come from to produce the album and to purchase the desirable diamond that now sat upon the third finger of her left hand – was it drugs money, Amelia wondered as she was suddenly inclined to remove the solitary jewel from her significant digit.

On each occasion when the break-ins had taken place thousands of pounds and precious artefacts had been stolen, Amelia recalled. Theirs was a large congregation and it was normal for over £25,000 to be collected in offering in just one well-attended Sunday service. The Sunday offering was kept in the safe in Bishop Manning's office, before being transported to the bank on Monday mornings.

At the first break in, it had taken some considerable force to open the safe – the lock had been blown off by a single bullet, apparently. On the second occasion there had been no lock to break.

After the first break-in security had been beefed up to digital and all the external doors of the church had been fitted with secret codes. But the digital security system had been somehow overridden. It occurred to Amelia that Yan might have been capable of carrying out such a task because she recalled him mentioning that he had studied and had extensive knowledge about computers and digital systems.

The question of whether Yan could have been so devious posed at the forefront of Amelia's mind and she tried but failed to shoo it away. And the doubt that had niggled at the fringes of Amelia's mind since Yan's arrest grew into certainty as she conceded that her trust had been misplaced? These ruminations caused her to become sad beyond consolation.

The ability to pray deserted Amelia again and she gave up trying as total confusion took control of her mind. She was bereft of guidance from the Holy Spirit – no still small voice or spiritual revelation told her what was happening or what she should do about it. And clearly no gift of discernment which she had once thought she possessed had warned her of this impending misfortune. The only thing that Amelia was certain of at this time was that she was becoming incredibly and inconsolably angry at God again, for His apparent abandonment of her. Common sense informed that she should try and call Avarel, who should know more about Yan so she called her friend, but was put through to voicemail. "Hi Avarel – hope you're okay", Amelia sighed heavily then continued "Please would you call me back – it's very important – I need to ask you something about Yan".

As she pressed "end call", the bitterness growing inside Amelia mutated into paranoia. An oppressive cloud of depression settled over her mind and hovered there. It remained in place until the next day when she awoke from a fitful night's sleep. She decided she was not well enough to go in to work and telephoned her workplace, informing them that she was under the weather. Then she switched off her 'phone and stayed locked inside her room. Having no inclination to pray she thought only of her misfortune. And days and nights passed. Amelia only left her room to pick at meals or to relieve herself. She effectively cut ties with the outside world, refusing to speak to anyone, even Bishop Manning.

Chapter 4

The pang of unrequited love stabbed at Avarel's heart as she listened to her friend's message that she wanted to talk about the man she had lost to her. She could not say which was hurting her most, whether it was the loss of Simon's love or the loss of the hope of a new love and with Yan. But the pain of loss was overwhelming and like a parasite, anger gained life from it. In a fit of rage Avarel called Amelia back on Monday evening with her own agenda. She wanted to give her a piece of her mind – to tell her that she was being insensitive. How could she expect that it would be okay to discuss Yan with her so soon? She became even more enraged when she was put straight through to voicemail. "Oooh", she fumed but didn't leave a message – she hung up with attitude, vowing that she would put some considerable distance between herself, Amelia and Yan for some good time. She had enough other problems on her plate to worry about.

Avarel's divorce proceedings had taken a bitter turn and she had discovered a side to Simon that she had never known before as he intensified his fight to retain exclusive custody of Davy. She could not make her "soon to be ex-husband" see that she needed more than just weekly visits with her only son. Lately she had been re-evaluating her life and realised for the first time just how precious a gift Davy really was. And she marvelled that she had taken him for granted in the past. But all that had now changed. Davy had become her sole reason for getting up in the mornings – her only hope for a brighter tomorrow.

Nectarous was not going well at all, because of everything that was happening in her life Avarel was lacking in inspiration. So she didn't need Amelia and Yan to keep reminding her that she was losing everything.

Chapter 5

Amelia was not herself – depression was distorting her mind. Joyce and Patrick fretted about their daughter and discussed taking her to the doctor. They decided against doing so just yet, but to put their trust in God and pray in the hope that she would shortly pull herself out of gloom. For their part, they had never been so embarrassed in their lives and they just hoped that they could live down the embarrassment that their daughter's association with Yan (or John) Kennelly had caused them.

On Thursday evening, Amelia became aware of a commotion at the front door. She overheard raised voices. She could hear Yan's voice pleading that he could explain everything, that he was innocent – that it was all a horrible mistake but she was not inclined to go down and defend him. She heard her father ask him to leave – Patrick diplomatically informed Yan that they were praying about the situation and ultimately it would be God that decided the way forward.

Amelia heard Yan speaking and even though she was angry and disappointed in him, the sound of his voice stirred something deep within her. Tears stung and spilt from her eyes as she listened

"Please would you ask Amelia to read through and sign these documents – they are required for the album launch", he said.

"Okay – leave them with me", Patrick replied.

That evening Amelia cried until her tear ducts were wrung dry.

On Friday evening Rita telephoned Joyce with and update – Yan had been charged with the offence of burglary but bailed, and Amelia faced the fact that she would have to call off the engagement. And as she removed the token from her finger, she was bereft of all emotion.

Friday and Saturday passed in a haze. On Sunday Amelia did not go to church – she only ventured out of her room to pick at her meal for a few minutes before returning to seclusion. Joyce and Patrick worried more about her. She had lost at least a stone in the week of her reclusion. And most worryingly, she continued to refuse to take Bishop Manning's calls, who hitherto had been her spiritual mentor. So Joyce and Patrick were happy to receive an impromptu visit from Bro Steve that afternoon. They had never in fact written him off as a potential suitor for their beloved daughter, and were optimistic that he might turn out to be Amelia's saviour.

"Hello Sister Joyce – I'll understand if you don't invite me in as you were not expecting me, but I was just in the neighbourhood and thought I'd drop by to see how Amelia is doing". "I wanted to ask you at church this morning but I missed you".

"Bro Steve – how nice of you to think of us, come in", Joyce said without hesitation.

"Are you sure – I will understand if you don't invite me in".

"No – it's okay – come on in", Joyce repeated.

Patrick rose to greet Steve as he entered the living room, "Hello Bro Steve – how are you?"

"Oh I'm not too bad", Steve's smile was bright, demonstrating his (expensive) newly polished teeth. He sat down where Joyce indicated and there followed a general chit chat between the three of them.

"Bro Steve – can I get you a cup of tea perhaps?" Joyce offered.

"Yes – that would be very nice thank you Sister Joyce".

Having filled the kettle Joyce went to knock at Amelia's bedroom door and inform her of Bro Steve's impromptu visit. Amelia was not in the mood to see anyone but for some strange reason she was touched deep inside that Bro Steve had cared enough to take the time to come and see if she was okay. And partly in gratitude, partly as an act of retaliation for Yan's actions, she fixed up and went down to say hello to Steve.

"Hello Bro Steve – how nice of you to drop by", Amelia said, adding "but you should have called first".

Bro Steve was taken aback by Amelia's forthrightness but kept his fixed smile in place. "I was in the neighbourhood – just around the corner ….." he stuttered.

"Oh, do you know someone in the area?

"Not exactly around the corner but I…. I .. was passing close by…".

"Well it still would have been courteous to call first – don't you have a mobile?" Amelia knew she was taking out her anger on Steve but she could not stop herself.

"Amelia dear – Bro Steve was concerned about your welfare, please be nice to him", Joyce intervened.

"Well it is good of you to consider me though", Amelia softened her tone.

"So how are you Sister Amelia?" Steve breathed out heavily as he spoke.

"I'm very well – thank you", Amelia replied and warmed towards Bro Steve as she accepted that his intentions were well meaning.

Joyce and Patrick left the two of them alone for a while and they talked, Steve making it clear that his intention towards Amelia was intact. And by the end of his visit Amelia was wondering whether she should give Steve a chance after all. After he had left she gave more thought to his open invitation and decided that she might just RSVP in the positive.

Joyce received frequent updates from Rita Harris on the situation and gathered that Yan had gone to see Bishop Manning that Wednesday to plead his innocence, but as far as Rita knew the evidence against him was damning, for they had found some of the church artefacts in his possession – stashed beneath the seat in his car and Rita was convinced that Yan whom she referred to as "the ole criminal" or "the ole cruff", was going down for sure. There was discontent throughout the church because Bishop Manning had agreed to receive a visit from the criminal. And depending on whom you spoke to, in this case Rita, rumour had it that Bishop Manning had even posted bail. Many brethren were up in arms that the Bishop was misusing the church funds to take care of the welfare of criminals but Bishop's attitude was that sinners should be forgiven in the same way that Christ had forgiven us.

Chapter 6

On Monday 15 January, Amelia returned to work. She barely spoke to anyone in the office and some commented that she still looked unwell and had perhaps returned to work too soon.

Deep in contemplation on her way home, Amelia did not see Yan as he emerged from a shop front and approached her as she waited for the bus on her way home. When she saw him she ignored him and refused to speak. Reaching into her handbag she took out the engagement ring and thrust it at him forcefully when he was close enough.

"Amelia – are you listening to me – I said I don't know anything about the incident – I am innocent", Yan remonstrated.

"Yeah right – John Kennelly – innocent indeed", Amelia mocked.

"Amelia – what are you talking about – why don't you believe what I'm saying? Yan sounded exasperated.

"Why should I Yan – just why should I?" Amelia shouted as the bus arrived and she boarded it.

"Because I'm telling you the truth – that's why", Yan said as he followed her on board.

"Look just leave me alone, right – I know who you are now and you are not my type – I don't fraternize active criminals", Amelia sneered.

"I am not a criminal", Yan said as all eyes on the crowded bus turned to stare at him. "Amelia – don't call me that again, right", he shouted angrily.

"Please be quiet on the bus", the bus driver interjected.

They fell quiet for a beat then Yan pleaded again. "Amelia, I don't know what you have heard about me, but none of it is true – I am not a criminal".

Amelia ignored Yan for the rest of the journey. She had known Sister Mona all her life and knew that she was not one to make things up, especially something so serious. Sister Mona was an old fashioned Christian lady who believed in "hell fire" and her word was her bond – she did not lie. And Amelia would rather doubt Yan's word than disbelieve Sister Mona.

When Amelia got off the bus Yan followed her. He continued to try and bend her ear. "Look Yan, if you don't leave me alone, I will call the Police – they are best placed to deal with unrepentant convicts like you", Amelia threatened, placing an emphasis on the word "convicts". The mention of the Police seemed to hit home as Yan fell silent. Then he said, "Amelia, it's all a mistake – I don't know anything about the break-ins – but obviously you do not trust me – okay, I'll leave you alone – I won't bother you again – I won't be around anyway", then he turned and walked dejectedly back towards the bus stop.

Those words struck hard upon the closed door of Amelia's mind – what if it was all a mistake? She wondered briefly. "No – there's no mistake – they found the goods in his possession – the Police don't charge people without good evidence". "And even if he is not guilty of this crime, I don't want to be involved with someone from such a notorious and unrepentant criminal family", Amelia mumbled to herself as she arrived home.

Bro Steve dropped by the Lanson household again the following Saturday evening (this time having telephoned first). Amelia was particularly depressed because tonight should have been the launch of her album, which she gathered had been cancelled by Yan at the last minute – he had left her a voicemail. She was glad to see Steve. He cheered her up with his endless show of interest in her and compliments about her beauty, and he encouraged her to come out to church the following day.

Steve touched Amelia's heart. Her opinion of and attitude towards him was slowly changing. She could now accept that whatever he had been before, he had turned a new page. The question of whether he was continuing his unjust lifestyle had been settled by his proven steadfastness in serving the church as a steward and general caretaker, and by his unerring philanthropic gestures. If God is willing to forgive those who are truly repentant who was she to hold it against Steve any longer? So that evening she agreed to accompany him to dinner the following Friday evening – she had made up her mind to give "them" a chance.

After Steve left, Bishop Manning also telephoned to encourage Amelia to come back to church the next day and she decided that it was time to face the shame. Bishop had also tried to talk her into forgiving Yan for anything that he might have done, but Amelia would not listen to his plea. She was simply not interested – there was no way she was taking their relationship forward, because he had deceived her and everyone else so mercilessly. Amelia hated deception – that was the reason why she had never entertained Steve – because she was not convinced that he had turned his back on his dishonest lifestyle. It had taken her this long to accept that Steve had indeed turned a new page – was a new creature who had truly repented of his previous sins, Yan on the other hand had barefacedly stolen from the house of the Lord. There was nothing lower than that – he had no doubt invited the wrath of God upon his destiny and Amelia wouldn't be around to share the Almighty's judgment with him.

As Amelia and her family entered the foyer of the sanctuary Bro Steve rushed over to usher them in. He fussed about them and treated Amelia like Sunday royalty. Sister Alice watched this display and seethed. She left the sanctuary and went to the ladies room where she cried for a long while. When she emerged her eyes were swollen and red. She returned into the sanctuary and made her way towards the altar where she gestured to Assistant Pastor Gentles. Pastor Gentles was happy to hear what Alice had to say – testimonies were always encouraged, but he informed her that she would need to wait until the evening service to give her testimony because the itinerary was full for the morning.

Word travelled fast at Born Again Church, especially now that Rita Harris was back, and in anticipation of the big testimony that Sister Alice had to give, many (including those who invariably only attended morning service), returned to evening service. When called forward Sister Alice took the stand and began to speak.

"Good evening brethren – let us praise God for all his goodness and grace", and the congregation obeyed with a rapturous "praise the Lord". Alice took a deep breath and continued, "I would first of all like to apologise for my duplicity over the past year, because I have deceived Bishop Manning and this congregation in an unacceptable and sinful way".

At that point the voice of one sister interjected "Clear your conscience my dear", followed by rumblings of agreement, then the crowd looked expectantly up at Alice who took her cue and continued, "I am so sorry for my rebellious ways", Sister Clancy spoke out then, "If God forgives you who are we to hold it against you", and another bout of mumbling filled the sanctuary.

Alice awaited relative quiet and then she carried on with her testimony. "Although it is not a good excuse, I ask you all to understand that my eyes were blinkered by what I thought was love but I can see clearly now and I have a confession to make".

"Say your heart my Sister", rang out from the balcony, and a rustle of agreement stirred the congregation yet again.

Alice coughed lightly and order was restored – she continued, "I have known for some time who carried out the break-ins of the church", Alice said to a hushed audience. "But I have kept this information to myself", she breathed in deeply then continued. "It is not the poor innocent soul that was arrested two weeks ago", a brief rumbling broke out amongst the congregation then the sanctuary fell deathly silent again. The hush was palpable as Alice continued, "Bro Yan is an innocent man, and was framed up by the same criminal who has deceived the Church Council and all this congregation all these years – Bro Steve". And she pointed straight at Steve who looked more shocked than anyone else present at the meeting. Then he began to laugh before speaking up in his defence. "She's mad – crazy – don't listen to her – she's completely mad", Steve said then chuckled again. The congregation looked at Alice with eyes that spoke disbelief – after all Bro Steve was their benefactor – everyone knew that. And many mumbled that she must indeed be losing her senses.

"No I am not mad, Steve – I have now come to my senses in fact – for a long time now I have known that it was you – I saw the items you stole at your home and at first I was going to tell Bishop and took away this goblet as evidence, but I just couldn't tell because I was so deeply in love with you", Alice raised the small golden communion goblet, one of a priceless set of 100, that had been stolen in the first burglary. Steve began to protest his innocence robustly and there was uproar at the rear of the sanctuary but Alice continued to speak commandingly into the microphone, drowning out the cacophony and chaos.

"But you never loved me in return and now my eyes are no longer blinded – I am free of you and that is why I have found the strength to speak out", Alice said as many members of the congregation looked on bemused and one man who had never liked Bro Steve egged her on "Yes Sister, speak out", the animated heckler shouted loudly.

Taking a very deep breath and shouting loudly Steve contested, "It must have been you who broke into the church and you are now trying to implicate me – but it won't work Alice", his anger was evident.

"You are nothing but a stupid ******* *****, Bro Steve spat out deadly Jamaican swear words like a venomous snake as he began to walk towards the altar. Audible gasps rang throughout the sanctuary as shocked brethren quickly re-evaluated Alice's revelation and switched sides. Bro Cyrus, the man who disliked Steve shouted triumphantly "You ole' thief – you ole criminal", and many voices joined in the accusations.

"No Steve – you did it – I have already gone to the Police this afternoon and they were very interested in what I had to say". "The Police told me that you are a person of great interest to them – that they have been watching you for some time because you are a known drug dealer who has been in prison for drugs before and they suspected that you have recently started dealing with drugs at a supplier level again – they are just about now raiding your home", Alice said acrimoniously.

"You see you, you are nothing but a ****, ****,*****, *****, Steve shouted even more lethal swear words than before, having obviously completely forgotten where he was. And as he rushed towards Alice on the pulpit, Bro Gustave who was sitting at the front and a burly usher ran to grab him on either side. As he was dragged away to the rear of the sanctuary, Steve sneered and looked menacingly at the congregation who mostly bore shocked expressions. But some were laughing and one bemused sister was heard to comment, "Oh my Lord – all kinda people come a church!".

"I'm sorry about that", Alice said simply after Steve had been dragged away into the back hall of the church. Bishop Manning had risen from his seat to place his body defensively in front of Alice, protecting her from any potential hurt by Steve. Now he stood back and allowed her to speak before taking the microphone from her hands. Bishop had received a revelation that this would happen some months earlier and had suspected since the second break-in who was behind it all, but without any proof he had been praying and waiting upon God to move as he knew He would.

The Policeman in charge approached Assistant Pastor Gentles and whispered into his ear. Pastor Gentles walked up to the podium and in turn whispered into Bishop Manning's ear, following which Bishop made a further announcement. "Would Sister Rita please speak with Pastor Gentles in the back hall". And as Sister Rita arose to answer the call Bishop Manning continued, "Brethren, let us be prayerful – Sister Amelia please come and lead us in the song "This is the House of God" – it is obvious that somebody needs reminding of that fact", Bishop Manning requested.

Still recovering from the shock, Amelia hurried towards the pulpit – she was overwhelmed with righteous indignation at Bro Steve's behaviour in the sanctuary and began singing "This is the House of God" militantly even before she took the microphone from Bishop Manning's hand. The band began to play military style as Amelia sang and the other worship leaders harmonized.

> "House of God, house of God – this is the house of God
> Tread with reverence and fear while you are here
> This is the House of God."

The refrain rang through the sanctuary as Amelia spurred the musicians on. The worship leaders also rose to the challenge and the anthem built more and more, until the cacophony of righteous indignation reached a pinnacle. Having reached a peak, Amelia changed the song and launched into a triumphant anthem.

> "God has scattered his enemies
> God has taken His stand
> God has scattered his enemies
> With his mighty hands
> Praises to the mighty God
> Glory to the triumphant One
> He has scattered – they are scattered
> They are scattered – He has scattered
> God has scattered His enemies
> With his mighty hand"

The Holy Spirit took control and for more than forty-five minutes there was a triumphant praise in the sanctuary as Amelia led the charge. When she had ended her ministration she burst into tears and fell at the altar where she gave praise to God for what had transpired. She arose to return to her seat and became aware, as did everyone else in the sanctuary, of another commotion at the back of the church as Bro Steve was led away by the Police. "Amelia – don't believe them – it's all a ******* load of lies", Bro Steve shouted as he caught sight of Amelia. And everyone could tell that he was losing his mind.

Sister Rita also went quietly to help the Police with their further investigations. Pastor Gentles had recently received a tip-off from a close relative of Rita's to say that she had siphoned away more than three thousand pounds of church funds over recent months, and was planning to continue this surreptitious criminal activity and this allegation had checked out without a shadow of a doubt. Bishop and Sister Manning each breathed a huge sigh of relief that Rita would no longer be an employee at the church because they had also become aware that Sister Rita was the source of many flames of virulent and malicious gossip about Bishop Manning – that he was apparently having illicit affairs with various sisters in the church and also in respect of fraudulent dealings with the church finances, all of which allegations were outright lies.

Amelia sat through the sermon without taking it in – she was numb. She was thankful to God for saving her from getting more involved with Steve. And she also contemplated the circumstances with Yan. If it had not been for the false accusations levied against him she might never have found out of his criminal connection. So she thanked God for all that had transpired. And though her heart was sad because she still did not have a husband, she resigned herself to be humbling accepting of God's will.

That night after they arrived home from church, Joyce and Patrick apologised to Amelia. "Amelia, we realise that we did try to force you to get involved with Bro Steve and we are very sorry for that", Patrick said.

"We should have realised that you are so close to God that he would guide you", Joyce said.

"Umphh", Amelia said and nodded.

"I suppose that we being human just looked at the gifts that he was offering without seeing his heart", Patrick added.

"I knew there was something wrong about Bro Steve", Amelia said then added, "I need to go and pray".

That night Amelia dreamt of Bro Al once again – they worshipped together and she awoke the next day spiritually refreshed. All throughout that week Amelia felt the presence of the Holy Spirit hover about her and her spirit was divinely connected with God.

Chapter Seven

On Friday evening Joyce received a telephone call. Amelia overheard her mother speaking to Sister Mona and left the dining room to go and stand next to her and eavesdrop.

"You saw John Kennelly?" Upon seeing Amelia Joyce flicked the speaker-phone switch.

"Yes, he looks so much like your daughter's fiancé, Yan but it's not him". "When I saw Martha Kennelly's son, John yesterday I could not believe it – he is mash up – he was begging at Wash House Market". "He looks terrible", Amelia heard Mona say and as the words *he looks so much like your daughter's fiancé but it's not him* registered and reverberated in her mind, her feet took on a life of their own. Grabbing her coat and keys she was out the door before Joyce knew it.

As Amelia set her car in motion there was only one question on her mind how would she begin to apologise to Yan for having mistrusted him so? Could any apology ever be enough? He had tried strenuously to convince her of his innocence but she had not listened to his pleas.

"Oh why didn't I listen to you – why didn't I trust you?" Amelia repeated over and again as she drove towards the offices of Astral Ventures International. Although she had never been to Yan's home, she had visited Astral's offices many times and was aware that his apartment was situated above. She thought of telephoning him to apologise but dismissed that idea, deciding that it was best to see him face to face so that he could appreciate her sincerity. She owed him that and much more.

As though rehearsing what she would say when she saw him, Amelia soliloquised, "I'm so sorry – oh Yan, you don't know just how sorry I am". And she shook her head from side to side as she thought of how she had wronged the man that God had sent to her in answer to her many prayers, and it pained her deep inside as she realised that she had been right about Steve Walters all along – he was an unrepentant criminal and the real culprit. The thought of Yan's innocence gripped her mind again and Amelia shook her head as though to try and clear it of confusion.

How might Yan behave towards her? Amelia's mind questioned. Would he accept her penitence? Would he refuse to give her an audience? Or would he listen to her and then reject her pleas as she had done to him? Or perhaps he would simply embrace her – Amelia hoped against hope that the latter would transpire.

The commercial district where Yan lived was almost deserted at 9.30 pm this Friday evening and Amelia felt a degree of vulnerability as she stood in front of the imposing five storey block. She pulled her coat about her as though seeking for protection and having located the correct buzzer pressed hard and waited. There was no response. She pushed the button again and waited. No response. She repeated the exercise several times more, but still there was no response. After 10 minutes she fished her mobile from her handbag and dialled Yan's number – she was put straight through to voicemail and left a short message that she needed to talk to him urgently. Then she reluctantly made her way home, her mind clouded by anxiety at Yan's possible rejection of her because of the way she had mistreated and mistrusted him.

Now that Amelia could see just how wrong she had been, with the benefit of hindsight she began to beat herself up. She should have stood by Yan – she should have given him a chance to explain properly – she should have believed him, but instead she had written him off as a criminal. How could he ever forgive her for that?

As the days progressed Amelia became more anxious. When she did not receive a call back from Yan on Friday night she waited until Saturday night then telephoned him again and left another voicemail. She repeated that exercise each night until Tuesday night, but still she heard nothing from Yan. That night was spent fretting that he had gone away for good – his last words to her, that he would leave her alone and that it would be the last time she would see him, haunted her and she tossed and turned until the light of morning.

Wednesday arrived on a new wave of anxiety. Amelia's moods swung between anxious one moment, and sad the next, then she felt desperate and despondent all at once. She could not shake this feeling and thought that she might be losing control as the torture pushed her towards the precipice of deep depression. She had also awoken with a clanging headache which meant yet another day off work.

For their part, Joyce and Patrick felt ashamed. They had the benefit of experience because they had been married for nearly 43 years and should have known better. They should have encouraged their daughter to stand by her man, especially in light of his protestations of innocence, and at least until there had been a final resolution of the situation. And they were ashamed too for having tried to force her to accept Bro Steve as a suitor, ashamed that they never had even an inkling of his continued criminality. And Joyce embarked upon a further 7-day fast, seeking for God's gift of spiritual discernment.

By Wednesday afternoon the clanger had lifted due mostly to over the counter medication and Amelia decided to seek spiritual guidance from Bishop Manning. She knew that the Bishop had gotten to know Yan pretty well and was hoping that they might still be in touch with each other So Amelia called the church office, where she knew Bishop Manning would be ensconced with his Bible, his computer and other seminary and theological material, ever learning more of God's words and ways.

"Hello Bishop – firstly, please accept my apology for not wanting to listen to what you had to say about Yan, but I was going through a lot Bishop and I didn't want to talk to anyone about it", Amelia launched straight into her mentally rehearsed speech.

"O hello Sister Amelia – how are you?"

"I'm okay Bishop – please accept my apology Bishop".

"I do understand what you have been through", Bishop sounded relaxed and sympathetic so Amelia went on.

"Bishop I have been so wrong in the way that I treated Yan and now he is avoiding me". "I called him so many times and left messages for him but he never takes my calls and does not call me back". "I know I must have hurt him so terribly when I disbelieved him that he was innocent, but now I just hope that he will find it in his heart to forgive me", Amelia sighed deeply.

"I know my dear – it's true that everyone treated that young man in an awful way and we are all hoping that he will forgive us".

"I was wondering whether he has been in touch with you Bishop, but from the sound of it, he hasn't".

"I spoke to him that Sunday night after the truth came to light and he told me he was going away – he didn't say where or how long for". "He just said he was happy that the true culprit had been identified, but he sounded very unhappy". "I telephoned him again yesterday, to check that he was okay – I left a message for him but he has not called me back either". "I hope he is alright – let's not worry though – let us pray and leave it to the Lord", Bishop surmised.

"Yes, please, please pray for me Bishop – I love Yan so very much and I don't know what I will do if I have lost him". "Please pray for me Bishop".

Amelia sounded like the most desperate of brethren to Bishop Manning's ears. In all the years that he had been the pastor of Born Again he had never had such a conversation with her and, receiving guidance from the Holy Spirit, he decided that he would do more than just pray – he would fast for the couple to be reconciled.

"Let us fast and pray for three days for God to bring a change of his heart, my dear" Bishop Manning said, and Amelia was happy to agree.

Later that evening Bishop Manning telephoned Joyce and requested that she also joined them in fasting and she confessed that she was already fasting in any case and would add the reconciliation prayer to the top of her list. And when Joyce told Patrick, he too wanted to take part. So the fast officially began at 6 am on Thursday morning. They fasted until 4 pm that day and prayed in earnest. They also fasted on Friday and on Saturday. Amelia resolved to continue fasting until she and Yan were reconciled.

When Amelia made her way to church on Sunday she was hopeful that God may have answered their prayers. But it was not to be – Yan was not in church.

On Monday Amelia was still fasting. She prayed in her spirit all day and went to the toilet to whisper a prayer at 4 pm, breaking the fast. As she left work that evening she was hoping that Yan would be outside waiting for her, but that wasn't to be and he still had not returned her numerous calls.

Less than an hour after arriving home from work Amelia bade her parents good night and retired to her room. There she cried out to God then rolled into bed and fell into a deep slumber. And she dreamed a beautifully simple dream that recurred 7 times during that night – in the dream she saw Yan and his face was radiant and he smiled. In the morning Amelia awoke with a feeling of wellbeing which bordered on euphoria. She felt in her spirit that all would be well and decided to conclude her fasting.

That morning as she walked to work she saw him standing outside her workplace and his countenance was as she had seen in her dream.

"I am so so sorry Yan, please forgive me", Amelia blabbered as she rushed towards him.

"I have already forgiven you my dear – God has shown me your heart", Yan replied immediately.

"What do you mean?" Amelia asked, she felt unworthy of his forgiveness, for surely she was undeserving of this show of grace.

"I fasted for the last 4 days and God gave me a dream and in it you were radiant like an angel – you simply smiled, and I knew it meant that your love for me is pure and true. We all make mistakes and I am happy to forgive you and I know you will learn from this and we can move forward knowing that we stand as one from here on", Yan said wisely.

"Yes Yan – I do love you – so very much and I will never again stand against you – no matter what – from now on we are one", Amelia replied and then they embraced, smiled into each other's eyes and said goodbye.

"I'm going over to see Bishop Manning now", Yan called back over his shoulders and smiled radiantly as he walked away.

"Yes, you do that – he is almost as worried as I have been", Amelia smiled radiantly back at him.

Chapter 8

Amelia could hardly concentrate all day – the butterflies in her stomach just wouldn't keep still. She was so excited to see Yan that evening and smile at him again that lunchtime came and went and she forgot to eat. They had spoken five times since their reconciliation that morning and the last time he had confirmed that he would be waiting for her outside her workplace at 5.30 pm. At 5.15 pm Amelia tidied her desk and she was the one waiting for Yan when he arrived at 5.25 pm. They embraced and entered their own world where it seemed that they alone existed.

Arriving at the Parque, they took their usual seats and remained cocooned in lovers' world as they perused menus.

"Yan, I love you sooooo very much", Amelia gushed, as she seemed to lose control of her tongue.

"I love you too, Lady Amelia", Yan reciprocated, and looked into Amelia's eyes.

They barely spoke for minutes after that, but their eyes spoke loudly of their special bond of love and all around them could sense the rapture.

Having put in their orders, Yan became pensive – he arose from his chair and knelt down, fished into his pocket and brought out the engagement ring, "Lady Amelia – may I place your ring back onto your finger?" And tears sprung up in the corners of Amelia eyes as she replied "Oh yes please Yan – thank you", she gripped his hand as though she would never let it go. The people at the surrounding tables cheered and congratulated them as Amelia's cheeks flushed dark cherry.

Taking his seat again, Yan said, "Thank you for agreeing to be my wife, Lady Amelia", and overhearing what he had said one inquisitive lady at the next table interjected, "Aaah – ain't he a perfect gentlemen – hold on to him tight luv or I'll be 'aving him", and all the others seated at their table roared with laughter. "You got a bruvva?" a blonde haired young girl at yet another table chipped in to a renewed roar of laughter.

Amelia and Yan smiled and Yan replied, "Unfortunately I do not", to an even bigger outbreak of raucous laughter. The couple made eyes at each other that spoke their thoughts *"it wasn't that funny"*, and was glad when everyone in the café returned to their own business so they could get on with bathing in their love stream undisturbed.

"Amelia now that we are to be married, I must tell you all about myself", Yan said and he cleared his throat with a small cough.

"As I have already told you, I am an orphan". "My father died instantly in a car accident when I was 5 years old – my sister Ella was 4 at the time". "My mother survived the accident but due to the poor healthcare available in the remote areas of Jamaica back in the seventies complications developed and she died two weeks after my father". "I can still remember that as the saddest day of my life". "My mother was all to me – I loved her so much – I can still remember how beautiful and caring she was – I remember everything about her, but strangely I can't remember a lot about my father, except that he was a light skinned man – that's how come I have light eyes but I inherited my mother's colouring". "My mother was dark and so beautiful like Avarel .... aahm – she was lovely", Yan stuttered.

Amelia's ear pricked up at the mention of Avarel's name, "What did you say about Avarel?" she asked.

"Oh nothing – I was going to say that my mother looked a lot like Avarel but thought I'd better not", Yan said.

"Oh – that's okay – so she was really beautiful then", Amelia said, understandingly.

"Yes – that's all I meant to say", Yan said and continued. "When my mum died we had to travel from Bogle Hill in St Elizabeth to May Cross in Clarendon where we went to live with our grandmother, my mother's mother. But after three months Granny became too sick to look after us and had to go into hospital. We had to go into a home for orphans run by the Glory Bound Church of God". "We were alone in the world – just me and Ella".

"The carers at the home tried their very best but they had very limited resources and too many mouths to feed". "They were entirely reliant upon hand-outs and a lot of the time we had to go without food – sometimes we were near starving". "Many times I gave what little food I received to Ella to stop her whining from hunger – it broke my heart to hear her cry". "I became so thin – just skin and bones really" Yan seemed to drift away as he shared his recollections.

"The house where we lived was becoming more and more crowded every day due to the fact that the Church had to take in as many orphans and strays as they could – they didn't like to turn anyone away into the cruel streets". "The carers searched for family members who would be willing to take us in but they found only my Aunt Betty who had a drunkard for a husband and 7 children of her own and she couldn't take us, although she tried her best to send food and clothes for us when she could afford to".

Yan spoke quietly and Amelia could sense the sadness within him as he recounted the early days of his life. A tiny tear threatened to spill down her face as she listened. "Some of the others were lucky though – they found family who were able to take them in and provide them with good homes but we had to stay in the orphanage".

"We had to work to bring in money to help out – we had to get up at 5 am every morning to wash clothes for local people in return for measly hand-outs". "And sometimes we had to go and help clean donors' houses – some of the donors were cruel and forced us to do strenuous work or abused us both verbally and physically". "I recall that one of the boys, Andy, was also sexual abused". "He was threatened by the perpetrator who said that he would kill him if he told anyone, but Andy was brave enough to tell one of the helpers at the home because he did not want the same thing to happen to any others of us". "And that wicked man, Mr Benson, was sent to prison for a long time", Yan shook his head from side to side as he spoke. "Thank God for Andy's courage".

"But some spoke kindly to us and would give us their very last dime". Amelia's heart began to break as she listened to the man she loved speak of his pain – the tiny tear became bigger and negotiated its way slowly down her cheek.

"Most times we had to work until very late into the night after we had finished our homework, ironing clothes in return for pitiful hand-outs". "We had no toys and our lives were frankly a living nightmare". "We wore clothes that were torn or too big or too small and had to go barefoot". "And when we went to school the other children and some teachers mistreated and teased us. Some children picked fights with us and cursed us that we nah ha nobody", Yan broke off into Jamaican twang as he was accustomed to doing occasionally.

"I can say that I have known real poverty, Lady Amelia – real hardship", Yan shook his head for emphasis as he looked deep into Amelia's eyes. Upon seeing her tears he took her hands into his own and rubbed them gently. "Are you okay?"

"Oh yes – don't mind the tears – I'm just a big softie – please go on I want to hear it all", Amelia replied. She withdrew her right hand and reached over to pat him lightly on his back as though he were a six foot four baby, then she returned her hand into his as Yan continued his sorry tale.

"For three long, long years we endured that inhumane way of living – three good long years which seemed more like a lifetime". "And each night we prayed together, Ella and I, that Granny would get better and we could go back and live with her, and if not, then that our Aunt Betty's situation would change – but that was never to be". "Others came and went but we stayed". "We gave up hope and became used to the suffering". "Our only pleasure was derived from talking about mum and dad". "I would tell Ella just how much our parents had loved us and of the way we used to live when they were alive and we would escape in dreams together". "We formulated reveries that our parents were not in fact dead but had gone away on a long journey and would return to get us soon", Yan chuckled lightly – his voice was a monotone. Then he fell silent as he shook his head gently from side to side.

"So what happened to you Yan? "I mean, how come you managed to escape such hardship and be where you are today?" Amelia asked gently.

"Oh you know Amelia – God is good – Lady Amelia God is good", Yan said and smiled as he nodded his head in affirmation of the statement.

"Amen", Amelia concurred.

Yan smiled and continued. "When I was 8 years two profound things happened. Firstly, my Grandmother passed away and all hopes that she would one day recover and we could go back and live with her died. We were grieving her passing two weeks earlier when the second thing happened. A couple came to visit the orphanage. "I still remember clearly the day that they first came – it was a Saturday and the sun was bearing down hard". "We children languished through hunger and exhaustion under the big mango tree in the yard after having finished washing huge bundles of clothes. I was wishing that it was mango season because we were all starving. As we watched the clothes blow in the hot breeze, the gripe of our stomachs could be heard in tune with the whines of the younger ones. Then one of the carers came out into the yard and called us all together into the living area of the house to tell us that we had received a great blessing that day – and truly we had been blessed".

"The couple – foreign visitors had called by and brought bags and bags of toys, an assortment of clothes and shoes – more than enough for all forty or so of us that were living at the eight bedroomed home at the time, and in spite of our hunger, we were all overwhelmed with great joy". "We all thanked the couple but apart from that did not pay them much attention that first time they came because we were more interested in the items that they had brought". "They didn't stay very long and I recall us rummaging through the bags and being disappointed that they had not brought any food".

"After the couple had left the carers told us that they had adopted all of us". "And later that evening we ate the best meal since our parents died". "After that we started to be properly fed – it was wonderful – we had breakfast in the mornings, lunch at school and a full dinner every evening". "We no longer had to get up at 5 am but were allowed to remain in our beds until 6.45 am". "And we no longer had to wash and iron other people's clothes in order to survive". "The carers were very happy because they also began to receive a proper salary for all their hard work".

"Six months after the couple's first visit they came back again". "They informed us that they were officially our new parents and would be coming to visit us more often in future". "Three months after that we were moved to a brand new development many miles away in Mandeville where we lived in dormitories each containing 4 beds and we each had our own bed, and properly functioning bathrooms and kitchens". "For the first time we also had televisions and telephones in the main communal living areas". "It was as though we had woken up in heaven". "The couple came to visit us at least three times a week and would speak to each one of us, asking how we were getting on at school and the like". "They treated each one of us as though they were truly interested in us as parents – as if we were truly their own children".

"Two months after our move to the new development the couple also came to live at the complex – they had been waiting for the building works to be completed to their quarters". "And after they moved in they fully assumed the roles of mother and father to every single one of us". "We still had live-in carers who took care of our daily needs, but when mum and dad were not away on their travels, they were always available if we needed them and we could talk to them about anything". "Over time our numbers increased to well over 100 and we all grew to love and cherish mum and dad very dearly – they were so loving – so kind". "They were devout Christians and instilled into us proper values and morals standards". "We went from impoverished waifs to being the envy of all the other children in school because we were dropped off each morning and collected each afternoon by luxury air conditioned vans or mini buses and always had immaculate clothing, shoes and the best study materials". Yan's mood visibly lightened as he spoke of his turn of fortune.

"When we finished school each of us went on to college – some who demonstrated an aptitude for learning continued on to university". "I came to study at Leicester University here in England and a year later my sister Ella joined me". "After my studies I liked it so much in England that I stayed on". "My sister Ella met her husband at university and returned to Canada with him where they married a year after their graduation". "We are still very close though – I go to visit her at least twice a year".

"And mum and dad kept on taking in more and more strays or orphaned children until mum passed away five years ago".

"Dad almost fell apart when mum died". "We were all devastated too". "He decided that he needed new surroundings and I was very happy when he decided to come to live in London for a while".

"Mum and dad were wonderful people – so loving – so kind". "But my father was the driving force though – he was the real philanthropist – he was the kindest most beautiful human being I have ever known".

Amelia noticed that Yan spoke of his adoptive father as though he was no more alive and asked, "So is your adoptive father still alive?"

"Alas, no – he passed away last year", Yan looked sad again,

"It was after he died that I learned of his connections to Born Again Church of God", Yan said. He noticed the perplexed look that crossed Amelia's face and before she could speak again, he continued.

"My father is better known to you as Bro Albert Cohen", Amelia gasped loudly as Yan said Bro Al's name.

"You mean, Bro Al?" she gushed incredulously.

"Yes – he was very unassuming – he liked to keep a low profile, but Albert Cohen – to all intents and purposes my father, was one of the wealthiest men that ever walked upon this planet". "And thank God for his philanthropic ways many unwanted orphans scattered all over the globe have been given a chance in life and have become somebody because of that dear kind man, just like me and Ella my sister, who is now a successful Dentist in Toronto".

"Bro Al – Bro Al – no wonder I loved him so much", Amelia confessed as tears welled up in the corners of her eyes.

"You did?" Yan asked as a look of surprise crossed his face.

"Yes – Bro Al was my worship mentor – I learnt so much about worship from simply observing him" Amelia reminisced with a bright smile". "I knew instinctively that he was my friend" her smile widened yet further as she recalled the few words exchanged between them during the three years of acquaintance.

"He thought a lot of you too Lady Amelia", Yan said. ""Lady Amelia" that was how he referred to you in his diary notes.

"Diary notes?"

"Yes – dad made notes about everything of interest to him – it was one of his foibles – and you were apparently of great interest to him – he had a section in his diary where he listed all your ministrations and he also kept a copy of every single one of the recordings". "He was probably your biggest fan", Yan chuckled and continued, "And he has passed that legacy down to me", and they both chuckled.

"When I read dad's diary after he died I was prompted to visit Born Again Church of God because I was intrigued to get to know you "Lady Amelia". "Dad loved you so much and he wrote about you as if you were one of his hundreds of beloved daughters". "He would have been very sad that you didn't accept his gift to you – of all people he wanted to bless you the most, Amelia", Yan said. Amelia listened, wondering what gift Yan was referring to. Then Yan spoke again, enlightening her. "Why didn't you accept the car, Amelia?"

"You mean Bro Al was the one who gave me the car?" "You mean Bro Al was the secret benefactor?" the penny suddenly dropped as did Amelia's bottom lip – then she burst inexplicably into tears.

"Why are you crying darling – please don't cry – I hate to see you cry and dad would definitely not like to see you unhappy", Yan said.

"I'm not unhappy, just sad", Amelia said then they both realised what she had said and burst into laughter again at the absurdity of the statement.

"Yes – dad was the secret benefactor – and that is another legacy that he has passed on to me and some of his many children who carry on his work", Yan said and continued, "Please do not tell anyone about this Amelia.

"No I won't, but it will be hard though", she promised.

"So were you the one who wrote me the letter about the motor car?"

"Yes – that was me – I had to try and convince you", Yan replied as Amelia nodded her understanding.

"After mum died, dad just didn't want to be in Jamaica without her any-more – he found the memories of her too painful". "He didn't want to return to South Africa, where he grew up either, or to go back to Israel where he was born". "They had always wanted to visit London together but had never gotten around to doing so, and so he came here for a visit, fell in love with London, and stayed".

"So your dad was truly Jewish then?" Amelia asked.

"Yes – dad was a full blooded Jewish man, skull cap and all", Yan said smiling at the memory of his father.

"So how did he come to end up in Jamaica – I didn't know there was a Jewish community there?"

"Yes man, there are a few Jewish people in Jamaica – in JA you can find every colour, every tongue and every creed", Yan broke off into twang again – then he looked pensive as he continued, "How he came to be living there is a long story".

Chapter 9

Albert Josiah Cohen was born in 1928 in a small town just outside Jerusalem. His family were not poor but they were not wealthy either. When he was 2 years old his parents decided to leave Israel and go to South Africa where his father had been invited by a friend to get involved in the lucrative diamond business. And that was where Albert grew up. He hated apartheid from his youth and gravitated towards the underprivileged in that society, whom he openly befriended.

His father, Josiah Cohen's diamond business excelled and over the years he amassed vast wealth. Albert was unhappy that his family were involved in the diamond business, even though their mines were operated on humane principles. Josiah Cohen was a philanthropist (from whom Albert inherited his heart for the poor and underprivileged), and was sympathetic to the plight of the poor people who worked in the mines. He paid more than double what other mine owners did and provided safe working conditions and decent housing and living conditions for his miners and other workers and their families. But, being fully aware of the pain and suffering inflicted upon mainly the black and "coloured" people who worked to extract diamonds from most of the other mines in South Africa, Albert could not dissociate his family's wealth made from diamonds, from the "blood money", made by other mine owners.

When Albert turned 21 years old, his father wanted him to get involved in the family business but the younger Cohen wasn't interested at all and showed signs of rebellion. He convinced his parents that he wanted to travel around the world for a few years and promised to return and take over the reins from his father, who was by then 69 years old. So they consented. Albert then travelled throughout the developing world – Africa, India, and South America. And he used his father's wealth, to which he had almost unlimited access as an only child, to do great things wherever he went – he established feeding programmes in schools he had built, he built hospitals, he provided money to thousands of poor farmers to buy land and cattle to help them build their lives, he built wells to provide sources of clean water in remote communities and established feeding and training programmes for disadvantaged adults in the poorest parts of the world.

Ten years passed and Albert's father implored him to return to South Africa and take over the business as his health had begun to fail. Albert agonised about doing so and in the end decided that he must keep the promise he had made to his parents to return. So he went back to South Africa. There he met Lydia, the daughter of one of his father's employees, and they fell deeply in love. Their relationship was taboo because Lydia was black and they had to keep their romance a secret – it was forbidden for them to marry. Albert made a vow to Lydia that he would never marry anyone unless it was her and he kept his promise.

As the Cohen fortune continued to grow so did Albert's concern for the plight of the poor and suffering in the world. Lydia shared his passion and sympathies towards the suffering of others, particularly the indigenous people of South Africa. In each other they found common ground for a strong union – one built upon compassion.

Albert's heart was never in the diamond business or the wealth it generated, and when his father died four years after his return and he inherited the vast empire, he decided to use his new found wealth to give back even more to the endless stream of disadvantaged, poor and destitute people. His sole purpose in life was to do good. He based himself in South Africa because of his mother but travelled to impoverished nations several times each year. On his first trip he arranged for Lydia to meet him in Ghana and there they were secretly married. Even his mother never knew of their nuptials. Lydia remained and settled in Ghana and Albert shared his time between his mother in South Africa and his wife in Ghana but whenever he travelled to any other part of the world Lydia accompanied him.

As he was away from South Africa so much Albert re-structured the company to function in his absence. He renamed it the JosCo Corporation. He was selective about whom he employed – he was careful to employ only whites who shared similar views on apartheid and he also employed black people and "coloureds" in positions that were prohibited at the time. This brought him into contention with certain South African authorities, but Albert was undeterred. He also established the JosCo Foundation, the charitable arm of the company, in honour of his father Josiah. That organisation was established with the main purpose of giving back to the impoverished native South Africans some of the wealth that Albert considered rightfully belonged to them. It is still in operation today under a different name. It is managed and staffed mainly by children adopted by Albert and Lydia and their adopted Grandchildren. And the profits from the JosCo Corporation still fund benevolent causes worldwide.

When Albert's mother passed away he was 41 years old. He had been very close to his mother and her death affected him a great deal. Now he was alone in the world except for his wife Lydia – Albert missed his family dearly. He and Lydia tried for many years to have children of their own but it wasn't to be, so they started to adopt, not one or two, but whole orphanages of children. The first was situated in South Africa. When they discovered it, it was an old dilapidated, overcrowded shack, where the children were loved but not properly nurtured due to a lack of resources. They adopted it and called the home the "Josco Children's Sanctuary", and 5 more offshoots of that organisation was soon established throughout Southern and Eastern Africa. There were two in South Africa, one in Zambia, one in Zimbabwe, one in Tanzania, one in Kenya. As the years passed Josco Children's Sanctuaries were established in other African countries – Ghana, Nigeria, Uganda, to name but a few.

Hundreds if not thousands of children escaped the grip of poverty and received a good education and a chance in life because of the work done at the JosCo Children's Sanctuaries. For ten years after his mother's death Albert and Lydia settled in Ghana, playing mum and dad to the children there and they would travel all over Africa working in the JosCo Children's Sanctuaries. Four or five times a year they also travelled to other parts of the world where they did great work with the under-privileged.

During their time living in Ghana Albert and Lydia met a Pentecostal Pastor called Kwaku Kwashi. Pastor Kwashi shared their philanthropic viewpoints and they were so impressed by the selfless attitude of this man that they grew to love and respect him greatly, and it was Pastor Kwashi who led them to faith in Jesus Christ.

After becoming Christians Albert and Lydia did not abandon Judaism but continued to observe the Jewish traditions. But they also treated Sunday as a day of worship and attended church every week without fail.

When Albert was filled with the Holy Spirit soon after his conversion, he began to receive guidance from the Lord in visions, leading him to various parts of the world where his help was greatly needed.

Chapter 10

"It was the miracle that me and my sister Ella had prayed for that brought mum and dad to Jamaica", Yan looked contemplative as he drew back the curtains on his childhood.

"Oh really?" Amelia asked.

"Yes – I firmly believe so, for dad told us that he had seen a vision of children praying for God to send them parents and in that recurring vision he saw the Jamaican flag flying above their heads like halos". "And I recall how me and Ella used to pray and cry out for help from God and I believe that He answered our prayers by sending those two Angels to rescue us from chronic, fierce, soul destroying poverty", Yan then fell silent. He looked near to tears and Amelia once again reached over and patted his back tenderly. Then she sat down again and the two fell silent, deep in thought.

After a few moments Amelia broke the silence, "Thank God for that Angel Bro Al and although I never knew her I also thank God for his dear wife Lydia".

"Amen to that", Yan concluded nodding his head as he also indicated by rising from his seat that it was time to go.

As he drove Amelia home Yan played the now completed album as Amelia inspected the cover proof, "I'm really happy with the way the tracks sound", he said smiling.

"Me too – thanks for making me sound that good – it must have been a hard job", Amelia chuckled.

"You must be joking – don't you realise that that is all you – we barely had to do any touch ups at all – you're truly blessed, Lady Amelia", and they both smiled.

"Oh good – you have written a tribute to Bro Al on the CD cover", Amelia observed.

"Yes – well it was all his idea after all – he left instructions that you should be recorded so that the whole world could discover the beauty of your gift – that was also part of the reason I came to visit Born Again", Yan said.

"Really?" Amelia asked.

"Yes, really – I'm telling you – dad was your biggest fan", and an overwhelming feeling of gratitude to God for having allowed her path to cross with Bro Al's overcame Amelia and she spoke out her emotion, "Father I thank you so very much for sending Bro Al into all our lives".

"Amen", Yan concurred.

"Ah what a wonderful man – and he also brought me the husband I have been praying for all these years", as the words left her lips Amelia wished she had not been so candid with her personal thoughts.

"And he led me to the wife I needed – would you believe that in one of dad's diary entries he actually mentioned how much he wished us to meet". "His exact words were *How I wish my son Marlon could meet Lady Amelia – he needs a good wife like her*", Yan glanced over at Amelia as he spoke.

"Truly?" Amelia asked and before Yan could answer she added "Marlon – is that your name?" and they chuckled.

"So now you know – yes my real name is Marlon – Yan is my pet name".

"Yan – is that a German name or something", Amelia asked still smiling widely.

"No, oh no – let me tell you how I got my pet name". "When Ella was little she couldn't say my name properly – she used to miss off the "Mar" and she couldn't pronounce the "L" or the "O" properly so she used to say "Yan" and everyone jus follow har an call me so", Yan said breaking into patois again. He continued, "You can call me Marlon if you prefer".

"No, I like Yan – "Mrs Yan Kennelly", and they both laughed happily again.

When they arrived at Amelia's home, Yan parked his car. He started missing Amelia already as a feeling of reluctance to be parted from her overcame him. He took her hands in his, looked deeply into her eyes and spoke his heart, "Amelia – when are we getting married then?" he asked, a question that Amelia did not expect or understand.

"We agreed that we would get married at the end of June, remember", she replied.

"Can't we get married right away – why do we need to wait until June?" Yan sounded like an impatient toddler.

"Because, because there is so much to plan and organise", Amelia replied and continued, "I want a big lavish wedding – I've been waiting a long time", and she smiled.

"Yes, sweetheart but do we need to have a big lavish wedding all the way in June – can't we have a smaller one with just the people we love most – wouldn't it be nice to get married on St Valentine's Day in 2 weeks' time instead", Yan sounded persuasive and he continued in an endearing voice, "Please Amelia – pretty please – I just want to be with you all the time – why do we need to wait?"

Amelia looked into his eyes and saw the sincerity, and she smiled, "Okay then", she just could not deny him anything, especially having just learned what he had been through in life. And anyway she was missing him already too.

"We can give all the thousands that we would have spent on the wedding to someone in need", Yan said.

When they had concluded their plans they exited the car. Yan made double certain that the car doors were locked before walking Amelia the short distance to her door.

"I will never again chance leaving my car doors open", he said recalling how Bro Steve had hidden the contraband article under his car seat.

"I don't blame you one bit – you never can tell what shady characters might be lurking around", Amelia concurred.

Joyce came into the hallway as Amelia opened the door and upon catching sight of Yan she enthused, "Oh Bro Yan – come in, come in", and he obeyed.

The joy of the Lord filled that home as they began to celebrate already the coming nuptials. Joyce wanted as large an affair as was possible at such short notice. She and Patrick offered to pay for the entire wedding too. But Amelia was happy to side with her future husband's suggestion of a smaller do.

"The money saved could be better utilised in donations to the poor and under-privileged in the world", Yan told Joyce and Patrick.

"I see you have genuine philanthropic ways", Joyce commented, deciding that it didn't need to be a lavish affair after all. She was simply overjoyed that her last child had now been settled.

When Yan left the Lanson household that night he was dancing to an inaudible tune – his heart was filled with inexplicable joy as he wafted on the highest cloud. He had at last found the Queen of his heart that he had been searching for, for so many years.

That night Amelia knelt and asked God to forgive her for ever doubting Him. Then she thanked God for His faithfulness and manifold blessings. Then it dawned upon her what the forgotten words were in the revelation that she had received so many years ago, "This is my son – he pleases me *with his philanthropic ways*". And she thanked God again and again for sending her a man after His and her own heart – one who loved God dearly, who evidently adored her and who had a big heart. She could not wait to begin to learn from him, more of his philanthropic ways.

That night Amelia had a dream – a vision in fact – she saw the face of Bro Al smiling at her radiantly through the clouds, then he disappeared and she saw golden hands reach out of the clouds and sprinkle confetti upon her head – a shower of gold, jewels and purest light.

Epilogue

"Wow – how time flies", Amelia was speaking to Carly as the two Angels sat in the park enjoying the warm early Summer sun on May Spring Bank Holiday 2013. Over the past year, since Carly's return home, they had rekindled their friendship and had made up for lost time. They were once more as close as they had ever been before their separation as teenagers, and it felt as though the years apart had never intervened.

"I know – I can't believe it's over a year already since you and Yan got married", Carly replied.

"It's one year and three months, one week and six days" Amelia observed and they both chuckled.

"How many hours?" Carly asked jokingly.

"Oh – 2 hours, 18 minutes", Amelia replied and the two chuckled happily again.

"And I couldn't be happier", she added when the laughter had subsided

"I am happier for you Amelia – you always deserved the very best and now you have it", Carly rocked the double cradle gently as they conversed. She did so in an effort to settle the twins who had stirred from sleep because of the yapping of a passing dog.

"You are such a good mother, Carly", Amelia smiled as she observed her friend's mothering skills.

"Well I've had plenty of practice Amelia but I never thought I would become a mother again so soon", Carly said as she looked adoringly at the two month old twins sleeping peacefully in their mobile cradle. Then she looked over towards the play area where her toddler twins were playing happily with other children. Her two oldest children were both working today, while the others had gone out with their father who had continued to take his fatherly duties seriously, probably due to the fact that his wife Alesha, with whom he had now reconciled made sure that he did not shirk them.

"They are so beautiful", Amelia said as she too looked admiringly at the babies.

Carly fished into the baby bag and came out with a bottle of feed which she placed into the mouth of Danette, who had woken up suddenly and begun to cry.

"Can I feed her?" Amelia asked.

"Yeah sure – come and catch your practise – come over to this side", Carly directed with a chuckle in her voice.

Amelia obeyed, excitedly taking hold of the bottle. She watched as the two month old beauty sucked greedily at the teat. A sense of privilege overcame her, at being allowed to feed this beautiful baby – no one would guess that it was her own, for since the birth of the twins her mother, Joyce, and

Carly had virtually taken over, sharing the role of surrogate mothers. Amelia didn't mind though, she was happy to share her two blessings with those that loved her best for she knew that her mother and friend were simply demonstrating love.

A wide smile crossed Amelia's face as she glanced at the little boy sleeping in the cradle below. The twins were not identical and, while Danette favoured Yan – a much prettier version though – Dan looked a lot like Patrick her father. Amelia smiled as she marvelled at the greatness of the Creator and worshipped within her heart.

Since they got married each day had been like a miracle for her and Yan. They remained cocooned in their love and even when they were apart they remained connected in their minds and spirits. They had travelled extensive in the year since getting married, mostly to satisfy the demand for Amelia to minister because the Album "Lady Amelia Kennelly – Touching Heaven" had proved to be an unprecedented hit in diverse parts of the world. They had been forced to curtail their travelling, however, when Amelia became too heavily pregnant 4 months ago. Yan was currently away in Jamaica, overseeing the Children's Sanctuary there. Amelia would like to have gone with him but they thought it best not to travel with the babies until they were at least six months old.

Yan and Amelia planned to relocate to Jamaica when the twins turned six months old, so that they could be raised in a stable rural environment, and they also intended to expand there, by opening two new Children's Sanctuary called AlCo Children's Sanctuary – one in Spanish Town and the other in Montego Bay. Yan was also setting up a state of the art recording studio which he envisaged would be one of the leading Christian recording facilities in the world, and plans were already in place for their move.

Danette began to wriggle around and cry and Carly sprang into action. "Come – give me har", she said and lifted the baby into her arms. The little girl nestled contentedly as Amelia watched and smiled.

"I don't know what I'm going to do without you and mum when we go off to JA".

"Don't worry – you'll be fine by then – anyway we will be coming to visit often", Carly hinted.

"And you will be most welcome", Amelia smiled. Each day she felt privileged to be enveloped in God's agape love and care and she thanked God that she also had the love of a wonderful husband family and friends. And each day she prayed that their lives would remain this blessed.

"I know, why don't you come and spend your honeymoon in JA – two weeks all expenses paid?" Amelia suggested.

"Sounds like an offer I cannot refuse", Carly chuckled.

Since returning to Born Again Carly had been praising God all day every day – she had a lot to thank Him for and never missed a chance to do so.

"Praise the Lord – I am so happy to be home", Carly enthused.

"Amen", Amelia concurred.

"I know I keep harping on about how thankful I am to God for drawing me back to Him, Amelia but it means so much to me – to feel God's presence in my spirit – to be embraced by His love, there is simply nothing like it", Carly sounded deeply sincere.

"Amen", Amelia repeated.

"God is truly faithful".

Carly nodded her head as she thought about God's love and care. He had provided for her in the most marvellous of ways, by giving her a husband – Brother Donald Syrenson. Donald had lost his wife 7 years ago. He was 20 years her senior but Carly did not mind that. She also overlooked his disfigurement due to the fact that he had been involved in a house fire two and a half years ago and was still undergoing a series of reconstructive surgeries, for she could see only Donald's beautiful heart – a heart of purest gold. Donald had embraced her large family as his very own, demonstrating the love of a true father to them and all the children adored him. He had only one adult daughter himself, who at 29, Donald had informed was "foot loose and fancy free". Donald said her name was Tricia and that he saw very little of her but everyday he prayed in earnest for his only daughter. Carly was hoping to finally get to meet Tricia at their wedding which was to take place in 6 weeks' time on 6 July 2013.

"I only wish I had not left it so long to come home, but at least I made it back in time", Carly said soberly.

At that moment the two friends' fell silent as their thoughts turned solemn – they were thinking about the third Angel. A tear arose in Amelia's eye as she recalled Avarel's lavish funeral six months earlier. No expense had been spared on the golden casket, the horse drawn carriage and the floral tributes. No eulogy sweeter had ever been spoken.

Although they said nothing, both Amelia's and Carly's thoughts concurred – *"Shame Avarel did not stay at home the second time".*

After her baptism Avarel had been resolute that she would stay saved, vowing within herself never to stray from God again and she had intended to change the course of her life completely, to turn back from the ways of the world and embrace Jesus Christ's ways fully. But although she had intended never to miss Sunday Morning service ever again, her work on *"Nectarous"* had gotten in the way. Then it was her obligations, for she was tied in to promoting the album – her contract demanded it of her. She had tried to stay connected to God, reading her Bible and praying every day, but the tide had proved too strong and before long she was sucked under again, deeper and deeper into the dangerous pit of her old sinful life.

Just one more riotous party had turned into just two more, then just three more.

And when *Nectarous* failed to "hit", Avarel had prayed, asking God to bless, but He could not because it had nothing to do with Him, for although she had intended not to do any more sexually explicit material, her record company had dug their heels in and insisted and she had eventually succumbed. Avarel was a stranger to failure, and she would win at any cost, even if it meant returning to the old ways taught to her by Brendon and recalling two of his favoured three-word sentences *"who will know?"* and *"live for now"*, she had succumbed to the temptation of the occult. And just one more candle lighted had burnt out too soon and just one more chant had been too short – another blasphemy against the Creator was needed – just one more, then another was needed, then another, and yet another. And before long, *Nectarous* was getting recognition and selling fast. She was in demand again but consequentially Avarel lost her soul. Overwhelmed by spiritual wickedness she had hit rock bottom, more of Satan's lies had distorted her mind, suggesting that just one more trip was the way out – but it was to be her last journey.

They had found her alone in the foetal position upon her living room floor cradling a Champagne bottle – next to her was the glass table with evidence of traces of cocaine on it. An almost empty bottle of narcotic based pills lay nearby – the verdict had been a colossal overdose. There was no suicide note and all agreed that she had had everything to live for. Those who had seen her last spoke of her excitement and optimism looking forward to the future. But a tragic misjudgement had led to the catastrophic accident that had stolen her soul and taken her out of the race for good.

And Avarel's parents and friends were left behind to grieve, to contemplate with hindsight the vanity of her wasted life, and all agreed that it would have been better if she had never left home in the first place.

"For what shall it profit a man to gain this whole world and lose his soul"?